PASSING SHADOWS

Passing Shadows

GENEVIEVE MASTERSON

Publisher: Genevieve Masterson

Contents

ACKNOWLEDGEMENTS

Prologue

    · Edmund Burke, *A Philosophical Enquiry Into The Origin Of Our Ideas Of The Sublime and Beautiful*

I keep having the same dream, one in which I am continually chased down an unending street, in a neighborhood known by heart. My pursuer is a phantom, his face shrouded by darkness, but I know the glint in his eyes and the shine of the street-lamp off his raven hair. I know the weight and feel of his hands, the callus of the pad of his left pinky finger, and the gin on his breath. I even know the staccato beat of his heart, the rat-a-tat-tat that drowns out the slap of my feet against the pavement. Safety is just ahead, but each step brings me no closer to refuge. Bile rises as his towering figure nears, and I've never felt so small in my life. She waits for me by the door, both out of place and right at home, tears streaming down her face. Her arms are outstretched, only to grasp air, and her body seems to grow smaller with every step of my own. A building comes in to view. A different man waits at the top of the stairs, always waiting for me to return home, but this man's home and hers are not the same. Which way do I choose? The dream plays on a never-ending loop. The intimate stranger's hand brushes the ends of my caramel brown ringlets, but I just manage to evade his grasp. One of these days, he'll catch me. The past will repeat itself. He'll make me pay for the mistakes I've made along the way. Wrath will bubble over, and I will pay the price. I will lose nearly everything before I gain anything. I won't be able to hide us anymore.

Chapter One

I look over the man sitting across from me. Matthew Clark is everything a woman could want. He's smart, polite, handsome, and he has lots of money. Close to six feet tall, with lean muscles, strawberry blonde hair slicked back, dark brown eyes, and a killer smile, he's a man few women would turn away. We met early in my freshman year of college. I went to visit my best friend, Claire, and went on a double date with her now-husband and one of his fraternity brothers. He asked me out on a second date, but I turned him down, my heart already longing for someone else. Imagine my surprise all these years later, when I walk into the restaurant for another blind date arranged by Claire and find him on the other side of the door. We've seen each other sporadically over the last few years but not often. Actually, if I recall correctly, this is my third time seeing him. Claire mentioned that he was traveling for work, giving seminars on real estate investment but cutting back on his travel. He grew up nearby like Claire's husband, Jesse, though they didn't meet until college. I didn't expect my interactions with him to extend past occasional run-ins when I was with Claire. The evening has been moments of bumbling conversation about his success in his inherited real estate investment business and my little flower shop, interrupted with long moments of silence. He even referred to my flower shop as my "hobby," which made me see red for a few minutes.

"I'm not really ready for a relationship," I blurt out when he begins talking about a second date. It's not a full truth or lie. I'm not sure if I'm ready for a relationship, or if I ever will be ready, but I'm not opposed to it with the right person. That said, I just don't see myself with him, not now or in the future. I need to shut this down fast, so I deliver the final nail in the coffin, "I'd like to remain friends."

That should do it, the kiss of death to any romantic inclinations. He looks at me blankly, as if stunned by my words, surprised that someone could turn him down. With the way he looks and his polished persona, he is probably rarely turned down for anything. He recovers quickly and says he understands. Claire and Jesse have seen so little of him since their college days that I don't think I'll see him again for a while. I don't know for sure how much they have shared with him in regards to my background. He probably knows some, but hopefully not all, of what led me to this exact moment in life. It's silent as we awkwardly and quickly swallow the remainder of our meals, and he hands our server money to cover the tab when she stops to offer dessert. Without waiting for any change, he gestures for me to rise and exit before him, then walks me to my ancient, gray Honda Civic that I nicknamed "Betty." I've had her for so long, I'm not sure how she's running anymore.

Ever the gentleman, he waits until I start to pull away before getting in his own car. Carrie Underwood comes on the radio singing the song of my life, and I crank it up as I maneuver the streets toward home, hoping to drown out my thoughts. A seed of doubt starts to work its way into my mind. What is my problem? He's successful and kind. Even if he did insult my profession a little, I doubt it was intentional. I miss having a partner around. It would be nice to have someone to help with the household tasks and parenting. Two blocks from home, the tears come. I pull over to compose myself, stopping my car under a faltering streetlight. If I'm honest with myself, I know the problem. Matthew simply isn't the one who holds my heart, even now, all these years after it was fractured. And he'd never be able to help fill in those pieces that are still missing. I think I've been ruined for the rest of my life.

When I finally make it home, I leave my phone in my purse, unwilling to force myself to let Claire know this latest setup is yet one more in a string of failures. She means well, but she doesn't understand how I can still struggle to let go, after everything I've been through. Personally, I don't know how much is not letting go and how much is just a fear to let someone get close. I don't think my heart could take a second blow like that. Claire wouldn't understand. She dated around in high school, and she is still happily married to the first guy with whom she had a serious relationship in college, while my first real relationship crashed and burned. After tossing and turning for an hour, my body finally reaches the point it can't stay awake any longer. Just before I fall asleep, thoughts of love and dead relationships heavy on my mind, I think of him.

I was eighteen, and it was freshman orientation at college. Claire and I were separated for the first time since we met. She chose to stay close to Boonville, going to the University of Missouri-Columbia for a Bachelor of Fine Arts degree on a scholarship. I moved to St. Louis for a business degree, wanting to be in a big city. She was, by far, the better student between the two of us, which she attributed to the knowledge that her grades would be her only way out of a small town and into a better life. Funny, she's still in a small town now. I always intended to get a Master's degree, hoping to someday break a glass ceiling at a major company.

Claire had been like a sister to me for so much of my life, from the day we met the first day of fifth grade. Emotions were battling to occupy the forefront of my mind: anxiety, excitement, loneliness, hope. I missed my grandmother and Claire. Truthfully, I wasn't sure I was ready for the change. Claire was always the more vivacious of us two. Everyone wanted to be her friend, and boys constantly asked her out. She was a buffer for me to the outside world, and I was only accepted within the in-crowd once she decided we were best friends. I'd have been just as happy holed up in a library with a fantasy book, lost in another world.

All the new students were gathered in the Quad, near Union Station, flitting from table to table with raucous laughter ringing through the air. I picked up my name tag from the check-in and breathed out my frustration that the torture of social interaction was mandatory. Surely, we could better prepare for life at college by getting a jump start on studying. Why didn't they send us our class syllabi ahead of time? There was a pungent floral smell, heavy in the humid air, and my curls were tangling in a giant knot with the breeze. While lifting my hair from my neck to cool down, I quickly looked over a few tables to give the appearance I was participating, all while hoping to sneak out silently without drawing much attention to myself. As I turned to leave, I saw him for the first time. He was standing at the booth for Writers' Club. I felt a tug at my core, drawing me closer to him, as if we were magnets. The sun beat down, reflecting off his golden hair, and I could see his turquoise eyes even from where I stood. He was much taller than me, not that it was a difficult feat, and his shirt hinted at muscles that don't belong on someone who spends their days writing. A new feeling began in my toes and expanded through my whole body. I knew in that moment that I would love this man forever.

With a lopsided grin, he extended his hand. "I'm Lucas. Are you interested in joining? Our first meeting is next week."

"What?" I was snapped from my reverie by the smoothness of his voice, like silk draped across my bare skin. A breath escaped me, one I didn't realize I had been holding. He let out a small laugh, sending shivers down my spine as I tried to recall the walk across the plaza to his booth. Afraid to look him in the eyes, I managed a small smile and opened my mouth to respond, but nothing came out. My cheeks instantly flushed, the brightness spreading down my neck and chest. Finally, I looked up to meet his eyes, and I felt found.

"Mommy, are you alive?" my daughter, Jolene, whispers next to my bed. She's named after my beloved grandmother, but I usually call her Jo. Her raven-black hair peeks over the edge of the bedspread, and I see the hint of her beautifully haunting, dark-green eyes. I smile, knowing it doesn't reach my eyes this morning, as I bend to lift her to my bed. As she snuggles in, a frown appears, and I know she can tell my smile isn't genuine this morning. Guilt floods me. "Why are you sad, Mommy?"

"I'm not sad, sweetie," I lie. "I'm just tired. I worked late last night. What did you do with Tina?" Jo loves her sitter, who is a student at a nearby college and a former cheerleader.

I hope the distraction will work. I've always used work as an excuse for every date I've let Claire arrange, not wanting Jo to get the wrong idea. There's no need for her to know about my dates unless they get serious. I breathe a small sigh of relief as

Jo moves into a drawn-out discussion of her evening. We move through our morning routine as she talks about playing *Zingo*, painting, *Dora the Explorer*, and the new cheerleading moves Tina taught her. Her life goal is to be a cheerleader.

After getting Jo settled at the table, I check my phone and realize it died overnight. Claire must be going crazy being unable to reach me. Maybe it'll be enough to get her to church this morning. Plugging it in, I whip together breakfast. By the time we eat scrambled eggs with sausage and pull up to the church, I think Jo has exhausted her vocabulary. Her love of big words definitely comes from me I think to myself as I study her climbing from the backseat. I don't know about the need for constant chatter. Unfortunately, as she gets older, she looks more like him. Her eyes bore into the soul and see the real you, underneath the layers put on to protect yourself from the truth. I'm ashamed to admit that in my nightmares, sometimes her eyes replace his. Appearances aren't everything, though. Children don't always look like their parents. It sounds like I don't love my daughter, but I do. I'd give my life for her.

The day I changed the course of our lives, I packed up Jo with our sparse belongings and moved closer to Claire, to home. Jo was just shy of six months old. Claire settled down when she married Jesse, truthfully from the moment she met him, moving out to the country to live on a farm with him. She was no longer the wild child I remember from our childhood, although she dropped out of college once Jesse graduated. Now she sells jewelry on Etsy, along with some artwork she does in her spare time. It gives her a meager income, but she loves it. Outside of the two of them and Jesse's family, no one else truly knows us here. We know the names of our neighbors, my employees, and several families at church, but it's a passing familiarity. They see what I want them to see about us and our life. There's safety in anonymity, and this was the perfect place. We have a small town feel but still maintain access to the city amenities. It's also big enough that we're just two more faces in a sea of many. Outside of those we allow in, no one knows any significant details about us, and we keep to ourselves. Staying in the background, we blend into the scenery. As Jo gets older, I worry about her opening up to kids at school and sharing personal information with the wrong kid's family. We already had an incident with a little boy at preschool teasing her about not having a dad. Jesse is great with her, but he's not her father. I know what I'll have to do if it ever happens, if the wrong person somehow finds us. It's nice to be close to Claire and Jesse, and near to where I grew up, but if push comes to shove, I'll drop Claire. I'll pretend I don't know her. If necessary, Jo and I will disappear into the wind and never look back. Jo will always be my priority. My hope is that we can stay here, be safe, and at peace.

After settling Jo into her classroom, I slide into a chair in the back, right corner, as usual. Claire isn't here, which isn't unexpected. The pastor begins the greeting, but my mind is already wandering. I feel in my bones that something is changing, about to reach a boiling point, and we will no longer be able to hide. I can't explain it. It just is. The blood coursing through my veins is poisoned with his scent. I'm struggling more every day to swallow my fears and anxieties and to focus on the present. I haven't told Claire of my fears. She tries to be supportive, but I can tell she thinks I'm paranoid anytime I've brought up concerns in the past. I know her well enough that she doesn't need to speak for me to know what's going through her mind. I've noticed the feeling of being watched, the hairs on the back of my neck standing straight several times the last few weeks. Any time I've tried to check my surroundings, I haven't seen anyone watching me, but I could swear someone is. One night, I closed up late and almost called Claire to see if Jesse could come walk me out to my car and follow me home. I worry that the time to leave may be coming sooner than I want.

The band begins playing a chart-topping Christian song, and halfway through, I feel a tingle at the nape of my neck, eyes on me. Glancing to my left, I expect to see mostly empty chairs with anyone seated in the row firmly watching the stage of the church, but a man I don't recognize is looking at me. He's not a regular attendee. I've never seen him here before, and we rarely miss church. The first thing I notice is his hair, as black as midnight on a starless night, and broad shoulders. I see warning signs flashing. Even seated, I can tell he would tower over me. He's here.

He notices that I see him and averts his gaze, but it's too late. My stomach starts cramping, and I feel sick, my heart pounding. I run from my seat, choking back bile, pick up Jo, and dash for the car. I need to calm down. It can't be my nightmare, but what if it is? I need to try to be rational here and not overreact. In all these years, I've never seen him here. Why would he show up now? Why would he try to find us? How is it possible he could be here this soon? My hands shake on the whole drive home as I swallow back hot saliva that tells me I'm about to be sick. I'm so rattled that when I pull into the driveway, I remember nothing of the drive. I know Jo is speaking to me on the way home, but I won't recall a single word she said.

Chapter Two

At home, safely behind a locked door, my panic begins to recede. My rational side comes out. There are countless men with dark hair in this suburb alone. I can talk to Claire. She'll help work through this, although I don't really want to see the look of pity on her face.

Claire always joins us for lunch on Sundays after church, whether she comes to service or not. Sometimes Jesse joins, but it's rare. He usually spends his Sundays tinkering around their farmhouse, fixing up odds and ends. He told Claire that Sundays are "girl time." Cooking is something I've enjoyed for a long time, and I appreciate the creative outlet. There's something special about putting a meal in front of someone you love, someone you cooked for with an open heart. While I cook, I forget about the troubles weighing on me. I am in the middle of chicken marsala, with a salad and Chenin Blanc, when Claire walks in. Jo is at the table shoveling buttery elbow macaroni into her mouth, her adventurous taste buds not quite developed, when my best friend appears around the corner.

"Aunt Claire!" Jo yells, as she peals from the table to jump into Claire's waiting arms.

"Hi, cuddle bug!" Claire exclaims, smothering Jo with kisses. As far as Jo is concerned, Claire and Jesse are her aunt and uncle, although she knows we're not really related.

The day Claire and I met, she was wearing holey jeans and a tee shirt far too big for her, and the soles of her shoes were nearly worn through. By contrast, I was dressed primly, in a long skirt and a short-sleeved blouse, with a cardigan over it. My shoes were black and shiny, well-used but clean. The resemblance to my grandmother was striking.

Physically, Claire and I are opposites. Claire is tall, around five-foot-nine, but I am lucky to break five-foot-four. Even at ten, she was already significantly taller than me. She's naturally thin and small-framed, while I spent most of my childhood being teased for being a bit pudgy. As I grew taller, my pudginess molded into curves, but I'm still self-conscious about my weight. Her hair is stick straight, the shade of blonde that women spend hundreds of dollars to achieve, and her skin has a naturally sun-kissed hue. My own hair is a mix of corkscrew curls and looser waves, my skin, a lovely shade of bland from working indoors. She also has gorgeous, pale-blue eyes. My eyes are a dull brown. Despite her ill-fitting and untidy clothes, she was beautiful, and I knew that she'd outshine me for life. But I couldn't help liking her. We both loved dogs, the color purple, and reading. Her positivity was infectious. There's no mistaking that we aren't really biological sisters.

My parents died in a car accident when I was barely older than Jo is now, and I was raised by my grandmother. My memories of my parents are fuzzy, at best, and most of the things I can recall are from stories I've been told rather than actual experiences. I was their first and only child. My mother had a sister, and I have a few cousins spread across several states, but my aunt wasn't in the position to take on an additional child. My father was an only child, and his parents passed away before his own death. Were it not for Grandma Jolene, I would have ended up in a foster home. Claire came from a family that defines dysfunctional, her mother a functioning addict with a revolving door of boyfriends. Her father had been in and out of jail for most of her young life, before passing away in a drug deal gone wrong. When he died, her mother moved the two of them to my hometown, and from the day we met, Claire spent more time at our house than her own. Grandma and Claire developed their own special relationship when Claire came to visit, only a week after our fateful, first meeting, and Grandma made sure that Claire had clean, proper clothes and good shoes from that day on.

Claire longs for a child but has been disappointed time and again. Yet, she still dotes on Jo and never lets her sorrow show. Jo and I left our home when Jo was still so young, and Claire and Jesse gave us a place to stay at his family's farm for a year. We lived there until I made enough money that I could afford payments on a decent, three bedroom, one and a half bath rental, without touching the sizable amount of money my grandmother left me. Originally, I thought it would cover a down payment on a house, but now I want to save what I still have for an emergency. I desperately want some normality and to give Jo a sense of home. If I'm honest, a small part of me thought a home of our own, even if I didn't own it outright, would somehow encapsulate us in safety. Real estate prices have been on the rise here since we moved too, and I doubt I could afford a home in a good neighborhood, even with a down payment. The landlord is a friend of Jesse's parents, and he's pretty much let me have free rein to do what I want with the house as long as I keep it in good shape.

Two hours later, we've polished off the wine, and Jo is sleeping soundly on the couch with her head in Claire's lap. Most of our conversation today has been silly, discussing movies coming out soon and which Hemsworth is better looking. Jo innocently added in her own opinion that someone on a Disney show, I can't recall which, is the cutest boy in the whole world. Heaven help me, I don't even want to think about her and boys for at least another thirty years. I know the ease of the conversation won't last, especially now that Jo's ears aren't listening in. Sure enough, Claire steers the conversation toward my date. She's twirling her hair around her finger when she finally asks, a habit she has whenever she knows a conversation isn't going to go well.

"What happened last night? I'm guessing since I didn't hear from you, he didn't wake up in your bed this morning. What's wrong with Matthew? I think you would have really hit it off back in college if you hadn't already met Lucas."

I can't pretend that the date ended nicely, and I definitely don't want to talk about Lucas.

"He's a little on the tall side and too perfect. No one is really that great in every way. He must have some deep, dark secret, and that's why he's agreeing to dates with single moms, particularly ones who shot him down in the past. If a guy like that needs a blind date, there HAS to be something seriously wrong with him." Shift the blame, a good motto for this type of situation, and my go-to method for diverting the conversation away from my own issues anytime we discuss a blind date I've had.

"Okay, first, it's not really a blind date. You've already met, and he asked Jesse about setting the two of you up on a date.

I'm sorry I didn't tell you, but in my defense, I knew you wouldn't go if you knew it was him. ...You're not giving him a fair chance. He's too tall? That's the lamest excuse I've ever heard," Claire replies. She's not done. "Everyone is tall to you. You're just short. What does being tall have to do with any of it? Lucas was tall. And Lucas wasn't perfect. Despite your romanticized recollections of him, he was an asshole. What's really going on? It's been years, Sammi, and Matthew is a good catch."

She's correct. Lucas and Matthew are about the same height. I'm intimidated by tall men, though, and I have been for years now, which means I'm intimidated a lot. Claire knows it, but I don't want the conversation to go in that direction. As for Lucas, I still don't think of him as a bad person, just a lost soul. I never really got over him, and I don't know if I will ever move past him. I'm certain I don't want him back. Even if he begged me, I'd turn him down, but he was a huge part of my life. That kind of love doesn't just disappear overnight, especially when it's entangled with a traumatic event. It's been years but same difference. I didn't really want to talk about him, but Claire, obviously, knows he's at the root of my hesitation, as always.

"I'm just not ready for a serious relationship," I snap back. "I doubt I'll ever see him again, unless he's at your house. It's just better this way."

My carefree act isn't selling, but I just don't mind if she's mad anymore. I'm mad too. I don't need a lecture from anyone. All I need is to be allowed to live my life on my schedule. I don't want to be forced into a relationship and pretending to love someone. It'll happen if it's meant to happen.

"Here's the thing, Claire. No more blind dates, please. No more playing the love doctor. I'm not looking to fall in love, and I definitely don't want any guys around Jo."

Again, it's a half-truth. Like I've said, I'm not actively looking for a relationship. I won't bring random guys around Jo, but if the right person came along, I'd be open to trying. It would take a long time for me to trust someone with my entire heart, though. Jo is always my reason for avoiding most social interaction. I need to protect her. Claire understands better than anyone about not introducing someone I'm casually dating to Jo. I can't even count how many times Claire slept at our house as a kid to avoid her mom's boyfriends. Jo's too young to know the truth about her dad. I don't know if I'll ever feel that she's ready to hear the story.

Not to mention, how would I even tell someone about my past if it ever got that serious? I don't want to get attached to someone, only for them to flee when they realize how mentally screwed up I am. At this point, the best thing I can do is change the subject before my mind delves too deeply into the past, my inconsistent feelings about my romantic future, or Jo missing a father.

"We missed you at church this morning, Claire," I say, trying to direct the conversation elsewhere.

She's not quite ready to let it go. "Well, you might see Matthew around because he's been hanging with Jesse more. They used to be really close friends, you know."

I do know how close they were in college. It seemed that every time Claire and I talked, Matthew was a part of whatever story she was telling. He was even Jesse's best man.

"Maybe just get to know him better, but that's all I'm going to say on the topic. I know you're changing the subject. I meant to come this morning, but Jesse and I had a previous commitment." Her face flushes a little when she mentions why she didn't make it to church.

I can assume what their prior commitment means. It comes every month. And every month, Claire fights through the disappointment and pretends she's okay. Usually, she acts like they're doing something scandalous, trying to hide her misery behind her sense of humor, but today she's somewhat withdrawn. Fertility treatments haven't helped yet, and they can't afford to continue them. Surgery hasn't helped either. They've started to discuss fostering and adoption. I know she'd make a great mom, and any kid would be lucky to be in her home. Jesse would be a good dad too. He works hard and does whatever he can to support Claire.

I should probably tell her about the scare I had at church, like I planned, but it's late, and I know she really doesn't want to hear it anymore. I don't really want to hear her opinion anymore either, if I'm honest. Even the short conversation we had about Matthew and Lucas is exhausting. Jo stirs from her nap just in time to help me avoid the awkward closure to our conversation, and Claire plays with her for a long time. After she leaves, I give Jo a bath and let her snuggle into my bed. Tonight, I am blissfully free from nightmares. Maybe my heart is finally listening to my logical mind. Maybe I'm doing better than I think at times. Maybe, just maybe, we really are safe.

The next day comes early, but my work week is uneventful. When we first moved out, I took a part-time job at a local flower shop, looking for something familiar and low stress. I figured I'd look for something better, but it would help me transition more easily in the meantime. The owner started cutting back on her own hours shortly after I started, increasing my hours, and to my surprise, she eventually offered to sell me the shop for an unreasonably low price. I was able to use part of my inheritance, saving plenty for my emergency fund. She had been widowed years prior and received a large life insurance payout on her husband. She could have sold the shop for much more but told me she wanted to "keep it in the family." Of all the people I've met here, she was the one new person I had really started to trust. Last I knew, she had moved down to Florida and remarried.

I kept the cheesy name, Nature's Beauty, and the one other part-time employee, Beatrice. After a few months, I hired Josef to work part-time as well. As a successful software engineer who works from home, he didn't really need the job. He just enjoys doing it, and it helps having an extra employee, especially as Beatrice began cutting back on her hours. We don't do as much business as bigger shops, but we do okay. It pays the bills.

We have a funeral, a few special orders, and a wedding this week. We prep as much as possible during the week when we have weddings, knowing Saturday will be mayhem. Josef usually covers the shop on Saturdays, and we're closed on Sundays, but I'm always there whenever we have weddings to do. With my Saturday all tied up already, I cut out early Monday to spend some extra time with Jo. Before I know it, she'll be fifteen, full of hormones, and leaving me wistful for the days I couldn't even use the restroom by myself. Better enjoy this stage while it lasts. I plan to be home each day when she gets out of morning preschool and stay home, rather than bring her with me to work, pack her off to Claire's, or leave her with Tina. We have so much fun together, and I go several days without any panic attacks and evenings without nightmares. It almost feels like we're normal, and the previous Sunday is far from my mind.

At least, it is until Thursday morning. Beatrice is working the floor, while I tackle our books in the office. She's in her sixties, and she moves a little slowly from her arthritis, but her mind is fast as a whip. She keeps her gray hair cut short and permed, her clothes are an assortment of long skirts and boho shirts, and her nails are always painted. My own grandma was made of a tougher stock, raised to be a "proper wife" someday, but being with Beatrice still reminds me of her. Inside, my grandma was a kindhearted woman. She watched over the house with strict rules, but she would have moved heaven and earth for her daughter's child. Beatrice shares that same passion and vibrancy. I hear the bell above the door ring and glance up to see Beatrice moving forward to speak with whoever entered the shop. I look back down to my work, but when I hear the two begin speaking, I look up again and choke back a surge of panic.

"How may I assist you today, sir?" Beatrice asks the man who I noticed watching me at church Sunday. It can't be a coincidence that he's here, of all the flower shops in the area. His voice easily reaches the office, and the sound tinkles in my ears, his voice deep and stretching through my core.

"I just need a dozen pink roses when you have a moment. Thank you."

"Yes, it will take just a minute," Beatrice replies, as she begins setting her materials on the counter to put the roses together. She works even slower than normal, but if the man is irritated, it doesn't show. His eyes flit about the shop as Beatrice shuffles toward the cooler. I hear her begin speaking again, in a louder than normal voice.

"I haven't seen you around before, but you look a little familiar. Are you new to this neighborhood? What brings you to this neck of the woods?"

I watch his face, studying him, and realize I'm anxious to hear his reply. I'd guess he's in his late twenties to early thirties. He must be at least six-foot-one, and his eyes are green, much like

Jo's. Through the glass of the office, I can see that the green in his eyes is a little softer and paler than Jo's. But it's close, and his hair is just as black as hers. It's long, curling around his ears, yet the look suits him. The beginning of a beard shadows his face. I admit to myself that he's attractive, but at the same time, the sight of him sends threads of fear though my veins. I can tell from here that before yesterday, I've definitely never seen him. I can see the differences between this stranger and my past. His eyes are gentle and kind, closer set, and his nose is narrower, but he still looks far too familiar for me to be comfortable.

I'm so focused on my examination of him from my office that when he looks over and meets my eyes through the glass, it's a moment before I realize it, a rosy glow spreading over my face and neck. He gives a small smile and responds to Beatrice's inquiry. "I am sort of new to the neighborhood. I grew up around here but left for a while. I just came back to be closer to my dad after my mam passed."

I look down at my desk, pretending to be engaged in my work, but my ears are listening for more conversation between this stranger and Beatrice. Their voices are so low now that I can barely hear them. Once she processes his credit card, she thanks him as "Mr. MacDonald". ...MacDonald sounds familiar. This stranger has drawn my interest. Who is he really, and why is he here? And then, I have to ask myself, why do I care?

I'm staring off into space when Beatrice pokes her head around the corner and startles me. "He was a dapper young man, wasn't he? You should ask him out."

I roll my eyes. Please, don't let Beatrice start hounding me too. She mostly leaves my love life alone since our first shift to-gether, when I told her I was recently divorced and better off for it. Occasionally, she makes a passing comment about how we're not meant to live alone for our entire lives, but I remind her I'm not alone when that comes up. I have Jo.

"I've never even met the man, Beatrice. I don't know who he is, and I definitely don't need to ask him on a date."

"Don't you recognize the last name, MacDonald? I bet his dad is Fergus MacDonald. They look alike. We did the flowers for Fergus's wife's funeral last year. I believe her name was Aileen, if I remember correctly. Their daughter, Fiona, took care of all of the arrangements. Such a sweet woman, it's a shame she's gone. She used to come in once a month and pick an arrangement from the cooler. Anyway, he was nice to look at, wasn't he? You can't deny that. Even his name is sexy, Ciaran." ... I don't ever want to hear the word, sexy, out of her mouth again.

Beatrice pauses for a moment, smirking, but when I don't reply, she goes back out to the front. I don't recall the funeral or someone named Aileen, but maybe she usually came in when I was off. My mind has been occupied with too many things lately, and I could just be forgetting. I start to zone out again, letting my past overtake me.

Not even two weeks into my freshman year, I had the opportunity to see Lucas again. His Writers' Club had its first meeting, and with a little sleuthing, I learned he was the Vice President. He was also two years ahead of me in school, the same age as the guy Claire had just met. When I got there, he and Megan, the President, launched into a discussion about the club and its goals. The idea was to have a safe place to share ideas and get constructive feedback from other members. Everyone also set their own goals for what they wanted to accomplish, and sharing it with the group would hopefully encourage them to accomplish those goals, although no one would be forced to share their work.

They had a monthly meeting to discuss everyone's current work, and people could get together at Union Station once a week to focus on writing. The weekly meetings were optional, but they were a good opportunity to be around other writers. I'd never been much of a writer, just a few short stories and poems for classes, but I figured I could float it if it meant I could be around Lucas more. I hadn't stopped thinking about him since the first time I saw him, and my grades would seriously suffer if I didn't stop daydreaming about him. They passed around a sign-up sheet and suggested we introduce ourselves to the group. I was mortified when my turn came. I gave my name, my major, and where I was from, then passed on to the next person. I was putting my note-book away at the end of the meeting when he approached me.

"I'm glad to finally know your name, 'Samantha but everyone calls me Sammi.' You didn't say much during introductions. I'm a business admin major too, if you need any advice on classes or professors."

The words slid from his mouth like liquid gold, and I held my breath for a fraction of a second, committing this moment to memory. My cheeks blushed with embarrassment. I needed to keep my cool.

"Sorry I didn't talk much. I'm a freshman." As soon as I said it, I realized how stupid I sounded. Obviously, I was a freshman. I tried to smile anyway, but I was sure it looked more like a grimace. He smiled and asked if I'd be coming back. He was close enough that I could smell his cologne, a woodland scent, and I'm pretty sure my eyes fluttered. I couldn't even speak. Just a nod would have to suffice.

"Awesome. It's getting dark out. Can I walk you home?" I hadn't even realized that the room emptied out in the few min-utes we were talking.

"Thanks," I said, giving him another nod, and he walked alongside me to my dorm. The sun set during the meeting, and the stars were hidden by clouds, portending storms on the horizon. Something in the air reeked of danger, and I was glad to have an escort. We made light conversation, and my dorm appeared far too soon for my liking. After he told me goodnight, I watched through the door as he faded into the night. Whispering, I told him I wish he'd stay, letting the words carry away through the nothingness.

Each week, for nearly the next three months, I went to the weekly writing sessions, working on a few short stories, followed by the monthly meetings. I was actually proud of some of what I'd written, much of it reflecting on growing up without my parents, and Lucas had given me helpful feedback on anything I'd shared. After each meeting, Lucas walked me home. Our conversations grew and became more personal.

I told him the details about my parents dying when I was five, beyond what I had shared in my writing, and about Grandma Jolene taking me in to raise me. He told me about his family, especially his younger sister, Amanda. Clearly, he adored his sister. I couldn't help but be envious. I barely remembered my parents, and it was lonely without having siblings. At least, it was until Claire came into my life. I only saw my aunt, uncle, and cousins at Christmas, and I never knew anything about my dad's side.

Lucas told me about his first passion – hockey. He played on a travelling hockey team while in high school, and the University of Wisconsin even recruited him. He chose to attend a local college to stay near his sister, but he still tried to play hockey as often as he could. Much to my chagrin, I also learned he had a girlfriend from high school, Rebecca, going to school a few hours away. Lucas dreamt of being an author, and I knew I'd never tell him that I only joined the club to get to know him, especially once I knew he had someone in his life. I thought that maybe him walking me home meant something, but perhaps all it meant was that he was a nice guy.

After the last meeting before the Thanksgiving holiday, Lucas walked me home and seemed jittery the entire way, chewing on his fingernails. It was a marked difference from the cool and collected persona he usually exuded. He lingered at the doorway, and I looked at him. "Are you okay? You seem anxious."

"Can I ask you something, Sammi?" His voice was hesitant and unsure.

I nodded, heady with a need to touch him, and thoughts about what he needed to ask pinged around my brain. I was hopeful it was something good, but maybe he figured out I was a fake.

"I was wondering if, maybe, you'd like to grab a meal sometime and go to a movie." I was stunned and excited. What happened to Rebecca?

I managed to stutter out a yes, and he suggested the evening we'd get back from Thanksgiving break for our date. Suddenly, he was standing right in front of me, looking down into my face. My eyelids lowered as I felt him lean in. His body pressed against me, and his lips brushed against mine. A heat exploded in my stomach, spreading through my limbs. I'd never felt this way before, and the foreign feeling was both stimulating and overwhelming. The kiss lasted only a moment, chaste and sweet on his part, and when he pulled away, my body screamed in withdrawal.

"I'll miss you over break, Sammi," he whispered, then he walked away.

Chapter Three

Time flies quickly, and before I know it, it's Halloween. Halloween is Jo's second favorite holiday, only falling to Christmas. I dropped the ball this year and forgot Halloween was even approaching. A couple days ago, we went to Target and somehow managed to find a few pieces she could use to go as a cheerleader. Her costume is modeled after Tina, her best friend forever. Tina is letting Jo borrow her old pom-poms. Someone must have been smiling down on me for the miracle of finding such a great babysitter. Her class schedule works well with our needs, and she's honestly like a big sister to Jo.

The work day passes quickly, and I head home Thursday to meet Tina and Jo and get my baby ready to go out. She's only four, but she's already planned out her route and where to get the candy she enjoys the most – a type A personality if I've ever seen one. She's singing as she uses the potty before putting on her costume, and I reflect back to my first Halloween on campus. I went as Molly Ringwald in the movie, *Pretty in Pink*. I was shocked some of the other girls in the dorm didn't even know who Molly Ringwald was. I grew up watching eighties movies with Claire and Grandma Jolene. The memory brings a smile to my face, which quickly fades as I start to recall other Halloweens, especially the one I'd rather forget.

It's odd that this holiday happens to be so high on Jo's love list. Halloween is central to our entire lives. But tonight is about her, and I push years old negativity from my mind as we head outside. The night is cool, and I make Jo put on her coat over her cheerleading costume. We stroll through the neighborhood, walking down to Boonville Road, the most popular spot in town for trick-or-treaters. After a few houses, Jo is already starting to wear down. We cross the street and head back, tucking into the safety of our familiar neighborhood. One reason I chose to live in this area of town is the proximity to a great pizza place, the elementary school Jo will attend, and my work. While I carry her home down the last street, my back screams at me that she's not so little anymore.

Once she's tucked safely into bed, I spend an hour reading a Shannon Mayer book before turning out my bedside lamp. Almost immediately, I'm sucked under and find myself dreaming of a different holiday – the first New Year's Eve in college. My desire to erase bad memories with good is particularly strong tonight. I went home for Christmas that year, 2011, but I came back to campus the day after, hoping to see Lucas before classes resumed. We had been spending a lot of time together since I returned from Thanksgiving break, and he had started referring to me as his girlfriend.

He had grown up in St. Louis, and he rented an apartment close to campus, his parents footing the bill for his portion of the rent. He was picking up extra schedules at the grocery store where he worked, and I barely saw him until New Year's Eve. Somehow, Lucas managed to get off early that night, with dinner plans in mind for the two of us.

"*Sammi, my love, what would you like to do tonight to ring in 2012?*"

I was still stuck on the phrase, "my love." I could have sat on the couch watching TV all night with him and still been happy. We hadn't said expressions of love yet, but I knew that I was in love with him, that I had been pretty much since the moment we met.

We decided to eat and just hang out, safely sequestered inside his home, away from the festivities sprinkling the neighborhoods around campus. After getting a quick bite to eat at the deli a few blocks down, we headed back to his empty apartment. His room-mates were either home for the holidays or out at the festivities, which we both wanted to avoid. While we'd spent a considerable amount of time there, I'd never stayed the night. We hadn't slept together or done much, besides make out. I had been hesitant to take further steps. I bought lingerie in case I needed it, but despite how much I wanted to be with him, I was still afraid of letting down my guard. The apartment was too quiet, as if it were a sentient being able to anticipate the need for quiet celebration, allowing the two of us to connect on a deeper level.

We sat down in the living room, on a worn, brown, leather sofa littered with torn fabric, and turned on old sitcoms to pass the time until the ball dropped. I was watching an episode of Friends, feeling Lucas's eyes on me the whole time, when he put his lips to my ears and whispered, "Sammi, I think I'm in love with you."

My heart felt like it stopped, and in that moment, I was suspended above us, watching my body radiate heat and love leak from my pores. He was finally telling me the words I'd felt so long but been afraid to say. I turned my head, leaning my forehead against his. "I love you too."

That's all it took. His lips crushed down on mine, more feverish than ever before. My hands were entwined in his hair, desire pulsing through me. He leaned me back against the couch, running his hands down my sides. When his hands touched my breasts, my whole body shuddered in anticipation of what I knew was coming. I'd been scared for this exact moment from the time Claire described losing her virginity to Chris Jones, in full awful detail. However, I'd still thought about it over and over. He pulled back, guiding me to my feet, and I knew this was it. Nothing would ever be the same again. He pressed his lips to mine once again, lifting me against him. I wrapped my legs around his waist as he walked to his bedroom, never breaking apart. He set me to my feet and stepped back for a moment. Expecting him to reach for the hem of my shirt, I decided to beat him to it, but he stopped my hands.

His breath was coming out in short pants, and I could see how much he wanted me. "I'm sorry. I got carried away. I should take you home now. Or if you still want to stay, we can just sleep."

I was stunned into open-mouthed silence, stuttering as I tried to respond while my mind played back snapshots of the last twenty minutes. "...I'm sorry. What did I do?"

My words were barely a whisper as I fought back the tears threatening to spill from my eyes. All the teasing from childhood flooded me, both about my appearance and my lack of worthiness of love. "I just don't understand. Is it me?"

His face was incredulous. "No, Sammi, but I don't want to force you into anything. I know you're a virgin, and I want you to be ready. I'm all in, and I want you to be too." I knew Lucas wasn't a virgin, but it never bothered me.

His concern for me made me even more sure that he was my person. What college-aged boy would turn down the opportunity to have sex? How many times had Claire told me about the boys she dated, trying to get in her pants from the first date? I thought of his words, that he was all in.

"I'm all in too, Lucas. I'm ready. I want this. I want you."

Those words propelled him forward. He wrapped his arms around me, his lips pressed to mine, and his tongue flicked out to meet my own. We were both lost in the moment. The slow, gentle manner in which we started was gone. I yanked his shirt from his body, and he lifted mine over my head. He pushed me back on the bed, pulling my leggings from my body, then stepped back to gaze at me in my red bra and panties, the special lingerie set bought in anticipation of this exact moment.

"You're beautiful," Lucas said, as he unbuttoned his jeans and pushed them down his legs.

He kissed me again and propped himself above me on the bed. His kisses moved over my face and neck as he licked the salt of my tears from my skin. When he unclasped my bra and his tongue flicked against my nipple, I nearly came undone. He raised to kiss my lips again, before moving his mouth down my stomach. When his mouth found my panty line, I was lost in bliss. He was my first kiss, the first man I ever loved, and he would be the first and only lover I'd ever have. Pressure began building with his tongue on me, and my muscles clenched deliciously. It was hard to breathe, feeling like my lungs couldn't draw in oxygen, and my limbs were already shaking. I finally managed a deep breath, and as I exhaled, my first orgasm overtook me. Electricity crackled through my body, and I cried out his name. When my trembling subsided, Lucas leaned over me, his eyes seeking permission. I pulled him down for a kiss to confirm my assent and felt like a scream would rupture from within when he entered me. He was slow and gentle, drawing in and out, moving faster as my breathing quickened. I'd never been so overwhelmed with sensation, the love I felt about *to explode out of me, shattering me into a million pieces. It didn't take long before I felt myself start to lose control, climaxing as I dug my fingernails into his back. He shoved into me again before releasing a groan and collapsing against me. We laid there, catching our breath and eyes growing heavy. The last thing I heard as I fell asleep was fireworks exploding outside. It was only the next morning when I woke up with him curled against me that I realized we didn't use any protection.*

I'm still dreaming of our first time, my relief when my period came like clockwork that month, and my initial appointment for birth control, when the alarm for the house invades my thoughts. For a brief moment, I struggle to wake up while trying to figure out how the alarm figures into such a moment. It's an incessant blaring in my ears that finally breaks through the fog of my intimate dream.

Panic sets in as soon as I realize I'm no longer dreaming, and I tear out of bed, running around the corner to Jo's bedroom. It's at the end of the hall, her window facing the street, as far from the stairwell as she can be. She's screaming before I reach her, and I'm terrified someone is already in the room with her. She's alone, thankfully, and I lock her door behind me. I had Jesse install a sliding lock high on the door when I moved into this house, one that I could reach without the worry of Jo accidentally locking herself in. I realize, too late, that my phone is in my room. All I can do now is wait for the alarm company to notify the police. I silence Jo as best as I can, tugging her into the closet with me and sliding the door closed behind us. In my mind, I can hear loud footsteps downstairs. It's hard to tell if I truly hear them over the shrill noise winding through the house or if they are only in my imagination. When I hear sirens draw near, I crack the closet door and see flashing lights through the windows. I tiptoe over, insisting Jo stay safely ensconced in the closet, and I open the window to yell down that we're upstairs, locked in a bedroom. The police find the window broken in the door to the back of the house and the lock turned. They enter through that doorway and search the house, checking the basement, closets, and rooms. Once they clear everything except the room we're in, they knock on our door and ask if I can open it. I do so hesitantly, waiting until the officer flashes his badge at me to grant him access. My heart is still beating out of control, and my hands are shaking from the post-adrenaline crash.

We settle in the living room, waiting for more officers to arrive while we discuss what happened. I try to be gentle and calm, so I don't further frighten Jo. She cuddles up next to me, and I can feel the tension leaving her body slowly, the presence of the officers a reassurance to her mind. The responding officers are quiet, trying to ask questions in a roundabout way. I'm grateful for their discretion. She finally manages to fall asleep on the couch, the exhaustion overtaking her. Even with the noise from the crime scene unit, arriving to dust for fingerprints and collect evidence, she continues to sleep, and I'm relieved that she can't hear our conversation.

Soon, another officer arrives. He introduces himself as Detective Chase and asks me if I know of any reason someone would break in. I lie and tell him, "No." There's no purpose in stirring the pot without need.

I'm not ready to spill my secrets, and I want to believe this is random. They're almost done when the sun peeks over the horizon. Detective Chase tells me that whoever broke the window did enter the house, as there are muddy foot prints on the floor. Aside from a few drawers in the kitchen that are dumped, nothing is out of order or missing. They're not finding much in the way of evidence, outside of the muddy footprints and the imprint outside. I have a feeling the only fingerprints they will find will belong to someone who is welcome in this house. He also informs me that he believes the break-in may have been kids, egged on by peers, or possibly someone looking for an easy payday.

While I'm still anxious, his reassurance makes me feel better about not telling him about the past. There's no reason for my past to come knocking now. He offers to have an officer stay while I call someone to come over, but I assure him it's okay. Once the house is closed again, I call Claire to ask if she and Jesse can come over. They agree, without hesitation. Less than two hours later, Jesse has covered the window, replaced the dead bolt, and installed an additional deadbolt higher on the door. Claire picked a good one. He's never hesitated to do anything for me, like the brother I never had. While Jesse works, Claire and I cook breakfast. We all settle around to eat once he's done. Jo is now awake and sidled up close to Claire's side. When the doorbell rings, panic must show on my face, and Jesse offers to answer it. He re-enters the kitchen with Matthew trailing behind.

"Sorry, I forgot to tell you I texted Matthew to see if he could help out with getting stuff cleaned and boarded up," Jesse mumbles out.

Matthews speaks, "Sorry, my phone was turned off. Looks like you are all set. I just wanted to pop in and make sure you're okay. Unless you need something else, I'll head out."

"Thank you for coming by, Matthew. Would you like to join us for breakfast?" I offer. It's the least I can do after his willingness to help secure the house.

A smile graces his face, and he settles down in the empty seat to my other side. Claire grabs him a plate and cutlery, while I pour him coffee. We all spend a quick breakfast listening to Claire tell about a customer order she recently had. Soon after the plates are cleared, Matthew thanks me and leaves. He's polite and gracious during the whole event.

Claire invites Jo and me to stay at their house for a few days, just to settle back into our routine, but I decline. When this rental worked out, I chose it because it felt safe from the first time we toured it. The owner had no problem with Jesse making additional security upgrades, which also helped me with my anxiety. Those upgrades included the installation of a superior security system, and I couldn't imagine anywhere safer. While my faith in that safety was shaken from the intrusion, Detective Chase was confident the break-in was a one-off, and I know I also have to fight my paranoia from taking control of my life and Jo's life. This was an anomaly. We are safe. No one has found us here.

...I just may need to remind myself of that a little more than usual over the next few days.

Chapter Four

Almost immediately, Jo is back to herself, as if nothing happened. We can return to our routine and welcome in November. I decide to take her to work with me and let her skip preschool, as we have a slow week, and I want extra time with her. It was a long night too, and she's still tired from her interrupted sleep. That doesn't even get into my lingering worry, despite the assurances of the police that the break-in was random. I know they're probably right, but I don't want her away from me.

During the day, she helps me make a few arrangements for display, napping after lunch, which Claire dropped off for us with a brief stop. The events of the previous evening are buried in the back of my mind with Jo's company and my work. We have a few customers come in the shop over time, and Jo enjoys helping me direct them toward what they need. Customers always love when she's there, and we even have a few regulars who recognize her by name. It's not lost on me that it's exactly this kind of familiarity I've always tried to avoid, but I also know we can't hide completely. I recognize that my mind is constantly battling between fear and wanting to overcome that fear.

Jo's disappointed when I close up around five in the evening, so I offer to take her out for pizza as a special treat. Thirty minutes later, we're walking down the street, headed toward her favorite pizza shop, Eat Your Pie, a ten-minute jaunt away. It's another five-minute walk from there to our house. I love being able to walk to work and for food when the weather is decent. It's a little crisp tonight, leaves of burnt orange and crimson fluttering to the ground around us, but it's refreshing. Suddenly, the feeling of needles prickles across my neck, and I glance around nervously, sure that someone is watching us from some hidden location. No one obvious comes in sight, and I chalk it up to the stress of the previous night. Nevertheless, I pick up Jo so I can increase the pace to reach our destination

The frantic pacing of my heart has sped up from my hasty gait, while holding a rapidly growing child. I wish we had driven today, my arms regaining feeling from a lingering numbness after I set Jo on her feet at Eat Your Pie. We order the usual, a large cheese pizza, and as I turn around to find my seat, I nearly collide with someone. He reaches out and grabs my elbow to steady me, his hands rough with callouses. When I see who touches me, I jerk out of his grasp. It's Ciaran, from church and the flower shop, holding a pizza box. What is he doing here? I know he told Beatrice he just recently moved back, but while the town is somewhat small, it's not that small. What are the odds of running into him in my neighborhood? Is it merely coincidence that I felt like we were being watched, and then we run into him? Maybe it wasn't just my usual anxiety setting in. I've spent years trying to overcome my fear, but it still has a healthy grip on me. It's hard letting go of paranoia when it's so deeply rooted into your mind, when it's been like an extension of you for so long.

"I'm so sorry," he says, looking flushed. "I wasn't watching where I was going, and I'm just a big oaf." I notice his eyes flick down, taking in Jo standing next to me, before looking me in the eyes. "You look familiar. Have we met?" His face is clean-shaven today, but he's still handsome.

I try to plaster on a carefree look while positioning myself between Jo and this man, reaching down to put my hand on her back. "I believe you came into my flower shop the other day. I'm Sammi." I even extend my hand to shake his. Claire would be so proud of me. The best way to overcome the constant distrust is to try to be as normal as possible. At least, that's what I tell myself.

"It's nice to meet you, Sammi. I'm Ciaran. You have a great shop there, good employee. She was very helpful. She actually recommended trying this place for pizza." He seems unsure what to say next, hesitating with his lips slightly parted, but he doesn't have enough time to come up with words. Jo picks that time to break out of her sudden shyness and tell Ciaran her life story.

She peeks out from behind my leg, "My name's Jo. Who are you? Are you my mommy's friend? How old are you? You're really tall. I'm four. I'm not as tall as you or my mommy. Do you go to school?" She finally stops to take a breath, and Ciaran lets out a small chuckle. He glances toward me, eyes seeking permission to respond to Jo's questions. I give him a hesitant nod, my hand sliding from her back to grasp her arm.

He bends down to squat, putting himself at eye level with her, and I tighten my grip slightly. "Hi, Jo. I'm Ciaran. I just met your mommy, but maybe we can become friends someday. I'm an old man, almost thirty! I grew up here, but I lived away for a long time. I just moved back here a few weeks ago, and I don't know what to do around here nowadays. Maybe you have some ideas of cool places you could tell me about? I should let you and your mommy go eat for now, but it's been so nice to meet you. I'm sure I'll see you around sometimes, especially if you like to eat here. Pizza is my favorite!" With his last sentence, he ruffles her hair, and I yank her back by the arm.

"Ow, Mommy!" she cries out. I feel bad, but it's instinctive. I have to protect her, always. He stands, looking both curious and a little ashamed. He can tell he's clearly crossed a boundary. Just at that moment, someone at the counter calls out my name.

"Well, that's us. Welcome to town, Ciaran," I say, already turning to grab our pizza. I ask the teenager at the counter to box it. We'll take it home instead. I glance around to be sure Ciaran has left. We watch him get into a Jeep and drive away before we walk out the door. The brief walk home is fraught with tension, the pizza under one arm and my other hand wrapped tightly around Jo's. My eyes observe my surroundings the whole way home. I don't feel eyes on me again, but I'm happy to enter our house, lock the deadbolts behind me, and reset the alarm.

Jo and I both pick at our pizza at the table. My stomach churns with anxiety over the break-in last night, the encounter with Ciaran, and the fact I know Jo's still mad at me and rightfully so. The grease sets heavy in my belly and leaves a sour taste on my tongue. We have plenty of leftovers by the time I clean up the table. When bedtime comes, I kiss her forehead and give her an apology for hurting her earlier. She gives me a huge hug in response, her anger from the encounter dissipating. I read her a story from *Frozen*, and she's asleep before I read the last sentence.

The kitchen is clean, but I need to finish setting up for breakfast. A pang of nostalgia hits me, and I open my junk drawer in the kitchen to look for a long-buried photo of me with Lucas. It's the only photo I've kept upstairs. The few remainders are safely boxed and hidden in the basement. Jo hates the basement, and I'm not worried about her finding the photos and asking questions that I'm not ready to answer. There are even a few, rare photos of her with Lucas in there, though I made sure those were all at the bottom of the box. I definitely don't want to explain the photos of a strange man holding her awkwardly, full of resentment.

...I can't find the photo. It was definitely here, buried under notepads and pens. I dump the whole drawer, sifting through the contents. There's still no picture. I know I'm not imagining things. The photo is gone. Who took it? Why did they take it? When did they take it? Was it there when someone broke in last night? I return the spilled contents to the drawer and slide it back into the counter. Before going to bed, I jot a note on a post-it with my questions. I double check every lock for each door and window in the house before I trudge upstairs. Once there, I pull the sleeping bag from the closet in the unfurnished guest room and grab my pillow, settling myself on Jo's floor. I know I won't sleep away from her tonight.

I decide the next day to tell Claire about the picture. Maybe she's the one who dug it out, and it would certainly make me feel a little better if she was. I don't know why someone would break in to take one photo. How would they even know where it is? Who would break in? The only person that comes to mind is Lucas, but why now?

The photo is from before we were married, one of my favorites. My head was turned to gaze at him as he laughed at a joke, his mouth open. A huge smile covers my face, and I remember feeling overwhelmed with love for him in that moment. His sister, Amanda, snapped it while spending time with us one day after the first New Year's together. What I wouldn't give to go back to that day just for a few minutes. Life with Jo is good, and I wouldn't give her up for anything, but I often miss that feeling of romantic love. I miss that version of Lucas, the version that stole my heart.

The next day is Saturday, and Josef is scheduled to work, as usual. He's on the short side, his wavy dishwater blonde hair always perfectly styled and his nails trimmed. He wears dress slacks and a button-down shirt to work every shift, but I managed to convince him to ditch the tie after his first month working for me. I had planned to come in, bringing Jo with me, to help with some late orders, so first, I call him to ask if he can manage the orders without me. As expected, he enthusiastically tells me to enjoy the weekend. With that settled, I call Tina and ask if she can watch Jo for an hour or two. Since it's last-minute, I offer extra pay to sweeten the pot. Tina asks for thirty minutes to wrap up something, so I send Claire a text asking if I can come over shortly. She responds almost immediately with a yes, and I pull into her driveway twenty minutes after Tina arrives.

Claire and Jesse live just outside of town, on a vast farm that Jesse and his father run together, although Jesse has done more of the work since they moved back to the farm. They live in the sprawling, yellow farmhouse where Jesse grew up, settling in when Jesse graduated college. After a couple years of cohabitating, Jesse's parents relocated to a smaller ranch just a mile down the road, wanting something simpler and easier to maintain. Claire is standing at the screen door watching for me, worry spilled across her face. Somehow, she always knows when something is bothering me, even when she hasn't seen me or spoken with me. It's like a sixth sense that twins experience, only we aren't twins.

The direct route is usually the best route with Claire. She's not one to beat around the bush, and she tends to be rather blunt when it comes to my worries, which isn't to say that she's without compassion. Once we're seated, both of us with a cup of hazelnut coffee in front of us, I ask her if she happened to take the picture from the drawer for any reason. She and Jesse are the only ones with an extra key to the house and the code for the alarm. She assures me she hasn't and tells me I probably put it somewhere else and forgot. I'm sure I didn't, but I can tell from the look on her face that she has no doubts about my recollection being faulty. For a minute, I even start to doubt myself. Maybe I'm wrong. Maybe I moved it. I can't even remember the last time I looked at the photo. It could have been a week, a month, or several months ago. But deep inside, I know I'm not remembering incorrectly. That photo has sat in that drawer since the day Jo and I moved into the house.

Suddenly, I feel an urgent need to leave. I love Claire, and she's usually pretty patient with me, but I'm tired of her thinking I'm overreacting to everything. I'm paranoid, but I'm not delusional. I tell Claire I have to get back because Tina has a prior commitment. She knows I'm lying, but she doesn't call me on it. I think I'm home free when she mentions seeing a therapist. I don't know why I've been so hesitant to go to one. Maybe it's because my grandmother never went to one, despite all the loss and heartbreak in her life. Maybe it's because I don't want to hear someone else tell me I'm irrational. Most likely, it's because I'm afraid of actually dealing with things. I don't know that therapy would convince me that we are safe. Maybe nothing ever will.

"I'm fine, Claire. My memory is just a little shaky. Not everything is a sign of psychosis. I'll talk to you later." I manage to bite back harsher words as I turn and run for the door. I decide I won't talk to Claire for a while about anything that might make her question my sanity, even in the slightest bit. I can't deal with her skepticism right now. She means well, but she doesn't understand the trauma I experienced, and she doesn't understand why I'm still afraid that he might find me, find Jo.

As I drive home, I decide Jo and I should do something fun today. Maybe we should go to the new aquarium in the city. When I suggest the trip, she enthusiastically agrees and runs for her bedroom to change her outfit. After paying Tina for the full two hours and the extra I promised, I put together a few items, and Jo and I head out. It's going to be a great day. And it is. As we explore the various sea creatures, all the troubles of late are far from my mind. We're anonymous, just ghosts trailing through the massive building. We end the day in the shop, and Jo picks a stuffed crab for a souvenir, due to her love of the book, *Hello, Crabby!* We both sleep soundly that night, her crab curled under her arm. My mind, for once, is not overflowing with dreams – good or bad.

While Saturday is a wonderful experience for us both, we're running late for church on Sunday. The seats are nearly full when I walk in, and I end up in a chair further up than normal. As I walk up the aisle, I see Ciaran in the same place as he was last week. I hear a voice in my head, my grandmother, telling me to be calm and just trust. It's not the first time I've heard her, and she is usually spot on with whatever her ghost is whispering in my ear. I've kept each experience to myself, not needing another reason for people to think I'm unhinged. My skin chills as I walk by Ciaran, and through my peripheral vision, I can see him glance up at me. I keep walking, refusing to acknowledge him. All through service, I can feel his eyes on me. It's unnerving. Yet at one point, a thrill runs through me. My body is sending mixed signals. This is a man I shouldn't trust, but I think of Grandma Jolene's voice as I walked past him. Was she talking about him, or am I projecting?

When service ends, I walk quickly toward the back and look at Ciaran from the corner of my vision. He's turned away from me, talking to the Campbells, an elderly couple with a penchant for gossip. I hope they're not talking about me. Who knows what they'll tell him? They'd probably tell them all about the unstable, single mom who won't tell anyone anything about her past, and her beautiful daughter she keeps secluded, except at church, of course.

Chapter Five

Claire doesn't show up for our weekly lunch and doesn't text me. I try calling but get her voicemail. She must be mad about our conversation yesterday. Oh well. She runs hot and cold, and she usually calms down given a little space. Jo settles on the couch, watching *The Little Mermaid* while I clean up the kitchen. Listening to Ariel singing from the other room, I zone out, thinking of when Claire and Jesse were married. It was a happy time, simpler than life today, though not necessarily better. After all, Jo didn't exist yet. When Claire told me Jesse proposed, I knew that this relationship was different for her. This wasn't a fleeting romance. It was here to stay.

Claire didn't want to wait to marry Jesse. He proposed to her the same night that I lost my virginity to Lucas. They decided to tie the knot quickly, right after our freshman year ended. With Claire's history of a revolving door of boyfriends, I was surprised to see her get serious about Jesse so quickly, but I wanted her to be happy. And I could see that things were unique this time around. He wasn't like the guys she dated before. He worked, commuted from his childhood home to college, and seemed to be pretty steady. They made a plan to rent a studio apartment close to campus for his final year. Then, they'd decide what to do for her final two years. Of course, she never made it back for those final years.

By that point, Lucas and I had been dating for six months, and I couldn't help imagining my own future with him. We'd settled into a comfortable routine of me staying the night when his roommates were gone and catching stolen moments when my socially distant roommate had classes. The thought of not being with him was unfathomable to me. I wouldn't let it root into my subconscious and become a self-fulfilling prophecy.

The weather for the wedding was beautiful, which is never a guarantee with a Midwest spring. There were tulips everywhere, in bright colors of red, pink, and orange. The ceremony was outside, at a botanical garden. Claire asked me to be her maid of honor. As I looked into the crowd, my lilac colored dress draped over my body, I saw Lucas watching me stand at the altar, with absolute love in his eyes.

I cried when Claire and Jesse were announced as "husband and wife," my tears a mixture of sadness at the inevitable change in my relationship with Claire and happiness for her, for the future she always wanted but would never allow before. Part of why Claire and I became such fast friends was our shared sorrow. We both felt the pain of losing a parent, both parents in my case. Claire's mother didn't even come to the wedding, stuck in rehab after another drunk driving arrest. Grandma Jolene was a kind woman but stern enough to be a guiding force for us both. She was exactly the kind of person Claire needed, a parental figure for her. Grandma was beaming from the front row as Jesse slipped a wedding band onto Claire's finger.

While Lucas and I were serious, the wedding was the first time I introduced him to Grandma Jolene. We hadn't avoided it, but it just never worked out before that day. At the reception, while Lu-

cas went for drink refills, she approached me, "Lucas seems like a nice young man."

I laughed, "Yes, Grandma, he is. He's really great."

"Do you love him?" she asked. I nodded. "Make sure you make smart choices..."

We looked up to see Lucas approaching. "I love you, my girl." With that, she walked off and struck up a conversation with one of Jesse's uncles.

Later that night, as Lucas and I danced, someone tapped on my shoulder, requesting to cut in for a song. Lucas looked to me, and my eyes told him it was okay.

"I'm going to go ask your grandma to dance, Sammi. I'll be back shortly." He pressed a kiss to my forehead before walking in her direction.

I hadn't seen Matthew since September, though I knew he had agreed to be Jesse's best man. He had his own date to the wedding, a gorgeous, tall, and willowy brunette, who looked like a model. I checked but didn't see her around. As the song played, I placed my hand in Matthew's, and he rested his hand against my waist. We made small talk, him telling me about his plans to join his father in business after graduation and of all the travel he'd be taking. I didn't say much. There wasn't silence for me to fill in the blanks, as Matthew was content to ramble on.

I could see Lucas dancing with my grandma, her laughing at something he must have said. When the song ended, he came back to find me, and the three of us walked from the dance floor together. I made the introductions between the two of them, and they shook hands before Matthew excused himself to return to his date.

Later that night, as we squeezed into my childhood twin bed, I asked Lucas what he and my grandmother discussed during their dance.

"Oh, not much. I told her about that time we went ice skating, and you kept falling. For some reason, she found your complete lack of coordination hilarious." He paused. "...So, did you date Matthew?"

I had to stop myself from laughing at his question. "Matthew? No, we went on one date the first month of school. It was a disaster. I told you I didn't really date before. Besides, I was already in love with someone else."

"Is that so?" he asked. "Lucky guy." He tugged me closer to him, and I leaned down to kiss him. He pulled back to take a breath. "You know he likes you, right? I saw the way he looked at you while the two of you were dancing."

I laughed wholeheartedly this time. "Did you see his date? Trust me, Matthew is not interested in me. Now, kiss me before I go crazy."

There in that tiny, twin bed, we made love, but something was different this time. I couldn't pinpoint what it was. As I drifted off to sleep later that night, exhaustion overtaking, I couldn't help wondering if Lucas was right about Matthew.

The song from *The Little Mermaid* cuts off, and I snap back to reality. Jo's dozed off on the couch in the few moments I was lost in my head. My phone chimes, and I take a peek to find a text from Claire, with an apology. Jesse's mom tripped and broke her ankle while Jesse and his dad were out of town at an auction, and Claire took her to the hospital. Turns out, Claire isn't mad after all. I should know better. She's never held a grudge in the entire time I've known her, except for when Billy Myer told me in seventh grade that I needed to go on a diet, or no one would ever want to date me, especially since I was an orphan already. She never did forgive him.

I decide to make a manicotti to take over later, for Jesse's parents. William "Bill" and Susan Knight were always kind to Jo and me, never questioning when we were included in their family's events. I'll make one for Claire too. She's always been there, anytime my grandmother was hurt or sick, or I needed her for anything else.

Shortly before Grandma Jolene passed, Lucas and I took a weekend trip to Branson, on a rare weekend we were both free. While we were gone, my grandmother fell while walking to the car and broke her hip. She never told me she was having balance issues, and I felt terrible that I was so far away from her. Thankfully, she had her cell phone to ring for help, and she had the hospital call Claire, after being brought to the emergency room via ambulance. Later, she told me that she didn't want to worry me or ruin my trip.

Claire called me anyway and insisted I finish the weekend vacation, per Grandma Jolene's request. I didn't, leaving Branson as soon as our bags were packed, urging Lucas to drive faster. I felt better on the drive back knowing Claire was already there, that she would do everything to take care of my grandmother.

I spent the first week after my grandma's fall watching over her, using her car to drive between her home and the hospital, then the rehabilitation center. Lucas had to return to St. Louis for work and classes, but my professors were surprisingly kind, allowing me to send in assignments via email. Even my boss told me to take whatever time I needed. Claire came to visit after her classes every day, returning to her tiny apartment late in the evening. I knew I'd have to get back to campus and regular life, and Claire assured me that she would take care of Grandma Jolene in my absence. My grandmother insisted I return to normal life, and it was with a heavy heart that I headed back to the big city. My plan was to come home to see her whenever I got a break with classes and my part-time job. Lucas and I discussed temporarily moving her in with us when she was released from the rehabilitation center. I didn't have a chance to broach that subject with her or even tell her that I had moved in with Lucas. She never left the rehabilitation center, an aneurysm killing her instantly before I could even make my first weekend trip back to see her.

Halfway through my sophomore year, Lucas had started talking more seriously about the future. One of his roommates had proposed to his girlfriend and wanted both Lucas and their third roommate to find somewhere else to live, so that his fiancée could move in. Lucas didn't want to move back in to his parents' house, but he wasn't sure what to do with one semester left. I remembered seeing a "For Rent" sign on a complex near my dorm that didn't look like it would be too expensive and mentioned it to him. It wasn't the fanciest place, but it would keep him close to finish out the year. He'd been working for several years at a grocery store a few blocks away, and they had already offered him an Assistant Manager position once he graduated and could commit to full-time. I had been picking up a few shifts at a floral shop across from campus. Since his parents had already warned him the financial support would end once he graduated, he'd need somewhere cheap to live soon. The cheapest places were near campus. He wouldn't be supporting himself as a full-time author as he dreamed, but he'd be able to write when he was off, with the goal of publishing his first book. I went with him to tour an apartment after my classes one day, and as we laid in his bed that night, he leaned up on one elbow to peer down at my face.

"Why don't you move in with me?" I stared at him, waiting for the sparkle of mirth in his eyes, but he was dead serious.

"Are you for real? Won't your parents freak out? We've been together over a year, but I've only been around them a handful of times, and they don't even like me. They still expect you to get back together with Rebecca." My relationship with his parents was rocky, at best. I wasn't sure how they'd feel about Lucas moving in with his girlfriend that was still in college and barely helping pay the bills.

Amanda had told me that Rebecca was engaged to someone slightly older, some sort of banker, but I hadn't told Lucas that I knew. It didn't mean that his parents didn't still want him to get back together with her. Surely, he could see the fault in this half-cocked plan. Elizabeth and Christopher ran in a different circle than me. To be fair, so did Lucas until he decided to make his own path.

"Oh yeah, I've been meaning to talk to you about that. My parents asked about all of us doing something this weekend, as in two days. I already told them we'd meet them for dinner on Saturday. I have the early shift that day. Hope that's okay. It's not that they don't like you. My parents are just different, reserved. But they've finally decided we're serious enough to make more of an effort to get to know you. Tell me you're cool with this," he pleads.

Amanda and I had hung out several times when Lucas was working. She was only sixteen, almost six years younger than Lucas, and she already had plans to follow in her big brother's footsteps after graduation. She had accepted me in his life, but his parents had never indicated any interest in getting to know me, more than a casual greeting and stilted interactions at family dinners and get-togethers. I figured I'd always be the outcast, even if

Lucas and I got married. I'd always be the poor girl without any parents. Oh well, there was no time like the present.

"Yes, to both," I replied. I already knew I wanted to marry this man. It was time to make nice with his parents. They'd be my in-laws after all, if things went the way I hoped.

"Awesome. I'll call them tomorrow and confirm. And I have good news. My application for the apartment was approved. I didn't want to tell you that I already looked at it and applied. I just went back today so you could see it. We can move in after New Year's."

I thought he was asking me to move in at the end of the school year. My grandmother would freak out, and my boarding expenses were already paid. I decided to keep my address at the dorm but unofficially move in with Lucas. I could tell her closer to the end of term that I'd be moving in with him, and she'd never have to know that I had been living, unwed, for months with him. Though, she wouldn't be happy about us living together in sin, regardless of when it happened. The fact we shared a bed when we went back for Claire's wedding was enough of a controversy.

A few weeks later, in early January, we moved into our very own third floor walk-up apartment. My roommate that year in the dorm was never home, just a random person who was assigned to the room, and I spent so much time with Lucas that I never really made any other friends. There was no one on campus to notice that I never slept there, and I simply picked up my mail between classes, using my dining card to eat meals when Lucas was at work. There was a slight odor of cigarettes that permeated the walls of our new home, and the pipes had a habit of groaning anytime someone in the building took a shower, but I couldn't care less. This was our first home together. It was the start of our new life.

Just a few months later, at the beginning of that March, was when Grandma Jolene had her fall. That little, first apartment is where I intended her to live with us. Lucas would have had to help her getting into or out of the building, but she'd have me there to take care of her. She wouldn't need to leave for anything. Lucas was surprisingly on board with the idea of her living there, although I had no idea how I was going to tell her that I was living with him in the first place.

I never had the chance to tell her. She never had a chance to see the apartment. I still wonder how she would have reacted to the news, if perhaps she would have been okay with it. During that trip to Branson, before I got the call from Claire late on Saturday, I felt a stirring in my bones, anticipation winding itself through my body. Without knowing why, I knew this was a change from simply living together to something more. What I didn't realize was that it was the beginning of the end. And every time I walked past the open door to the second bedroom where I had envisioned my grandmother sleeping, until the day I left, I thought of her.

Lucas finished out the year, earning his Bachelor of Science in Business Administration as his father demanded, while still pursuing a minor in creative writing, much to his father's chagrin. With my grandmother gone, I stopped going by the dorm or using my meal plan, and I picked up more hours at work to help pay the bills. She left me her house, but Lucas helped me sell it, and I used the proceeds to help pay for my last two years of college. Boonville was no longer my life. My life was in St. Louis, with Lucas.

Chapter Six

The next week passes predictably. Jo goes to preschool each day, and I work open to close each weekday. Tina helps out until I get home every night, even cooking dinner several evenings for Jo and me. To my surprise, Claire shows up to church on Sunday. We're a little early, meeting her at the door. As people filter in, I spy Ciaran as he walks next to a woman who looks remarkably like him. This must be his sister, Fiona, that Beatrice mentioned. She has beautiful, long, black hair hanging down to her hips, with the same shade of green eyes that highlight Ciaran's face. An emerald-green wrap dress accents her full-figured body and brings out her eyes. Claire sees me staring like an idiot and turns to look.

"Who is that? Do you know her? Good heavens, Jo looks exactly like her!" Claire blurts out.

Ouch. I don't want to think about the similarity between Ciaran, his sister, and Jo. It hits a little too close to home for me. I hesitate, thinking before replying, "Um, I don't really see it. Ciaran, the man with her, came in the shop the other day. Beatrice told me about his family. I think she's his sister."

My voice turns up a little at the end, like I'm asking a question. As a pang of jealousy hits me, I have to admit that I want this woman to be his sister. I'm not prepared to think about what that means. I'm not attracted to Ciaran, am I? ...Okay, yes, I do find him attractive, but I'm not even sure what that means. Where is Grandma Jolene's voice when I need her input?

All Claire manages to get out before service starts is, "Ciaran, huh? He's cute." I know she must be biting back what she really wants to say, a smirk crossing over her face. He is more than cute. If I picture him, parts of my body light up, which have long been dark.

It takes a tremendous amount more effort than I anticipate to avoid turning around to look at Ciaran and Fiona. Throughout the service, I can feel his eyes on me once again, and my body tingles. There's Grandma Jolene's voice now, distracting me and telling me, once again, to trust. Trust who? Myself? Ciaran? She needs to give me a little more information.

Today is a special day, and my baby girl, along with other kids from Sunday school, comes in toward the end to sing a few songs they've been practicing. Ciaran slips from my mind when I see Jo standing on the stage, joy radiating from her. My heart swells to near bursting. She's so much more outgoing and sociable than I ever was, something she could easily have in common with Lucas. She smiles out at the crowd. A few moments later, she lifts her hand in a wave. I raise my own to wave back, but I realize she's not looking at me. When I follow her line of sight behind me, I find Ciaran beaming at her, giving her a return wave. This is going to be trouble. I don't know him well enough to trust him, whether Grandma is whispering in my ear about it or not. My body may be a traitor, responding to him in ways that have been deeply buried, but my mind says to slow down. Jo's never once asked about her dad, other than the incident at school, but even at four, she has to realize how similar she looks to Ciaran, how different from me. She's never seen a picture of Lucas, and while I've never hidden that I was married, it's never really been discussed between us either. I have no engagement ring or wedding band hidden away for her to find, both left on the dresser the day I walked out. My gaze flicks over to Fiona, and I see her look between Ciaran's face and Jo's shrewdly. Then, her head turns, and she locks eyes with me, a smile dancing across her features. It's not unkind, but her eyes are wise, telling me she sees things that most people would miss. I flush and smoothly whip back around just as the music begins. Maybe Ciaran pointed Jo and me out when the kids came in to the auditorium. There's no doubt that Fiona has some idea of who I am.

Even though all the children are singing together, I can hear Jo's voice ringing through the building. I'd be able to pick out her voice anywhere. Even when she was a baby and would cry around other babies, I could always tell which cry was hers. We are linked, she and I. When the children finish singing, we bow our heads to pray. Then, the children are slowly released to their parents in the audience, staff members aware of which child belongs with which parents. That's the thing about a town like this. You're only completely anonymous in large crowds. Jo leaps into my arms, while Claire and I pour praise onto her for her performance. She glows, rightfully proud of herself. I set her down, the two of us shrugging on our coats. As we turn to leave, Ciaran walks up behind us, but I don't even notice his approach until he speaks.

"Sammi, right? And Jo? You did an amazing job up there. You're a natural performer."

"Hi, Ciaran!" Jo replies, stumbling slightly over his name, pronouncing it as "Key-wren". He obviously made an impression on her at Eat Your Pie. "This is my Auntie Claire," she nearly shouts, reaching out her arms for Claire to hold her now. She turns to Fiona and blurts out, "Wow, you're really pretty. Are you Ciaran's girlfriend?" ...That's my girl, no filter whatsoever.

Ciaran chuckles and coughs, "It's nice to meet you, Auntie Claire. Jo, this is my sister, Fiona. Fiona, Sammi owns the flower shop that did Mam's funeral, and this is her daughter, Jo."

Fiona shakes hands with all of us, a broad smile on her face as she exchanges pleasantries. "It's nice to meet all of you. Sammi, you did a wonderful job with the flowers for Mam's funeral. It meant so much to us. And Jo, you're too sweet. You're a great singer. I hope you keep performing." Jo seems enraptured with her. She's just as polite as she is beautiful. I can see the beginning of lines around her mouth and eyes. I'm guessing she's slightly older than her brother.

Claire interjects as she's shaking Ciaran's hand, "It's nice to meet you both." I expect more from her, but she doesn't continue.

There's a beat of awkward silence, and I take it as my cue. "Well, it was nice to see you again, Ciaran, and to meet you, Fiona. We have to get to lunch, but I'm sure we'll see you around town." We all bid our goodbyes, and Claire heads for the door in front of me, Jo still in her arms. She's been suspiciously quiet, which usually means her brain is firing on all cylinders. I can only imagine what she's thinking, but something tells me I'll find out soon enough.

Claire follows us back to the house in her own car. When we arrive, Jesse is waiting in the driveway. I forgot he was going to come over and join us for lunch today. Someone else opens the passenger door, and as he straightens, I realize Matthew has come along as well. He wasn't invited, but I don't want to be rude. He was perfectly polite the other day and there was no hint of any unreciprocated romantic feelings between us. Since he's been around so much, maybe I need to make more of an effort to actually be friends with him.

Jo asks Jesse if he'd like to play *Zingo* with her, her current favorite, and then invites Matthew to join them. While they're busy, Claire helps me in the kitchen, and I observe through the entryway, silently noticing how easily Matthew gets along with Jo. I didn't really expect us to be friends, but maybe we can be. He could be another positive male influence in her life.

It's times like this that I am both most grateful for my friends and most miss having a partner. Turning my attention fully to lunch, I pull out the prepared spinach and artichoke chicken bake that Claire had popped into the oven to warm. Matthew sticks his head in the kitchen and graciously offers to set the table, then says a prayer before we eat. For a brief moment, it almost feels like he's a part of the family.

We're silent as we dig in to the meal, Jesse shoveling in several mouthfuls like he hasn't eaten in days. Claire is a good cook, but she tells me all the time that Jesse loves when she brings him food that I've cooked. He pipes up a few bites in to the meal, "How was church today? Sorry I couldn't make it. I had to help mom with a few things since she can't walk." Jesse rarely comes to church, but it's never been an issue for me.

I open my mouth to respond, but Claire beats me to the punch. "We ran into some guy that I think has a little crush on our Sammi. He's a doll. I think she should ask him on a date." I can't believe she brought him up. Even though Matthew seems okay with the way things are between us, it rubs me as callous.

His head whips up from his plate at this news. "Who is this guy? Do any of us know him?" When we all look at him curiously, he adds, "Sammi's got to be careful, you know, having Jo and all." It's a logical thought, but I still get the feeling a part of his reaction is jealousy.

Jo pipes up, "Ciaran is SO nice. I'm so glad he's my friend now."

I need to nip this conversation in the bud, before Jo gets the wrong idea about Ciaran. He is not her friend. We've barely spoken to him. And Matthew's outburst isn't helping. I don't want her to get the wrong impression about him either.

"He came in to the shop the other day, and we ran into him at Eat Your Pie. Claire's being dramatic. He's just a nice guy. He does not have a crush on me. We barely know each other." For Jo's ears, I add, "We're not even friends at this point. Now, can we talk about something else? Claire, you said you needed to talk to me about something."

Jesse interjects, "I know who he is... Ciaran MacDonald. Ciaran isn't exactly a common name around here. I've actually met him. He was down at the feed store the other day, and I was having trouble loading the truck. He was walking by and offered to help. Didn't talk to him much, but he seems like a decent guy. He used to play basketball in high school, you know? I didn't recognize him at first since he's a little older, but he played for the Catholic school." Jesse pauses before continuing. "But yeah, Claire and I do need to talk to both of you. Claire, you want to jump in here?" He returns to his meal, his brief contribution to the conversation over. He always has been a man of few words.

Looking over, I see Claire is positively radiant, and my heartbeat speeds up, recognizing good news is on the horizon.

"Well, you know Jesse and I have been trying to have a baby for a long time. It's been difficult for me to accept, but even I have to admit at this point that it's not likely to happen for us, not biologically. That's why we decided to look in to adoption. ...We finally got our application approved!"

She mentioned about a month ago that they had started the process quite some time before, but she hasn't said much about it since then, and she's cut off any attempts I've made to bring it up. She's been pretty quiet about the whole thing, afraid of jinxing herself.

She continues, "We met with a mother last week. I didn't say anything because I was afraid of being disappointed again. We got a call yesterday. She picked us! We're going to have a baby, a boy, around Christmas!" Claire is crying now, and even Jesse looks like he's on the verge of tears. He's silent and stoic most of the time, but I know how much he adores this woman who is so much like a sister to me.

Jo starts screaming about having a cousin, and I offer my congratulations, my own tears brimming over the surface. Claire has wanted a child for so long, and her dream is finally coming to fruition. I jump up to hug her, and she chokes back a sob, speaking again, "The reason we wanted to have lunch with both of you today is to ask the two of you to be Godparents to the baby. If anything happens to us, we want him to always feel loved and special. Jesse's parents are getting up there to have a young child, and we couldn't think of anyone we'd trust more with our child."

"Of course, Claire!" I feel like I'm overflowing with excitement. Almost immediately, as I move to hug her again, another thought hits me. What if we don't stay around here? Would Claire ever forgive me?

Matthew moves over to give Claire a hug of his own. "Jesse, Claire, I'm honored you would ask. Of course, Sammi and I will be the Godparents. We'll treat your son like our own."

Claire is still beaming, and Jo is hugging Jesse, but I can't help being perturbed that Matthew answered as if he was speaking for both of us. I'm sure I'm being overly sensitive. It just rubs me the wrong way. Once the initial excitement dies down, Claire spends the rest of lunch telling us her plans for a nursery and some of the names they are considering. With her chatter, time flies.

As I start to clean up plates, Claire asks if I care if she leaves. They have plans to go to Jesse's parents' next and share their happy news. I'm surprised they haven't told them, but I am touched that Claire wanted to tell me first. I'm not bothered that they leave, but Matthew offers to stick around to help clean up. He doesn't have a vehicle here. I assure him he's okay to go with them, but he insists he can call an Uber.

We spend the next hour cleaning dishes, sweeping up crumbs, and tidying the rest of the kitchen. I put some Margo Price on my phone and let it play, reducing the need for meaningless chatter. I have to admit, it's nice to have the help. Now that Matthew and I will be Godparents, I need to continue making an effort to establish a solid friendship with him. Jo sits at the table and colors while we're busy. When the last dish is dried and put away, I turn to offer Matthew a ride. It's a small gesture of kindness after he stayed behind to help. I got my shirt wet while doing dishes and run upstairs to change. When I return, Matthew is holding a picture of a butterfly that Jo drew for him, promising her it will have a special place on his fridge.

Once I load Jo into the car, I follow his verbal instructions to find his house. It's about ten minutes away, in a nice but moderately priced area of town. When I pull into the driveway of a two-story Craftsman style house, I'm more than a little surprised. I never took him for the type to live in a place like this, figuring he'd have a fancy condo somewhere or a McMansion in the hills. I got the impression on our date that he was a bit of a snob about his success, but maybe I misinterpreted. I put the car in park, leaving it running.

"Do you want to come in for a coffee? It's still early. We can talk a little more," he suggests, with a hopeful note in his voice. "I can let Jo pick a spot on the fridge for her picture."

It's not late, but I'm not quite ready for our friendship to include a visit to his house, especially when Jo is with me. "Oh, thank you. I appreciate the help and the offer, but we need to get home so Jo can follow her evening routine. She's a creature of habit, you know." I trail off, uncomfortable with this turn in the conversation. He seems a little disappointed, but he maintains his polite demeanor.

"I understand. Thanks for lunch, Sammi. You're a great cook. I'm glad we're getting to be friends. I'll see you later. Bye, Jo," he calls as he opens the door.

"Bye, Matthew," I say as he's shutting the door. Friends? I hope so.

Chapter Seven

The next two weeks are hectic. We have an uptick in orders leading up to Thanksgiving, which is normal. It's not our busiest time of year, but it keeps us active enough. Jo's preschool is still in session, and I'm thankful more than ever for Tina, as I find myself running late nearly every night.

The first week goes quietly and smoothly, but on the weekend, Jo comes down sick. The pediatrician squeezes her in on Saturday, and she diagnoses Jo with an ear infection and a cold. It seems like this is a recurrent event around the same time every year for us. We miss church Sunday for the first time in a long time, and I cancel our weekly lunch with Claire. Thankfully, Beatrice and Josef both say they can cover Monday, so I can be home with Jo an extra day. She's a tough kid, but she seems to struggle to recover anytime she's under the weather.

Claire comes to my aid on Tuesday and Wednesday, staying at my house with Jo, who still seems exceptionally tired. This bout with illness has really taken it out of her, but she's lively enough to go back to school on Thursday and Friday. Other than still being a bit on the fatigued side, she's pretty much back to herself, with no other lingering symptoms. We spend the weekend buying materials for crafts for Claire's annual

Thanksgiving dinner. Jo likes to use the craft kits she finds in the store to make small tokens for everyone. Her love language is definitely gifts.

Despite Jo's illness and the busier than normal schedule, it manages to be a pleasant two weeks. My stress level is way down, and things feel normal, at least, as normal as they can ever be. Once again, we skip church on Sunday. I don't want to risk Jo catching something else and ruining her holiday. Jesse and Claire have plans to go to lunch today with Jesse's older brother. He lives in Colorado and doesn't stay in touch much with the family. He comes into town once a year, right around Thanksgiving, and they all do an uncomfortable family meal. The age difference between the two brothers is fifteen years. Jesse was an unplanned, late in life baby.

Before I know it, it's the Tuesday before Thanksgiving. Jo's preschool is on a holiday break, and Tina can't watch her this week. She's headed home to spend the holiday with her parents, so Jo spent yesterday with Claire out at the farm. She's with me today, though. Claire has to take Susan for an appointment this afternoon. She pops into the shop early to pick up a wreath for Susan before the appointment. While there, she strikes up a conversation with Josef. Beatrice is off this week to spend the holiday in New York with her daughter. The bell dings, and I leave Jo in my office to help the newly arrived customer. Their face is hidden in a shadow from the sun shifting behind clouds. He turns when I step from the hallway, and I find myself looking into Ciaran's eyes. I haven't seen him since our last run-in at church. My heart skips a beat in excitement before I recover, stepping forward to greet him. Pull yourself together, Sammi. Down girl.

As I stumble over a hello, the bell rings again. Josef breaks off from Claire to greet one of our regular customers, and Claire saunters over to stand next to me.

"Hi, Ciaran. It's nice to see you again, been awhile. I heard you helped out my husband a few weeks ago. Do you remember Jesse Knight?"

"Auntie Claire, nice to see you too. I do remember your husband. He seemed like a nice guy. He told me the best place to get a Guinness around here." He smiles at this and turns to me, "Sammi, how are you? I just need to get a small arrangement. I'm taking my dad to see Mam's grave today."

I don't even have a chance to speak. Claire takes over any conversation as if she's worked here for years. "Of course, I'm so sorry about your mother. Is Fiona going with you all?" Alarm bells are ringing in my head. She's up to something.

"No, Fiona has decided to take a weeklong vacation to Playa del Carmen with her boyfriend. She came into town this past weekend for an early Thanksgiving, but we won't see her again until Christmas. She lives about an hour away." His face tells me all I need to know. Fiona's absence for Thanksgiving is an issue between them and likely has been for quite some time.

"Well, I'm hosting Thanksgiving this year. We have a little farm just outside of town. You should come. Your dad is welcome too. My in-laws will be there, and Sammi and Jo, of course. Our friend, Matthew, is also coming with his girlfriend. It'll be a huge celebration." She shoots me an apologetic glance. Not only is this the first time I'm hearing that Matthew is coming with a girlfriend I didn't know about, she just invited a near stranger to Thanksgiving.

"Wow, that's a really nice offer. I'd need to ask my dad, but I'm sure he'd be happy to come. Is there anything we can bring?"

He accepted her invitation? Maybe I should cancel and stay home with Jo. I can fake a cold. I turn to walk back to the cooler, while Claire and Ciaran discuss the meal. I pause as I see Jo standing silently in the entry to the hallway. She has an odd look on her face as she watches the three of us, and I know I can't cancel. Jo thrives on being around other people, and she loves Thanksgiving at Claire's. We've gone every year since we moved here. It's our tradition. Even if she didn't hear Claire's invitation or Ciaran's acceptance, she wants to go. I can't break her heart. It's just one meal, and we'll be surrounded by other people.

After ringing up Ciaran's purchase, he gets directions from Claire, and they both leave. I don't get a chance to bring up her impromptu invitation with her as she laughs on her way out and calls back to me, "He's got it bad for you, girl."

I'm taking off this afternoon to get groceries for my taro root stuffing and Dutch apple pie. Josef has no problem closing up, and we're only open a half day tomorrow. We drove today given the chillier weather, and Jo and I make the trip to the other side of town to go to Whole Foods. As I drive, a small, dark pick-up truck follows me, too close for me to be comfortable. The tint on the windows prevents me from seeing the driver, but I feel a chill. Half convinced I'm right to be concerned and half convinced I'm paranoid, I pull into the lot of the shopping complex. I won't stop if the pick-up turns in behind me. I'm convinced it's a man. The truck screams of testosterone. He's been behind me – turn for turn, for blocks, and I can't see the plates. When the driver passes the turn into the complex, I let out a breath. Paranoia for the win... I need to get a grip.

An hour and a quick snack at the in-store café later, Jo and I are in the car, prepared to leave. As I'm pulling out of my parking spot, I see a small, dark pick-up idling in a spot at the end of the row. From this angle, I can't see the plates on the vehicle, and I don't want to get close enough to look. My sixth sense is screaming at me to get out of there. The truck definitely wasn't there when we went in to the store, and I can see the exhaust dispersing into the air. Something tells me not to pass whoever it is, so I pull out the opposite way. The truck tears out of the spot in the other direction, and I think I'm overreacting again until it pulls in behind me to approach the turn from the complex. I'm already committed to turning right, back in the direction of our home. I hold my breath until I see the truck move into the lane to turn left toward the interstate. Despite the relief flooding my body, I still find myself pushing down on the accelerator. I've got to calm myself down. We're in a suburb of a large city. How many dark pick-up trucks are registered in this county alone? It's just a coincidence.

I push it from my mind and don't think about it again until Thanksgiving morning. I've already loaded the stuffing and pie, cushioned into my trunk and carefully buffeted by towels to prevent them moving around. The car is sitting in the driveway, instead of the garage. Jo and I walk out the front door to head to Claire's farm, locking the door behind us, and I notice something sitting on my porch – a bottle of La Marca Prosecco. It's the same prosecco I glanced at in the store, but I returned to the shelf. I feel like I can't breathe, my eyes darting around for an intruder, but the street is eerily quiet. There's not another soul in sight.

Hastily, I let Jo into the car with her backpack and leave her to fasten her own buckle, hopping into my seat. I slam the door and hit the locks. I need to get away from here, right NOW! Going back into the house doesn't feel safe. From the security of the car, I use my phone camera's zoom feature to snap a photo of the bottle, before hitting the gas to back out of the driveway. It wasn't there when I loaded the car, and only a brief, few minutes had passed. When did someone drop it off? I stopped short of putting up outside cameras when upgrading the security of the house, and now I'm wishing I hadn't.

My hands shake the whole way to Claire's, my eyes continuously flashing between my mirrors, watching for a dark pickup truck or any other questionable vehicles. My bagel from this morning threatens to make a second appearance, and I have to take deep breaths the entire drive there, thankful that Jo is distracted with *Frozen* on her DVD player.

Jesse is outside when we pull in, about to head over to his parents'. He needs to help them with a few tasks and wants to make sure his mom gets to their car without any problems. I feel an instant sense of relief when I see him. I didn't spot anyone appearing to follow me. However, if there was someone, they surely wouldn't stop with Jesse standing in the drive. Before he leaves, he unloads Jo and carries her inside, while I grab the food. We're still in the entryway when a small beagle runs up to us, jumping on our legs and trying to lick Jo with a pale-pink, wriggly tongue.

"Sorry," Jesse says as he pulls the puppy back. "Surprise! This is Oliver. What do you think, Jo?"

"Hi, Oliver!... I love him, Uncle Jesse. Can I play with him?"

Jo is more than happy to entertain the new pet, and Jesse slips out again as Claire comes around the corner from the kitchen. A Looney Tunes apron, made years ago in our junior high home economics class, is tied around her waist.

"Will she be okay in here playing with the dog?" I ask. Claire tells me not to worry and motions for me to follow her into the kitchen. I hesitate a moment, but decide that it will be okay for a couple minutes. It's only a few steps from the room where Jo is playing to the kitchen. I can still hear Jo's laughter and the excited yips from Oliver. "When did you get a dog?"

"Surprised? Me too. Jesse brought him home Tuesday. They were waiting when I got here from dropping Susan back at her house. It's amazing how easily he's woven himself into our lives." She pauses, reflection and amusement written on her face. "What's up? You seem troubled," she adds.

I know I had decided not to tell Claire about anything that might make her question my grip on reality, but it seems like the truck and the prosecco are worth mentioning.

"I've had a weird week... Jo and I went to Whole Foods on Tuesday to get some groceries. The whole way there, some asshole in a pick-up was riding my tail." I'm watching her face as I speak, and I can see that she's questioning my point.

Taking a breath, I continue, "I chalked it up to a shitty driver, but when we left, there was an identical or very similar truck, idling at the end of the row I parked in. They left when we did, but they turned the other way, toward the interstate."

She's still distracted, fluttering around and moving things in the kitchen. She doesn't think anything is serious at this point.

"While at the store, I looked at some prosecco. I thought it might be nice to have for today, for all of us to toast new beginnings. But I put it back. No big deal. Then, this morning, the exact same brand of prosecco was sitting on the porch. It was left sometime between me loading the food and us actually leaving the house. It was maybe ten minutes, at most." At this, her attention snaps back to me. I hold up my phone, flashing her the photo of my front porch.

She opens her mouth, but it's a moment before she begins to speak. "There was no note or anything with it? Are you sure it was the same kind? Maybe you just remember seeing it and convinced yourself it was the same. Or maybe a neighbor dropped it by for the holiday, and it's just a coincidence." Her tone is flat. She's trying to come across as calm and collected, but this freaks her out a little bit. For once, maybe she doesn't think it's all in my head.

"No, it was just sitting there. I didn't see anyone around. I barely talk to the neighbors, but wouldn't they just ring the doorbell? It's creepy. ...What if someone was really following me? What are the chances of the exact same kind of wine being left on my porch?" My voice spirals higher and higher, louder and louder, and I cringe, not wanting Jo to overhear.

"Let me talk to Jesse and get his opinion. You know that he would do anything to keep you and Jo safe. If he's worried, then we'll figure out next steps. Maybe you and Jo should stay here tonight, just to be safe. It would probably make you feel better. I can make up the bed in the guest room."

I consider her offer. I'm stubborn. Sure, I'm majorly shaken right now, but there's a small part of me that fights back. It's a new sensation, this need to defend what's mine, beyond protecting my daughter. I've never been so determined to stay before, and I have the fleeting thought that perhaps Ciaran has something to do with this sudden change in my personality. I've spent my whole life being passive, but I don't want to be that person anymore. Besides, I don't have any clothes or toiletries, and I have to work tomorrow morning. Jo was supposed to come spend the day with Claire, so maybe it would be good for her to have a night here. I can go home and think about everything on my own. If I have a panic attack later, Jo wouldn't be home to witness it. Claire keeps a few extra outfits and some toiletries for Jo, for when she stays over. I agree to at least talk to Jesse later and ask if we can focus on something else, so we spend the next hour cooking together.

Jo comes in to join us. After she washes her hands, Claire sets her down to roll out and cut cookies. I'm feeling calmer already. Claire's presence and the comfort of cooking cause me to lose track of time until the doorbell rings. There's a hitch in my breathing. My fear is ever-present, but until the doorbell, it was simply simmering in the background. Claire steps away to answer, and I hold my breath. A minute later, I hear her welcome Matthew, followed by Ciaran and his dad. They must have all arrived around the same time. I motion Jo to join me, and we round the corner to extend our own greetings.

Claire makes awkward introductions, "Matthew, Ciaran, hi. Have you two met?"

The men shake hands, Ciaran's face an open book. He's friendly and approachable, seemingly eager at the opportunity to make a new friend. Matthew's face is a different story. He's polite, but it's clear he has no interest in Ciaran's presence. It's uncomfortable, but Ciaran doesn't seem to be bothered.

Matthew speaks up and gestures to the woman next to him. She's not much taller than me, full-figured but athletic. Her hair is clearly dyed blond, her dark eyebrows standing out against the color, and she has a deep tan that screams of a spray bottle. There's no denying that she's pretty, but it's not really the type of person I expected Matthew to bring.

"Ladies, this is my girlfriend, Vanessa. Vanessa, this is Claire, Jesse's wife. Back there is Sammi, and the little one is her daughter, Jo." Vanessa smiles and moves forward to shake hands." Matthew looks at Ciaran again. "It's nice to meet you, Ciaran," he says.

Ciaran smiles in return, "Everyone, this is my father, Fergus MacDonald. Dad, this is everyone."

He glances up at me, locking eyes, "Hi, Sammi." His singling me out doesn't go unnoticed, and a dark look flashes across Matthew's face, but he remains silent.

I look to the man next to Ciaran. They look similar, though Fergus is much shorter than Ciaran, perhaps five-foot-nine, around Claire's height, which is also close in height to Matthew. Fergus has dark hair, sprinkled with salt and pepper, and his dark brown eyes speak volumes, reflecting a life full of happiness but also loneliness. He wears a huge grin as he looks from face to face. ...I'm glad they came. I have the feeling that Fergus needs this interaction more than any of us.

"Please, call me Fergus, or Pop, or anything else you want, just not Mr. MacDonald. Oh, and I have cake!" He laughs as he says this, holding the cake up for us to see, and it's a deep, throaty laugh. His pronunciation is perfect, but you can hear the lilt of somewhere overseas in his speech.

Jo was still cutting out cookies when the doorbell rang and asks Fergus if he'd like to help her. She's clearly latched on to him from the beginning. They settle down at the table, and Jo speaks to him as if she's known him her whole life, referring to him as "Papa." I find it a little odd, but I don't tell her to call him something different. I don't want her getting too attached to Fergus. We've just met the man, but I also know she wishes she had grandparents around.

I haven't spoken to Lucas's mother since before I left, and truthfully, she only saw Jo twice when we were still there. She never really accepted her. Matthew and Ciaran both offer assistance in the kitchen, but Claire shoos them into the other room to watch football. I can only imagine what they'll discuss on their own, particularly without Jesse to mediate, if they even talk. I can't hear any conversation. Vanessa slinks into the room behind Matthew without asking what she can do to help with the meal.

The Dundee cake that Ciaran and Fergus brought looks delicious. I set it out on the dessert table, and Claire and I get back to work. Thirty minutes later, Jesse has returned with his parents. Jo has set the table, with the help of her new best friend, while the cookies bake and the finishing touches to the meal are done.

Once we fill our plates, I find that Jo has set out place cards she must have made at home, with pictures she drew of us, instead of names. Jesse is at the head of the large farm table, Claire to his left, with Bill and Susan next to her. That side ends with Matthew's date, which Jo drew in pencil – no colors to give a clear indication of who the place card depicts.

On Jesse's right side, there is a drawing that looks like it could be Ciaran but with glasses. It's not a bad guess for Fergus, minus the glasses, and she directs him to his seat, plopping herself next to him. Only three seats remain, and she has placed her drawing of me on her right side. With two places left, the drawing of Ciaran is clear, his dark hair a dead giveaway, placed on my right. Matthew is at the end of the table, his hair red in her drawing. I wonder when she decided where to place each attendant.

I glance around as we sit, and Matthew's face is like a stone mask. He notices my observation and smiles at me. Jo wiggles around in her seat, and I lean my body away to give her more room. As I do, my arm brushes against Ciaran's, and a shiver plays down my spine. Instantly, I jerk back, crimson staining my cheeks, but no one else seems to have noticed the effect of our touch, which has now spread throughout my body. I'm drawn to him, but am I ready to see where that leads?... Jesse says a prayer, then carves the turkey as we begin to pass around the sides.

"Did you make these cards, Jo?" Fergus asks, and she beams with pride, nodding her head. "You did such a good job. You're a talented artist."

It turns out Bill and Fergus have a passing acquaintance with one another. They begin talking about all the changes in their lives, since they've last run into each other. I'm focused on my meal and Jo's while they talk.

When my grandmother passed, I felt lost. I didn't know how to function, throwing myself into finishing the semester and working as much as possible. Lucas took care of me while I grieved. I spent the summer in a daze, but I needed to pull myself together before classes started. My grandma never really got over losing my mother, and I knew that the one thing I could do for her was go on to achieve my dreams and be happy.

Things slowly regained some normalcy. Sex between Lucas and I had become more sporadic with both of us exhausted, the weight of my grief hanging over us. But as we regained that normalcy, I found security in intimacy with him again. Things were different, but they were okay. I still knew I wanted to marry him, and I thought he felt it too.

Before I knew it, Thanksgiving arrived – our first Thanksgiving while living together. I couldn't believe my grandmother wouldn't be around. It hit me that all I had left was Lucas and Claire. With Grandma gone, my aunt wasn't really a part of my life nor were my cousins. Claire was with Jesse's family for the holiday, so Lucas invited his parents and sister to our apartment. It would be the first Thanksgiving I would cook for him, and in spite of our close proximity, it would also be Elizabeth and Christopher's first visit to our home. They preferred meeting on their own turf, in their palatial estate. Our table was cramped. We all bumped elbows and squeezed together at the tiny table meant for four. I burned the turkey, but everyone politely ate. His parents still hadn't warmed to me, but I was hopeful that would change soon.

When the meal was done and everyone had gone, Lucas and I had our first real fight, over the stupid meal I'd painstakingly prepared. It wasn't good enough for his parents. Couldn't I have done more with our meager budget? All I heard as Lucas spoke was that I wasn't good enough for his parents ...and by extension, him.

"Earth to Sammi... Did you hear me?" Claire's voice intrudes on the thoughts running through my head, and I realize everyone is watching me. I have no idea how much time has passed since I drifted into my own thoughts or since she started talking to me.

"Huh? Sorry, I was zoned out there for a minute. Just thinking about how much Grandma Jolene would have loved to see us all together. I wish she was here."

Claire smiles. "Yeah, I miss her too. She was something else." She lets out a chuckle. "Anyway, we were just talking about the baby, and everyone was giving opinions on names. I think we're going to go with William and call him Will."

"I think that's perfect, you guys," I reply, genuinely meaning it.

We spend the rest of the meal mostly quiet, Fergus telling us about growing up in Scotland and moving over with his wife, Aileen, right after they were married. I keep waiting for him to throw in some Scottish terms, but his vocabulary is surprisingly formal. He's hilarious, though, and it feels like I've known him forever. As we wind down the meal, Jo asks if she can play Chutes and Ladders with Fergus, and I give her the okay. Bill and Susan excuse themselves. She's still struggling with pain and wants to go lay down. Claire brings out a pot of coffee, and we all sit around with our mugs, the meal still waiting to be cleared from the center of the table. ...I can tell the food coma is beginning to set in with everyone.

Claire decides to break the silence. "So, I think this would be a good time to talk about what we discussed earlier, Sammi. You can get everyone's opinions."

...Seriously, Claire? I thought we were going to talk to Jesse, privately.

Jesse asks, "What were you discussing? Why does something tell me that, whatever it is, it won't be a good thing?"

Everyone is watching me. "It's stupid, really. I thought there was someone following me the other day. Today, I came out to my front porch to find some prosecco. It just gave me a little startle."

"Don't downplay it," Claire says. "What Sammi didn't say is that she happened to look at the exact same brand of prosecco at the store, the day she thought she was followed. I told her it's probably a fluke, but you know why it would make her nervous."

She gives Jesse a meaningful glance as she says this. I glimpse at Ciaran, and he's looking back at me with concern. Matthew appears embarrassed, and his date seems bored, examining her nails. I wonder if Claire or Jesse told Matthew more about my life in St. Louis, with Lucas, than I know about. Either way, it's not what I want to discuss, not in front of everyone seated at the table.

I expect Jesse to answer, but it's Matthew who speaks up. "I'm sorry, Sammi. That was me that left it. It was purely coincidence, I promise. ...I was talking to someone at work about getting something to celebrate, and they suggested that brand. I thought you'd like it. It was just a friendly gesture. Honestly, I figured you'd bring it with you today."

I'm staring, open-mouthed, at him – with, no doubt, a dumbfounded look on my face. I'm not sure how to respond to him. Why wouldn't he bring it himself?

"I'm sorry I startled you," he says.

I realize everyone is watching me, to see how I react. I wish someone else would say something, but everyone is quiet. I don't want to be dramatic, though. I bite my tongue and respond politely.

"Oh, um, thanks. It really wasn't necessary, but it's a thoughtful gesture."

He smiles at me in response. A few moments of silence pass before Claire jumps in to change the subject.

"Well, that mystery is solved. The truck was just a coincidence, driven by some asshole overcompensating for something. Matthew, don't be an idiot next time. ...So, Ciaran, tell us more about you. You moved away, didn't you? When did you come back? What brought you back to this area?"

The tension at the table breaks, and it's as if everyone sitting has let out a collective sigh of relief.

"Yes, I did move away. I went out to UC Berkley for my journalism degree. Ended up staying out there for a girl, but it didn't work out. When my mam passed a few months ago, I decided to come home. Just needed to find an apartment before I could move. I wanted to be able to spend some more time with my dad, and California is so far away. I've been back about six weeks now." His answer is honest and to the point.

"Journalism, huh? So, do you like work for a newspaper?"

"No," he laughs. "Actually, I ended up doing graphic design. It's all from home, so I didn't need to stay on the west coast."

I've been quiet since they started talking, but I ask now, "Do you and Fiona have any other siblings?"

"No, it's just the two of us. I think we were enough work for my folks, especially Fiona. She was a firecracker, and she tried her best to get me to grow up to be just like her. How about you, Sammi? Do you and Claire have any other siblings?"

"No, it was just me, with my grandmother. Claire and I aren't really related. Claire spent enough time at our house, she may as well have been my sister. We've known each other since we were ten. We grew up, side by side."

"Oh," he replies. "Jo called her 'Auntie Claire,' so I assumed you two were sisters. What about other family?"

"Again, no. I have some extended family, but we're not in touch. It's just Jo and me. Claire doesn't have any siblings either, but she's family to us." I smile at her.

He doesn't respond, but he nods. Everyone is quiet until Ciaran offers to help clean up the kitchen. I shoo Claire off to the living room with Jesse, Matthew, and the remarkably silent Vanessa. While Ciaran and I stack dishes in the sink, I can hear everyone laughing together. This is what family should feel like. I'm still not sure about Ciaran, old habits trying to gain a foothold in our interactions, but I felt completely comfortable around Fergus by the end of the meal. We work together easily, with Ciaran rinsing dishes and me placing them in the dishwasher.

"Can I ask you something personal, Sammi?" I'm hesitant when Ciaran asks, but I also am curious what he wants to know and nod my head. "Matthew isn't Jo's dad, is he?"

I choke reflexively when he asks, my mind spinning with an answer and all the implications of the question.

"Well, that was a little more personal than I expected. Uh, Matthew is definitely not her father. We've never dated, never... well, you know, and Jo's dad isn't in the picture anymore. He hasn't been for a long time..." I trail off, wanting to keep some things private.

"Sorry, I didn't mean to be rude. He and I were talking earlier, and he implied that the two of you had history. He seemed very protective of you and Jo."

"Absolutely not," I reply. "We went on two dates, and they didn't go well. He's not really my type. We're just friends." I expect him to prod more about Jo's dad, but he doesn't.

"Cool. So, if he isn't your type, what is your type?" He's grinning ear to ear now.

There's a small part of me that wants to throw myself at his feet and scream, "take me now," but there's a larger part of me that goes into my fight or flight response. "Look, Ciaran, you seem like a great guy. But between Jo and my business, I'm pretty busy." I can't tell him I'm not looking to date, unless I look away to hide the lie, because I'm more interested in dating him than I want to admit, despite my uncertainties toward him.

He doesn't miss a beat. "No problem. I was just teasing. Friends, right?"

"Sure," I say. "Friends, I can do that."

It's the end of the conversation. Once the dishes are done, Fergus and Ciaran head home. While weird and tense, at times, it was still a pretty great Thanksgiving. I'm surprised that my heart feels so light, even after the conversation with Ciaran. Without a doubt, I need to figure out what to do about him. Do I give him a chance? Or do I go with my usual routine and shut him out? I already brushed him off, so going with the latter would be easy. Clearly, Claire wants me to give him a chance. Kissing Jo goodnight, I head home, thoughts of Ciaran dancing through my mind.

When I get home, the prosecco still sits on the porch. I leave it for now, breaking out my laptop. I google Lucas's name, and a hit comes back for Facebook. But without an account of my own, I can't look at it. Further down, I see his name pop up again, with an obituary for a grandparent I met only once, at our wedding, but there's nothing to indicate where he is now.

Giving up, I retrieve the prosecco from outside. I examine the bottle and see a sticker on the bottom from Whole Foods. Something still feels sinister about it, even though I know that it was completely innocent. I uncork the bottle and let the wine slide down the drain before tossing the bottle into the recycling can. Disposal of it helps purge built-up tension, and I feel like I can breathe again.

Chapter Eight

The day after Thanksgiving, Lucas and I both had to work early in the morning, but it was extremely slow at the shop. My manager told me to go home at noon. Even though I didn't want to spend the afternoon alone, I couldn't argue with her about it. Lucas was scheduled to work until three, so I ran by the store to pick up a few Black Friday deals before heading home to study.

I was shocked to walk in and find Lucas sitting on the couch, staring at nothing and catatonic. At first, he didn't respond when I called his name. I moved closer to him and repeated his name, at which point he startled, looked into my eyes, and immediately started to sob. Between his tears and frantic gulps of air, he told me Amanda called him at work. His dad killed himself, early in the morning. My heart broke for him, and just as he had carried me through the loss of my grandmother, I would carry him through this vacuum of grief. I was oblivious to the way his grief would completely consume him as we moved forward, changing the course of the rest of our lives.

I open the shop early and make a quick phone call to Claire. I need to hear Jo's voice. She doesn't sound like she misses me, even a little bit. Josef is coming in at noon, so I ask if Claire cares if I go by the store before picking up Jo that afternoon. She tells me to take my time and enjoy shopping.

I need to start buying gifts for the baby, not to mention Christmas. Claire doesn't want a baby shower. She's afraid of jinxing the adoption, and I'll respect her wishes. That doesn't mean I can't spoil little Will.

It's a slow morning. The shop is quiet, with only a few stragglers wandering in from the other stores on the street. We usually have this type of lull the day after Thanksgiving. Most shoppers head out to hit big box stores with deep discounts. During a particularly silent period, I feel eyes on me, and a shiver runs down my spine. I look out the shop windows, but even the street is empty right now. I turn back to my work, the chill that settled over me never fading. I shoot off a quick text to Claire to check on Jo, but they're fine. They're busy shopping online together for baby furniture.

When Josef comes in, I head toward Target on the other side of town. For a reason I don't want to acknowledge, I can't help watching my rearview mirror for a dark pick-up truck. The last few weeks have really gotten under my skin, and the prosecco from Matthew was just the icing on the cake. I don't notice anyone unusual, and I am relieved when I pull into Target.

My relief quickly subsides when I actually enter the store. I hate crowds like this, but I'm certain that earlier this morning would have been much busier. I'm already here and don't want to waste the opportunity to finish some shopping, despite my discomfort.

On my way in, I stop at the ridiculously long line for Starbucks for a caffeine boost. I'm standing in line to wait when someone, only a few people ahead of me, turns around and locks eyes with me. It's Ciaran, and his whole face lights up when he sees me. He calls out to ask me what I want, and when I start to decline his offer, he insists. Once he gets our drinks, he comes over, an Americano in hand for me.

"Thank you, Ciaran. You didn't need to do that." It's a sweet gesture.

"It's no problem. I was closer in line. No need for you to wait." He's looking at me with alarm, and I can't help but wonder if I have something on my face. "Hey, are you okay? You seem a little shaken."

I am shaken, but it's just from the busyness of the store. "Yes, I'm okay. I just don't like large crowds of people. I need to get some Christmas shopping done, though, while Jo is with Claire."

"Do you want some company?" In response to the questioning look on my face, he adds, "Just as a friend? ...I can run interference if anyone gets pushy. I need to do some shopping myself."

At first, I want to decline his offer. I still haven't decided if I'm ready to risk opening myself up to him. Then, I hear my Grandma Jolene in my head, telling me to live a little. Between her encouragement and my heart telling me to throw caution to the wind for once, I agree. I grab a cart, and he offers to push it as we walk toward the toys.

"Listen, Sammi, I don't want to make things weird, but would it be okay if Dad and I picked up something for Jo, for Christmas? She's a sweet kid, and she really made an impression on old Fergus."

What am I supposed to say to that? We don't know each other that well, but Jo seemed taken with Fergus at Thanksgiving, and something about Fergus makes me trust him wholeheartedly. Ciaran senses my hesitation.

"Forget I asked. It is weird." He acts like it is no big deal, but I can hear a twinge of disappointment in his voice.

"No, it's okay. I'm sorry. I'm just not used to having a lot of people around. It's been just us, Claire, and Jesse, pretty much her whole life. I'm not used to other people caring. As long as we're still just friends, it's okay." Liar. No matter how much I fight it, I don't want to be his friend.

"I get it, Sammi. I won't lie... Something about you intrigues me, but I'm okay with being friends. Most of my old buddies have moved away. So, it's nice to have some new people in my life. If, someday, you decide to give me a chance, I'd be interested. But I won't push it."

If only he knew the thoughts that go through my head every time I so much as think about him. My mind and my heart are always at odds with one another. But for now, I'm good with friends. It would be nice to have more, and I think Jo would love having Fergus in her life. My brain says it would be easier to leave, though still painful, if I keep this relationship to friends only.

We spend the next thirty minutes strolling the toy aisles, and I help him pick a cheerleading doll for Jo, along with some new *Frozen* books. Thankfully, I'm able to get everything I need for Jo while there. When I mention I need to go by the baby section, he comes along without discussion. I pick up a few baby toys and place them in the cart, then guide us toward the clothes. As we turn the corner, I bump into someone. Looking up, I see Matthew, who had stopped to look at some sleepers. He smiles until he sees Ciaran come up behind me. Right now, I feel like fading into nothing, so I can avoid the inevitable awkwardness of this interaction.

He recovers quickly. "Hey, Sammi! It's so good to see you! Ciaran." Matthew extends a hand to Ciaran, then reaches to hug me. I give him a half-hearted hug in return. "What are you guys doing here together?"

"I came to do some shopping and ran into Ciaran at Starbucks. We were just chatting while I picked up some things." I remind myself I don't have to explain anything to him. "It was nice to meet Vanessa the other day. She was kind of quiet, but she seems nice."

"Yeah, she's great. A little bit too serious about us, though. I'm not quite ready for marriage and babies myself, you know? I was just here, looking for some gifts for Claire and Jesse. It's actually good I ran into you. I wanted to ask you about going in on a big gift together, like a car seat. Figured as Godparents, we should do something a little above and beyond, but I realized I don't have your number."

"Yeah, that's a great idea. I'll give you my number." Truthfully, it would be nice to be able to split the cost on an expensive gift, even if it is a little couple-like. I glance over to Ciaran as I rattle off my number to Matthew. His face is expressionless, his arms crossed as he openly stares. There's no questioning how he feels toward Matthew. It's a big change from the little bit I saw them interacting yesterday. Before our conversation in the kitchen, Ciaran seemed amicable toward Matthew.

I try to steer the conversation and unexpected meeting to a quick ending. "I'm really excited for them. Claire has wanted a baby for so long."

"Me too," says Matthew. "...uh, I'm happy for them, I mean. It's not really my cup of tea, but I think they'll be good parents."

It's the second time he's mentioned not being ready for or wanting kids. I'm a little taken aback and look over to Ciaran again, to gauge his reaction. He still hasn't spoken, his greeting to Matthew limited to the handshake. His arms remain crossed, and it's easy to see him bristling at Matthew. I'm not the only one uncomfortable. I better extricate myself from this situation quickly, though a part of me thrills at the overprotective stance Ciaran has taken. There's my heart making its opinion known again.

"Well, I need to finish up this shopping and go pick up Jo. Text me about the car seat. I'll try to look online at pricing."

"Sure, we can talk later." He glances at his watch, "I better head out myself, or I'll be late for a meeting. Nice seeing you again."

He squeezes my shoulder as he walks away, but I see him glance back several times, no merchandise in hand. I turn to Ciaran, and his posture has softened.

"It's my turn to ask if you're okay. You seem a little tense." I chuckle lightly and look at the clothing on the nearest rack. There's an adorable onesie that Claire would love for Will.

"Listen, Sammi... how well do you know him?" I'm not watching his face, but at his words, I look up and see only concern in his eyes.

"I don't know him that well. I told you, we went on two dates. Our first one was back in college, but I was already interested in someone else. Then, Claire set us up on a pseudo-blind date before Halloween, but I just don't feel a spark with him. I think the only other time I've seen him was at Claire's wedding. He seems nice enough. He's always polite. But he's just a friend. Besides, I never thought I'd date anyone again, ever."

As soon as I finish, I realize I should have left the last sentence off. Ciaran is looking at me peculiarly.

"I hope you don't close yourself off to the possibility of something great coming into your life. I don't know what happened to you to make you so afraid of ever being in a relationship again, and I'm not going to push you for it. You'll tell me if and when you're ready. You know that I'm attracted to you; I have been since the first moment I saw you at church. But I'll respect your desire to just be friends. I hope, someday, you give love a chance, even if it isn't with me. Just please, not Matthew. There's something about him I don't trust." His face is earnest, and I know that while he may be speaking partially out of jealousy, that's not all of it. That said, I don't know what it is about Matthew that bothers him. Matthew seems to have a big ego, but I really don't think he's a bad guy.

"Matthew is okay. Jesse has known him for a long time, and I trust Jesse's intuition about people. I think Matthew is just very different than you or me. He was born with a silver spoon in his mouth, and I don't know about you, but I definitely wasn't." Matthew's upbringing likely wasn't all that different from Lucas's. That similarity isn't lost on me.

I place a onesie in the cart and throw in a sleeper I've been admiring. "Thanks for your concern. As for why I'm hesitant about dating, I don't want to get into all the details about it, but I've been married before. Suffice to say, it didn't end well. I just don't want to go through that again. I don't want to put Jo through getting attached to someone and having her heart broken if it doesn't work out." My breath painfully hitches in my chest.

I was hoping the next question wouldn't come, but I'm not surprised when it does. "Oh? Is your ex-husband Jo's dad?" It's a fair question, but it doesn't mean it doesn't hurt.

"He and I were together when Jo was born. He hasn't been in our lives since Jo was a baby." I conveniently don't answer his question directly, crossing my fingers that he doesn't pick up on that. By the look on his face, I'm guessing it didn't slip his notice, but he doesn't call me on it.

"Well, he's missing out. Jo seems like a great kid. She's pretty outgoing, funny, creative." He pauses, studying my face for a moment before continuing. "But listen, I've got to get going. Dad is waiting on me. Are you ready to go? Or do you have more shopping to do?"

I'm ready to go see my girl. We head toward the registers, and I think about the conversation. I didn't really plan on telling him even that much about my marriage and divorce. Sometimes, the past is best left buried. I've spent nearly Jo's entire life trying to keep us safe by keeping our circle small, and it's growing faster than I anticipated. Maybe it's a mistake to tell him that he and Fergus can give Jo presents, but I don't know how to broach the topic with him, and he's already separating his items from mine on the conveyor belt. The safest thing would be to cut him out of our lives completely, but I don't really want to do that either. I want to have him in my life in some way.

Ciaran walks me to my car and loads my bags in the trunk for me. He makes sure I'm safely in the driver's seat before speaking, handing me a business card for his graphic design. "That's my cell on there. Call me anytime, for anything. I really mean it when I say I'm okay with just being your friend."

"Thanks, Ciaran. I will."

He closes the door, and I watch him walk away, a part of me wishing he was going home with me. I sit there for a few minutes, composing myself before I go to face my daughter and the best friend who can read me like an open book.

A few weeks after the funeral for Christopher, Lucas was still struggling with day-to-day life. Christmas was coming soon, and I worried about how his whole family would deal with the first holiday without his dad. His boss called and told him politely, but forcefully, that he needed him back at work. If Lucas didn't return to work, he'd lose his job. They were running on a skeleton staff as it was, with the kids preparing for finals and to go home for the holidays. He went back reluctantly, but when he came home every night, he was angry and sullen. Finally, over dinner, I suggested that he go see a grief counselor. His face turned red, and he exploded. He yelled at me that I wasn't helping him, before storming out of the house. I was unnerved by his reaction and sat there stunned for several minutes. Finally, I rose to clean up dinner, while crying silently. I felt like if I allowed myself to make even the slightest noise, the house of cards in which I found myself would come crashing down.

After the dishes were put away, Lucas still wasn't home. I felt like I couldn't stay there anymore. My phone kept dinging with text messages from Claire, checking in with her extrasensory knowledge that something was wrong, but I ignored them. It was cold, a week before Christmas, but I put on snow boots and a coat and left the apartment on foot anyway. As I walked down the street, I felt the sensation of being watched and looked around anxiously. The street was bare in front of me, and I turned around, but the only person I saw was someone walking away from me, back in the direction of home. I could see them holding a leash, a small dog trotting ahead of them, and I felt relief. Nevertheless, the tingles along the nape of my neck became so intense, I rushed back to the apartment, the dog walker no longer in sight. I allowed myself to relax once I'd locked the door behind me.

I was surprised to find Lucas in bed, already asleep. He didn't even wait up for me to come home or try to text me to see where I was. I slid off my jeans, crawling in next to him, and slid my body against his. He stirred, his arm snaking out to reach around me, holding me tight to him. Then, his lips pressed down on me, and he pushed me onto my back, sliding into me with a roughness I didn't recognize. I couldn't help it. I started to sob, and I kept repeating to myself, "We're okay. I'm safe."

If only the lies we tell ourselves could become the truth.

Chapter Nine

It's Sunday. We go back to church, but I don't see Ciaran. I'm not about to call him, leaving his business card buried in my purse. I find myself disappointed to miss him, but I'm grateful that both Claire and Jesse show up. Afterward, we all head back to the house for lunch. Over lasagna, Claire talks more about her plans for the nursery and a mural she is going to paint over the crib. I try to prod, to see if she has any specific car seats in mind, but she doesn't give me any indication. She doesn't even give me a hint. As usual, Jesse sits quietly while he eats. He can be quite animated at times, but mostly, he's happy to observe and let Claire lead. They don't stay long after lunch, with plans to go over to his parents' and help with some of the work around the house. All in all, it ends up being a pretty decent holiday weekend, but I'm happy to get back into our routine.

Monday, Jo is back in preschool, and Tina is back in town to help with babysitting. Beatrice won't return from New York until tomorrow, so Josef opens the shop for me. When I come in a few hours after opening, he descends on me like a hawk.

"Sammi, someone came to see you this morning. He said his name is Ciaran. He's so dreamy. I told him you'd be in late and offered to give you a message, but he told me he'd try to drop back over lunch. So, spill. Who is Ciaran? Give me all the details."

Josef is a great employee, but he's a terrible gossip. The fact he's stopped talking for me to respond just goes to show how much he's hoping for a piece of juicy news to pass along.

"Ciaran is just a friend, nothing else," I reply, but I can't help the smile on my lips. A smirk plays across Josef's face. "Now, can you put the final touches on the order for the memorial wreath the Manger family ordered? They're supposed to pick it up this afternoon, and I need to do a little paperwork."

"Right," he replies, drawing it out slowly. "I'll get it done."

I head back to the office, and we both work quietly for a couple hours. He leaves for the day at noon. People have been filtering out of the nearby offices to head to lunch, and my stomach growls in protest of my skipped breakfast this morning. I'm debating closing down for thirty minutes to grab Chinese take-out from down the street when Ciaran walks in. I feel lighter just seeing him and a little giddy when I see a bag for my favorite Italian restaurant in his hand. If that isn't for me, the universe is playing a cruel joke.

"Hey, Sammi. How are you doing today? I thought I'd bring you some lunch. If you've eaten, you can save it for dinner."

"Hi, Ciaran. Sorry that I missed you earlier. I'm famished. Did you bring something for yourself?"

"Not today. I don't have long. We're working on a new website for a start-up, and I'm under a deadline. I wanted to stop in to apologize for last Friday, at the store. I didn't mean to cross the line. It's not any of my business who you date or don't date. We still friends?" I nod and smile at him. "With that said, I do need some roses. I'm headed out to see my mam, before I wrap up my project."

He looks so troubled as he says this, and I feel a weight in my own heart, as if I'm experiencing his emotions with him. "I know it's been awhile, but I am truly sorry about your mom. You must miss her. It's a pain that never really goes away. You learn to live with it, but it's still there, simmering below the surface."

"Thanks, Sammi. That means a lot. You know, you never told me what happened to your parents, just that you grew up with your grandmother."

My face falls, but I still answer him. "They passed away when I was young. I was five, actually. It was a car accident. Honestly, I don't really remember them, and that bothers me. I feel like their faces should still be fresh in my mind, that I should still be able to recall their voices."

"Understandable," he replies. "I'm sorry, Sammi. I can't imagine what it must have been like growing up without them."

I can't respond and simply nod my head once, swallowing back a lump in my throat. I occupy myself with trimming some thorns and wrapping the roses, and Ciaran respects my silence. As he hands me his credit card, he starts speaking again.

"Listen, my dad decided he'd like to throw a Christmas party this year. He wants to do it early, so that Fiona can come. She and her current boyfriend are taking another vacation over the holidays, and they invited my dad. She didn't tell him that they invited her boyfriend's widowed aunt to come along too. I swear, all they do is travel. Must be nice to be independently wealthy." He laughs at this, and I can't disagree. "I know it's last-minute, but it will be this weekend. He asked me to invite you, Jo, Claire, Jesse, and even Matthew."

I want to say yes, more than I want to admit. But I don't want to appear too eager to spend more time with him, still unsure what I should do about my burgeoning feelings. Let the wall down or keep up a fence? "Wow, thanks for the invite, Ciaran, but I don't want to intrude," I begin, but he cuts me off.

"Please come. It's not intruding. I already called Jesse. I extended an invitation to them and asked him to invite Matthew, even though I think he's an ass. I'll be nice to him, since he's your friend. Jesse texted me just before I got here and said they're all in. Matthew is bringing Vanessa. We're only missing you and Jo. Some of Mam and Dad's friends will be there, plus Fiona invited a few of her high school friends."

"What about you? Did you invite your high school friends, the ones that still live around here?"

"That would be a no. I invited you. I'll give you the address. It's at six in the evening, and we'll have hors d'oeuvres and some desserts. You don't need to bring anything, just yourselves." There's no way for me to outright deny him with the pleading look in his eyes.

"Okay, okay, we'll stop by for a little bit. But I've got to get Jo home at a decent hour for bed. Why don't I give you my number, and you can text me the directions?" His whole face lights up, and it lifts my heart to see it. I'm in so much trouble. Right now, my heart is definitely winning. He hands me his phone, and I add myself to his contacts. He texts me before leaving to make sure it comes through. I still have his credit card and hand it to him as he turns to leave. His hand brushes against the top of mine. It's so light and brief, it's barely felt, but electricity still zings through my body. Definitely trouble.

The rest of the week passes in a blur until Friday. Ciaran ends up texting me a few times, and we exchange some innocent "how are you" messages, but I don't see him again. I don't see Claire either, which is unusual for us, but we chat a couple times. I know she's busy getting the nursery ready and shopping for furniture. I get a text from Matthew, letting me know he's looking into car seats.

On Friday, I discover an error in the books, and I need to get it corrected before going home for the night. I've never been able to put off things like that for the next day. Since it will be late, I call Claire and ask her to pick up Jo from the house, where Tina is watching her.

When I finally get ready to lock up, the sun has disappeared beneath the horizon, and the moon's light does little to illuminate anything. I head toward the darkened front and glance out the window, startling when I see a figure outside. They're staring into the shop. At least, they're trying to see inside. With the dark interior, I doubt whoever it is can actually see me, but I can see them, dimly lit by a street lamp. At first, I can only discern their outline, and I hesitate, unsure if I should call the police, hiding behind the locked door until they arrive. Before it's in sight, I hear a car rumbling down the street, in need of a muffler. Its headlights briefly illuminate the face on the sidewalk. In those few seconds, I swear I see Lucas, the same posture I'm so used to seeing, feet braced apart and arms loose at his sides. I count my breaths to three, giving myself a moment to decide what to do before committing to confronting him. I dash to the door and fumble the lock open, but when I step out, the figure is gone.

Looking around frantically, my breaths coming in fast pants now, I see a car's lights come on across the street. I take three steps in that direction before the car pulls away, and its lights fade from sight. My heart is thumping so hard, I'd think it possible to see it pulsing outside my body. It's been years without a single word from Lucas. There've been no letters, no phone calls, no attempts, whatsoever, to connect with either Jo or myself. I sent him a text message with my new phone number after we moved, and he's never used it. The events of the last few weeks must be playing tricks with my mind. I've been too burdened and anxious. It wasn't Lucas.

Despite assurances to myself, I still feel nervous. Locking the door to the shop, I run to my car, but my key fob won't unlock the doors. I use the manual locks, but the car won't turn over. The stranger earlier pops into my mind, and my body tingles. At this point, I have no choice but to call someone for a ride. I won't call Uber. I don't trust strangers. My first calls are to Claire and Jesse, but oddly, neither one answers. I try again a few minutes later, and the calls still ring through. Next, I try to call Ciaran, and his phone goes to voicemail too. My breathing becomes thinner and more desperate. I feel the need to flee. I can't stay here much longer, or I'll have a full panic attack. Shit, shit, shit. I don't feel right calling Jesse's parents, and the only other contact I have is Matthew. Desperate, I dial his number, and he answers immediately. He says he's in the area and will be right over, but I'm still surprised when he knocks on my window five minutes later.

"Thank goodness you're here. I appreciate you coming out on short notice, Matthew," I say, opening my door. I pop the hood on his request, and he insists I sit in the passenger seat of his running car while he looks at my engine. After a couple minutes, he slides into the driver's seat of his silver Audi.

"Your battery was unhooked. Probably some kids playing a prank on you. I've heard some people are having issues around here with that kind of stuff. If you want to give me your keys, I can try to start it, make sure that's all that was going on with the car." The stranger flashes in my mind again, but maybe Matthew's right. I vaguely recall overhearing someone at church talking about pranks from some neighborhood teenagers a few weeks ago.

Relief floods me as I hand him the keys and watch as he starts up Betty. I definitely could not have paid for repairs if something was truly wrong with her. I run over to my car and without thinking, give him a hug. "Thank you so much. You're a lifesaver."

He looks a little stunned but smiles broadly. "No problem. I'm glad I could help. Where are you headed? I should follow you, just to make sure you get there okay. I want to make sure the car doesn't act up."

"That's okay. I think it's fine now. Seems likely it was just the battery, like you said. I do really appreciate your help. You're a good friend."

"Right. Thanks. Uh, you're coming tomorrow to the party, right? Jesse said Ciaran was inviting the whole crew." For the briefest of moments, the party had slipped my mind.

"Sure, we'll be there for a little while. I heard Vanessa will be joining you. That will be lovely. Jo will be excited to see Fergus. He really made an impression on her."

"Cool. So, are you, like, dating that guy now?" Is he talking about Ciaran? He's trying to come off casually, but I can tell the possibility of Ciaran and me irks him.

"Ciaran? No, I'm not dating anyone. We're just friends. I'm happy to just do the single thing right now. Thanks again, Matthew. I appreciate it." I move to get into my car. This situation has become uncomfortable.

He smiles at me. "Sure thing. I'll see you tomorrow." He watches as I close the door behind me, and I wait until he's back in his car before easing away from the curb. I'm thinking about Ciaran as I drive. We're not dating, but do I want to date him?

Yes, I think I do. But maybe I shouldn't rush into it. I'll talk to Claire. I can get her opinion, aside from the fact she thinks I'm overdue for a roll in the hay.

Something is changing inside me. The wall around my heart is crumbling. It's exhausting, being torn between this fear that has been a constant part of my life for over four years and this desire for something more. Before I know it, I'm almost to the turn off for Claire's when headlights pop up in my rearview mirror. As I turn off, I could swear the outline of the car passing the turn looks like an Audi.

Chapter Ten

Our first Christmas in the apartment, in 2013, was somber. Lucas and his family were lost without the anchor of Christopher. We went to his parents' home for lunch, and Lucas drank one beer after another, leaving me to nervously maneuver us home in the dark that night. He passed out, fully clothed, on the couch as soon as we got home, but amazingly, he got up the next day and went to work. He was quiet the next few days, but he seemed excited by the time New Year's Eve rolled around. It was the first time I'd seen light in his eyes since his dad passed, and I felt relief, followed by guilt for feeling for that relief. It gave me hope that things were going to get better. We were going to be okay.

In the morning on New Year's Eve, he told me to dress up for the evening. We were going out to dinner. I pulled out a periwinkle wrap dress I found on clearance and had been holding on to forever, waiting for the right moment. I also spent extra time pinning my curls up into a loose chignon, leaving a few curls hanging free to frame my face. My look was complete with a pair of sky-high, black pumps. Examining myself in the mirror, I felt pretty for the first time in a long time. When Lucas saw me, his whole face lit up.

"Wow, Sammi, you look.... amazing. I am a lucky, lucky man." His praise filled me with a bubbly excitement. He was always handsome, but he looked exceptionally nice himself, his hair styled with a slight spike and his favorite charcoal grey suit, finished off with actual dress shoes. He was always so casual when outside of work. The look overwhelmed me at first.

"Thank you. You look incredibly handsome. I'm the lucky one," I responded, leaning up for a quick but steamy kiss.

Lucas drove, his left knee jiggling the whole way until we pulled into a small and intimate restaurant – The Sycamore. I'd never been there. It was far too expensive, but Lucas seemed to know everyone when we walked inside, seated almost immediately at a quaint table in the corner, candlelight illuminating our faces. Lucas still seemed nervous. He kept wiping his hands on his pants, and they were sweat-covered every time he reached for me. The waiter brought over a bottle of champagne, something we surely couldn't afford. I was confused. We hadn't ordered, and when I looked to Lucas, he was grinning.

"I already took care of ordering. Just enjoy." He was beaming, and I was left even more perplexed. The behavior was so out of character for him.

I took a sip of the champagne and a moment to savor the crisp flavor before opening my mouth. The waiter returned with chopped salads before I could formulate my response. I started in on my meal, but Lucas continued to sit back, watching me.

"Sammi, I have big news, and I just can't keep it in. Back in high school, my dad opened a bank account for me, in both our names. He made regular deposits to it. The rule was that I couldn't touch it until after I graduated. I'm sorry I haven't told you before. Honestly, I didn't think about it until now. His lawyer brought it up after he died, and it's a decent sized amount. ...So, you know that

my dream has always been to write a book. With the money from that account, I can afford to quit my job and focus on my writing!"

I stopped with my fork halfway to my mouth. How was I supposed to respond to that? I knew we weren't married, but we were committed, and I didn't understand how he could quit his job without talking to me first. And how much money? Rent was cheap, but I hoped we wouldn't live there forever. I only had a year and a half left of school, and I didn't want to live in apartments typically rented by students after I graduated. But the look on his face was so full of hope. I didn't want to ruin it for him, not after he'd been depressed for the last month.

"Wow, Lucas, that's amazing," I managed to squeak out. "Um, just out of curiosity, how much money are we talking about? And what about your book? Do you have a new project in mind, or are you going to finish one of the drafts you already started?"

His face fell. It's not the response he wanted or expected. "Why aren't you more excited for me? It doesn't matter how much, Sammi. It's more than enough for us. Rent is cheap, and you'll still be working to help it stretch farther. This is going to be a good thing."

"I'm sorry, Lucas. You just surprised me. Tell me about your book." I didn't want to fight tonight, or ever. Things seemed better before that moment, and I wanted to hold on to it.

He seemed content with my response that time, like my first lackluster response had never occurred. "Do you remember that book I started to write back when we were first dating, about the kidnapped boy and his father, who everyone believes really killed his son? I was thinking I might finish that." That book was the first of his several attempts to write something while we were dating. I'd forgotten about it, long buried and neglected.

The waiter returned to clear our salad plates and deliver our meals. We both had fresh lobster tail with sides of asparagus. I hate asparagus. Lucas knew that, but I guessed he forgot in his excitement over the night. He liked it, so it was possible he just ordered identical dishes. He paused for a few minutes while we both took bites of our meal, and I couldn't help letting a groan escape my lips as I tasted the succulent lobster. It was the first time I had ever had lobster, and I was pleasantly surprised by the flavor.

Lucas practically inhaled his meal and started talking again. He told me all about his plans for the book, the characters and the plot, while I ate. I could tell how happy he was, but I hoped he didn't ask my opinion. His book didn't sound like one I would ever read. I preferred fantasies over the evils of real life, and I didn't want to lie. Despite this, I couldn't help being infected by his enthusiasm. He was like the Lucas I met when I first came to college, someone I'd been missing terribly even before his father passed away.

The waiter brought out dessert, a chocolate lava cake that looked and smelled divine. The first bite was almost sinful. I choked, coughing, when Lucas stood only to get down on one knee.

"Sammi, you have been there for me, for two years, through thick and through thin. You inspire me and motivate me to be a better man, and I can't imagine my life without you. Would you do me the honor of being my wife?" It was short and sweet, and the ring was a stunning full karat, pear cut solitaire. It must have cost a fortune. Maybe he had more money than I thought. I realized he was waiting for me to respond, eyes from the tables around us glued to his proposal.

"Of course, Lucas. I love you, always." I was crying, smearing my mascara, and vaguely registered applause around us. I was going to be his wife, Mrs. Samantha Atwater.

Beatrice's voice pulls me out of my memories. Josef requested off for the day, and Beatrice offered to close up to give me time to get ready for Fergus's party. "You better get going, honey. Give that handsome man of yours a kiss for me." I roll my eyes and remind her that Ciaran is not my boyfriend. At least, not yet...

A few hours later, pulling up to Fergus's house, I instantly fall in love with the small cottage residence. The pale-green exterior is highlighted by evergreen shutters, and leaves from the old trees that surround it blanket the lawn. It's homey and radiates emotional warmth. The house is perfect. I can picture Ciaran growing up here. I look around, but I don't see Claire's car or Jesse's truck. Matthew's Audi is parked in the double driveway, and I pull in next to him. As we approach the door, Jo places her small hand in mine, and I'm swept with both love for her and a weird sort of anticipation. With the thawing of my heart, I'm looking forward to seeing Ciaran.

Fergus answers the door, and Jo immediately jumps into his arms for a hug. He laughs, and I'm hit with a feeling of family, a feeling that has been fleeting, outside of Claire, Jesse, and Jo, for years. Fergus's joy is like a grandparent's, and I know that regardless of what happens or doesn't happen with Ciaran, Fergus needs to remain in our lives. We're still standing in the doorway when Ciaran walks up, putting his hand on my shoulder to welcome me into the house. As I look around, I see Matthew standing in the corner with Vanessa, speaking with an older couple, but his eyes are locked on us. I offer a small wave, and he gives me a nod in return. I take in more of our surroundings and immediately notice this house is bursting with love and joy. There are framed photos everywhere, with bright light filling the space and laughter ringing through the house.

Ciaran and Fergus excuse themselves as the doorbell rings again, and I take Jo's hand, walking around to look at photos. There's a beautiful picture of Fergus with an auburn-haired woman who I assume must be Ciaran's mother, Aileen. Ciaran and Fiona have their father's hair and complexion, but they both have the same beautiful, green eyes as their mother. There are pictures of Ciaran and Fiona as babies, then small children. I can't help but grin at a picture of a teenage Ciaran, with his arm around a blonde teenager at a dance. As I move further along, there's a picture of Fiona, arms entangled with a handsome older man. He looks to be in his late fifties, a little younger than Fergus, but his hair and beard are peppered with gray, and lines frame his eyes. She looks happy. Matthew comes up behind me and taps my shoulder, right as Fiona appears around the corner with the man from the photo.

She leans in for an unexpected hug, "Samantha, so good to see you. This is my partner, Richard. Richard, this is Ciaran's friend, Samantha, her daughter Jo, and..." Her eyes flicker to Matthew, eyebrows raised. I heard the emphasis on friend in her introduction.

"It's nice to meet you, Richard, and see you again, Fiona. This is Matthew. He's an old friend. And this is his girlfriend, Vanessa."

Matthew leans over to shake hands, and I see a look pass over Fiona's face, the overprotectiveness and skepticism of an older sister.

"Matthew and I have known each other since college," I add, hoping it's clear that there's nothing there.

A woman that appears close in age to Fiona interrupts, and Fiona excuses herself and Richard, while Matthew stays behind. I send up a silent thank you when Claire and Jesse approach, Jesse quickly engaging Matthew in a conversation. Claire tries, without much luck, to find a discussion point with Vanessa. Ciaran returns and points out two couples as his parents' oldest friends. He motions to a group of women, who keep sneaking glances at both him and Matthew, as Fiona's friends.

"What about you? Are we really the only friends you invited?" I ask with a grin. I'm curious to know more about him.

"Uh, well, yeah. I was gone over ten years." He seems uncomfortable, and I realize I put my foot in my mouth. Unsure how to respond, I just smile at him, and he returns the grin.

Our small group stays together, picking over the appetizers. Ciaran comes and goes several times, trying to mingle with the other attendees. Every time he comes by, his arm brushes against me, and a tickle spreads through my body. Vanessa clings to Matthew and laughs constantly at everything he says, as if he's a comedian. She's an odd one. As everyone starts to settle down, Fergus sits on the couch to chat with one of the couples Ciaran pointed out earlier, and Jo climbs into his lap, her eyes drifting closed. I should get her home, but when I offer to lift her, Fergus shoos me away. Ciaran leans down to whisper in his dad's ear, and they both glance up at me, before his dad nods, and Ciaran walks in my direction.

"Can I show you something? My dad said he'll keep Jo with him for a minute, if you're okay with it." I know I've just barely met Fergus, but I trust him. Something tells me he'd take a bullet for Jo, despite our lack of familiarity with each other. Besides, Claire and Jesse are on the other side of the room talking with Fiona.

I nod to Ciaran. He takes my hand, guiding me down the stairs to the basement. Half the room is full of boxes, and the other half looks like a shrine to Ciaran's teenage self. A full-size bed is pushed against the wall, bare of sheets, and a bookshelf is next to it, crowded with tattered paperbacks and basketball trophies. There's an old writing desk in the opposite corner, with a globe atop, and a small door that leads to a tiny bathroom. Drawing pads are stacked on the desk, and I flip open the top one. There's a beautiful drawing of a bridge, surrounded by full trees.

"Did you draw this?" I ask Ciaran, in awe of his ability.

"Yeah, it was kind of my thing, outside of basketball and newspaper. My mom was an artist, and she taught how to draw and paint. I don't do much art for myself anymore. Everything for work is on the computer." He sits on the bed as I continue looking at the drawing. "As you can probably guess, this is my old bedroom."

"It's really good. You know, Claire is an artist too. You should see some of her work. She sells it sometimes on Etsy." Placing the drawing pad back on the desk, I notice a framed photo and pick it up. It's a sweaty, teenage Ciaran in a basketball jersey, with Aileen next to him, her hand on his shoulder. I move to sit beside him, holding the picture frame.

"That's my mam. I was seventeen in that photo," Ciaran begins. "We had just lost our final game of the season, missing out on a championship game, but she was still so proud. She always said it was one of her favorite photos of us."

"It's a nice picture, Ciaran. You can see how proud she was. She must have really loved you and Fiona. Your mom was beautiful. You and Fiona have her eyes."

He smiles and wistfully replies, "Yeah, she always told us how glad she was we inherited at least one thing from her." He pauses a moment. "Anyway, I just thought I'd show you where I grew up, give you a chance to see what I was like as a kid. Since we're friends and all."

He says this with a mischievous grin that tells me he's fully aware of the effect he has on me, regardless of how much I deny it. A wink would have been less obvious. An impulse comes over me. I lean forward and touch my lips to his, which are soft and gentle. I pull back quickly, shocked by my own behavior.

"I'm sorry, Ciaran. I don't know what came over me. I tell you I just want to be friends, then I do something like that." I bury my face in my hands, embarrassed and confused.

He wraps an arm around my shoulders in a friendly gesture. "Sammi, it's okay. I won't pretend I didn't like it, but I'm also not going to push you into anything. Let me just ask you a question. Do you like me?" There's a hopeful tone to his voice.

I look up at him, my face burning, "Yes. I just don't know if I'm ready."

He looks serious as he responds, "Let's just take it slow. Why don't we go back upstairs and check on Jo for now? I know you were wanting to get home before it got too late, but I'm not rushing you. Stay as long as you want." He's right. I do need to get home.

He stands, offering me his hand and pulling me up from the bed. I set the picture back on the desk and swallow the lump in my throat. Before we climb the stairs, he wraps both arms around me and presses his lips to the top of my head. Butterflies dance in the air around me. I'm falling fast and hard. I can't help but think about Lucas and how quickly I knew I was in love with him. Am I rushing into this too soon? I don't want to make the same mistake.

When we return upstairs, I thank Fergus for the invitation. Jo is still asleep, but she's spread out on the rest of the couch and lying next to Fergus, rather than on his shoulder. Claire and Jesse must have snuck away while we were downstairs, and I don't see Matthew or Vanessa. Ciaran offers to carry Jo to the car for me and easily lifts her into his arms. As we walk out the door, I look back one last time. Matthew is suddenly there, watching me leave. He waves, and I return it with a smile. Once Jo is fastened into her car seat, I turn to thank Ciaran again for the invitation.

"Thanks again for inviting us. I've been really stressed lately and needed a night with good company."

"Anytime. If you need help with anything, you'll let me know, right?"

"Sure," I reply, and he leans in to me but doesn't press his lips to mine. I stand on my tiptoes and finish the kiss, wrapping my arms around his neck. He snakes his own arms around my waist, and my body presses against his. It lasts longer than the one downstairs, but he pulls away before I'm ready, and I'm left with weak knees and a pounding pulse.

He opens my door and closes it behind me, then watches as I back out of the driveway. As I start to pull away, I wave at him, but I see Matthew and Vanessa standing behind him. I guess the cat is out of the bag. Just yesterday, I just told Matthew that Ciaran and I aren't dating, and today, he's caught me kissing Ciaran. I shouldn't feel guilty. I've always been clear with Matthew about being friends, but I still don't want to hurt his feelings. I definitely need some time to think things through, my shifting emotions and attraction leading me down a road that I'm still not sure I'm ready to travel. As I drive, I hear Grandma Jolene's voice, as clear as day, telling me it's about time.

Chapter Eleven

I skip church the next day, exhaustion deep in my bones, but Claire still comes over for lunch. I haven't decided what I really want. This is the first time I've been truly attracted to anyone since Lucas, despite her best efforts to set me up on dates over the years, and I'm starting to question my sanity. Do I really like him, or is the stress and uncertainty recently making me act uncharacteristically? I put on a DVD for Jo after lunch, so I can talk to Claire in the kitchen for a few minutes.

"Don't freak out, but I need to tell you something." She raises her eyebrows. "I kissed Ciaran yesterday."

I can't even look her in the face, closing my eyes in anticipation of her response.

"Why are you acting so weird? It's about time, Sammi. For heaven's sake, you've been divorced for years. It's time you woke up from the living dead." I know she's wanted me to move on from the past forever, but it's easier said than done. "So, what's the problem? Was he a bad kisser? Bad breath?"

The smile on my face is involuntary as I think of his lips. "Keep your voice down. And no, he's a great kisser. But you know me, I never thought I'd date again. I have Jo to think about. Getting involved with anyone is a terrible idea. I don't want her to get her heart broken. And haven't you noticed how similar he looks to someone else?" The words spill from my lips before I can stop them, and I worry I've said too much.

Claire has a quick response ready, as if she knew exactly what I'd say. "Sammi, listen to me. You're not marrying the guy. It was one kiss. Even people who get married split up sometimes. You can't avoid men just to try to keep Jo from ever getting attached to someone. Besides, I'd guess she's already attached, whether you like it or not. He's hot and smart, and he seems like a decent guy, any similarities in appearance be damned. They're not that similar anyway. I think you need to go for it."

"You always think I need to go for it, Claire," I reply.

"True. The difference is, this is the first time I think you've ever considered listening to me. Just take things slow and see what happens."

"Okay," I mutter. "Oh, and it was two kisses." Her only response to that is a laugh, and I feel like I'm floating on air. I'm going to give this a try, slow and low pressure.

That night, and the next two, Ciaran calls me. We talk for a few minutes about nothing serious, but I don't see him. I haven't heard anything else from Matthew, but I need to get in touch with him soon about the car seat for William. I don't know why I'm worried about Matthew's feelings. He's with Vanessa. There's no spark there for me, but I've always been the type to put other people's feelings first, sometimes to the detriment of myself. Lucas is a perfect example.

Wednesday rolls around, and I'm manning the shop on my own all day. Even worse, we're running late in the morning, and I don't have a chance to put a lunch together for myself. I barely manage to remember cupcakes for Jo's class.

Jo's been excited all week, talking about her big party with Fergus. She's asking when we can see him and Ciaran again, but I haven't given her an answer yet. At some point, I need to explain to her that I'm going to be spending more time with Ciaran, but it doesn't mean we'll be running off to get married or anything. During a lull, I send a text to Matthew about the car seat. While awaiting a response, I keep myself occupied with putting together several arrangements. Maybe I'll get lucky, and Claire will take pity on me and drop off some food. By the time lunchtime arrives, my stomach is screaming at me. I decide to get something delivered with the last twenty dollars in my wallet, but a regular customer comes in to the shop and wants to stand around to chat. When she finally leaves, I turn around to walk to the phone when the bell over the door rings. ...Perfect. Another delay. I spin around and find myself staring at Ciaran.

"Hey, Sammi. I brought lunch. A little birdie told me you were on your own today. Sorry I'm late. I can't believe how crowded it was." He laughs and runs a hand through his hair, which is significantly shorter than it was on Saturday. He also has a shadow on his face again, and I decide not to comment on how incredibly attractive it is. He should definitely go with the beard.

"You got your hair cut. It looks good," I tell him.

"Yeah, my dad was on me to get it cut, so I thought I'd trim it and make him happy." He holds up a bag from Five Guys, and my mouth begins watering. "Claire mentioned you like cheeseburgers. I hope that's okay." He grimaces... "And now you know who the little birdie was."

I can't help chuckling. "I kind of figured it was her. What about you? Did you bring yourself something this time? If you have time for lunch, you're welcome to sit around and eat. It's been pretty dead here today." I'm hoping he'll stick around for a bit, realizing I've missed him despite seeing him a few days ago.

"That'd be nice," he answers. We drag a couple chairs from the office and sit down by the counter to eat, so I can better watch the store. For a few minutes, we sit quietly, sharing the large fries that Ciaran set down between us. I've made it halfway through my burger, grateful that Ciaran didn't include my usual onions, when he shifts. I have a feeling he's about to start an awkward conversation. I need to speak first, need to control the way this goes.

"Ciaran, I'm sorry for my behavior this weekend. I'm feeling very conflicted lately, and I just want you to know that I do like you. You know, when I got divorced, I pretty much swore off men forever. I've gone on some dates, but I haven't really been in a relationship since then. I'm not ready to be serious, but maybe we can go on a date. I hope...." my words die out as I glance up and notice someone looking in the window of the shop. I must look truly panicked, as Ciaran jumps up immediately and spins around, but the person has already moved on.

He turns back to me. "You look like you're about to pass out. Are you okay?" he asks.

It takes me a minute to calm myself enough to speak. "Yeah, sorry. I thought I saw my ex-husband. It's the second time in less than a week, and it just startled me." Even I know that my response isn't convincing. Anyone could tell I'm scared, even someone who's never met me. "I'm sure it's just someone who looks like him. How many guys out there share the same color hair?" I laugh, but it's a lie. It's possible it could be someone else, even likely, but I'd know Lucas anywhere. I know his gait, his posture, even his aura. I would bet money that it's him. If I'm right, what is he doing here now? Is it pure coincidence, or is he looking for me? Or even worse, is he looking for Jo?

Ciaran glances out the window again, walking over to look down the street. When he looks back at me, concern is clearly written in his expression. "Are you sure you're okay? You're still awfully pale." He pauses for a moment as he studies me, and I can see the war behind his eyes. He's debating whether or not to continue, and I know the moment he decides that he needs to ask the questions that come next. "I have to ask you, why are you so scared of your ex-husband, Sammi? Do you think he'd hurt you or Jo? Has he hurt you before?"

"No, he hasn't hurt me, not physically. He'd never do something like that. To be honest, I haven't heard from him since the divorce was finalized. I just don't understand why he'd be here now. But like I said, it's probably not him. He has no reason to be here." I can tell he sees through me. I don't know who I'm trying to convince more – him or myself.

"Maybe I should hang out here for a bit. I can stay out of the way, not interfere with your work," he offers. I'm touched by his thoughtfulness, but I need some time alone, our earlier conversation all but forgotten.

"Thanks for the offer, but really, I'm okay. I have some orders that I need to work on. Thanks for lunch too. I really appreciate it. I'll call you?"

If he senses my brush-off, he lets it slide. "I look forward to it." He picks up his trash and puts it back in the bag. "I almost forgot. Do you have any poinsettias? It's my mam's birthday, and she always wanted a poinsettia for the holidays." I'm thankful he doesn't press to finish what we started earlier. My nerves are too raw to handle it right now.

Of course, I have poinsettias. He checks out, brushing a light kiss against my lips before heading outside and looking around, as if he'll be able to spot and recognize a man he's never seen. He glances back at me through the glass of the door before he leaves, and I wave. His shoulders are slumped as he walks away. I should be nervous about the possibility of a date, but I'm not. I'm anxious about the possibility of change, but I feel safe around Ciaran ever since the other night.

I'm briefly overcome with longing for my grandma, and I wonder what she'd think about Ciaran. I can make a pretty safe assumption, based on the whispers in my ear from her ghost. Now, I just need to figure out why Lucas could possibly be here. If I'm right, and it was him, I've seen him twice now. I should talk to Claire about this, but I'm too much of a coward to talk to her in person, or even via phone. I finger the buttons, contemplating the best way to tell her my suspicions.

Before I knew it, June arrived, and Lucas and I were getting married. He was adamant about having our nuptials before I went back for my senior year of college, and I felt ready for it, even though it was a short engagement. While planning, he tried to insist on a big and lavish wedding, but I wanted something small and intimate. We finally agreed to getting married in his mother's backyard and having a small reception under some tents.

Most of my friends were the girlfriends of his friends from college, and I didn't have any family left, outside of Claire and Jesse. Biologically, my aunt and cousins hadn't talked to me since the funeral for my grandma, and I hardly considered them family anymore. Nevertheless, I still invited them, but they told me they couldn't make it, as I had expected.

For the latter half of June, the weather was surprisingly pleasant, a bit cooler than it usually is that time of year. Claire took her time pinning back the front of my hair, with only a few tendrils around my face and curls cascading down my back. My dress was beautiful, with a sweetheart neckline and lace cap sleeves. The lace wrapped around the low-cut back, which was otherwise open to the small of my back. The beading on the bodice and train was simple but elegant. She wove the stem of a purple stargazer lily through the twist that pinned back the front and sides of my hair. She was radiant herself, in a rich purple dress with deep vees and a short skirt to keep her cool. She'd styled her blond locks into a loose French braid. I asked if Jesse would walk me down the aisle, and he'd happily agreed. He was the closest thing I had to a brother, and it meant so much to me to have Claire waiting for me as my matron of honor as he escorted me up the aisle.

When I saw Lucas for the first time, I had to choke back tears. I dreamed of our moment from the first time he kissed me, and it felt surreal to have it finally happening. I only wished my grandma could be there to see it. He was wearing a black tuxedo, with a simple spray of purple on his chest. He had his hair trimmed recently, and the sun reflected shades of red within the blonde. His skin had the same sun-kissed tone it always held, and I didn't know if he had ever looked more handsome. It was a moment I wanted to hold onto forever, that image of him standing at the end of the aisle, beaming at me. I needed that memory to carry me through the next few months, though I didn't know that yet. My life was changing, just not in a way that I expected.

We spent our honeymoon in Jamaica, wrapped around each other. Things felt like they did back when we first started dating, when Lucas still wanted to be with me all the time. He was patient and tender with me, nothing rushed or forced. It was bliss. I wish now that I had taken more time to soak in the experience and let it imprint on me.

It didn't take long for things to deteriorate once we got back from the honeymoon. Lucas started spending more time at the bar in the evenings, and whenever I questioned his progress on his book, he told me not to worry. I was nervous about our income, but he continually assured me that we had plenty. We weren't in financial distress.

We had combined our bank accounts when we got married, and he took care of balancing the checkbook. I had no idea how little money we had put away. With Lucas gone more, I picked up extra shifts when I could, and I started taking a walk around the neighborhood nearly every day. Finally, I asked him why we were still living in a shabby apartment when we had so much money from his dad. He told me that we'd move once he found a publisher for his book. What book? I had yet to see proof of its progress.

He went out the night I questioned him, and Claire called me while he was gone. She said she had a feeling something was wrong. I assured her that we just had a fight, but it would be okay. She offered to come visit for a few days, but I shrugged her off, too embarrassed to tell her what was going on. Lucas stumbled in sometime after midnight, liquor from his breath heavy in the air. I tried to roll away from him, but he pawed at me clumsily. Finally, I gave up and laid there until he was spent. Once I heard his snores, I cried myself to sleep.

Lucas is heavy on my mind this evening as Jo and I sit down to a late dinner. Once again, Tina proves why she is the best, cooking up some stir-fry with ingredients she found in the fridge. I don't know what I'd do without her help. If we ever left, what would I do? I certainly wouldn't be able to work long hours with no one around to help with Jo. Even when she was in kindergarten, I'd still need to be home to get her on and off the bus, not to mention what I'd do if she was home sick. I wouldn't necessarily be in a big rush to buy a business again, so I'd be subject to someone else's rules. I get the familiar itch of something on the horizon but stuff it down. Not only am I likely just paranoid after seeing someone that looks like Lucas, Jo will sense my worry and get herself worked up. Besides, even if it was Lucas, I don't believe in my heart that he would hurt us any more than he already has. My phone rings, and I look down to see Claire's name on the display.

She starts talking before I even greet her. "What's wrong? I can sense your anxiety from here." There's that link between us again.

"Nothing is wrong. We're just finishing up dinner." The doorbell rings. I'm not expecting anyone, and my heart stops for a beat. Claire hears the doorbell and doesn't speak as I peek out the window. "Hey, Matthew is here. Can I call you back?" I hang up before she responds.

Opening the door, I politely greet him, "Hi, Matthew! Nice surprise to see you. I wasn't expecting you this evening."

"Um, you invited me to come by and hang out, remember? I brought beer," he says, holding up a six-pack of IPA. I don't remember inviting him over. Why would I invite him on a weeknight, when Jo will be up early the next morning? Though, I've been so overwhelmed lately, it's possible I just forgot. He senses my hesitation and adds, "Back on Saturday, at the party. I can tell you forgot. I'll just go. We can do it another time."

"Truthfully, I don't remember, but it's okay. Jo and I are just finishing our meal. Why don't you come in? I need to read to Jo before bed, but I can join you downstairs after."

He offers to tidy up in the kitchen, and I'm thankful for the help. My long day is wearing on me, and I'm not sure how I'm going to stay up much longer. Maybe I can find a way to cut this short. After I finish reading and kiss Jo goodnight, I head downstairs, but I don't see Matthew anywhere. His car is still in the driveway, and then I hear footsteps above me. Is Jo out of bed? I climb the stairs, rushing to her room to peek in on her, but she's sound asleep. My heart starts to thud against my chest. I pull my cell phone from my pocket, ready to dial 911 as I tiptoe back down the hallway, logic fleeing and panic taking its familiar place. I pass the bathroom and turn the corner into my room to find Matthew looking around. My initial reaction is anger. This is my private space.

"What are you doing in here?" I ask, unable to keep a hint of my frustration from my voice.

He jumps. "Sorry, I was looking for the bathroom and walked in here instead. I got distracted by the artwork on the walls." Framed photos of Jo, my grandmother, Claire, and me hang on the walls, along with several drawings and paintings Jo has made over her short life. I also have a large framed drawing of snow falling onto evergreen trees that Claire made. I loved it from the moment I saw it and begged Claire to let me have it. It's so serene and beautiful, bringing me a certain kind of peace. What Matthew tells me sounds reasonable, though we have a half bath on the first floor.

"Oh, there's a restroom downstairs. I can show you." My heartbeat slowly returns to normal as I lead the way. He follows me, and I point out the tiny room in the hallway when we reach the bottom. While he's occupied, I return to the kitchen to see that our waste is in the trash bin, and it even looks like he's wiped down the counters. I can hear the toilet flush, and he comes around the corner a minute later. I hand him a beer but grab a bottle of water for myself.

"No beer?" he asks. I shake my head, shunning beer since one horrible experience in high school, and we walk to the living room, settling down on opposite ends of the couch. "Sammi, I want to apologize. When we went on our date, I acted like a jerk. I really liked you and reacted poorly when you said you didn't want a relationship. It hurt, but I mean it when I say I'm okay with just being friends. I hope you'll give me the chance to prove to you that I'm actually not a jackass."

This is a different side of Matthew. He always seems so well put together and even a little arrogant. I like this softer side of him. "It's okay. I get it, but I appreciate your willingness to give the whole friend thing a try. I'm sorry I forgot that I invited you over. I've been so tired lately."

"No problem. I think you were a bit distracted." He pauses, watching my face, but I don't respond. I know he's prodding me, and I'm not going to take the bait. "So, I thought you weren't dating Ciaran, but I guess things changed. How is that going?" I was hoping if I didn't offer, he wouldn't ask, but I can't avoid it now.

"Yeah, we're not really dating. Are you sure you're okay talking about this?" Even if he's okay with it, I'm not comfortable. But how do I avoid the subject without being rude?

"Yes, that's what friends do. It's cool," he replies.

Okay, I guess we're really talking about this. "Like I said, we're not really dating. We're just kind of.... I don't know, getting to know each other. What about you and Vanessa? You're still together?"

"Yeah, she's something else. We have fun together. As long as we keep it casual, I'm good with it."

"I see." He gives off the most conflicting vibes. One minute he seems like he wants to settle down with someone, and the next, he seems like he just wants to get lucky. He says he's not into having kids, but he wanted to go on a date with me, knowing I'm a mother. I don't really know what to make of it.

After that, we settle into a comfortable conversation about everything from our childhoods, to embarrassing moments as a teenager, and leading up to my marriage. When we reach that point, I clam up, and Matthew can tell the conversation isn't going anywhere. We sit in awkward silence for a few minutes.

"Well, thanks for the company tonight. I had a good time, but I should get out of your hair."

"Thanks, I actually enjoyed myself," I tell him, picking up his single empty bottle. I hand him the remainder of the pack of beer from the refrigerator.

"I'll see you later, Sammi." He gives me a hug, and I genuinely hug him back. With that, he walks out the door.

Once his taillights fade from sight out the window, I call Claire back. It's already late, but she's a night owl. How that will change when Will arrives.

"What did Matthew want?" she barks out as a greeting.

"Gee, hi, Sammi. Thanks for calling me back." She doesn't respond to me. She's not in the mood tonight. "He said I invited him to come by and hang out, but honestly, I don't remember asking him. Either way, it was nice. I think the friend thing may actually work out."

"Sammi, you're oblivious to how beautiful you are, but I hope you're right. Do you want to tell me what was bothering you earlier?"

I don't, but I do need to talk to her about things. I can't keep putting it off. "Nothing earlier, but I did need to talk to you. You remember when I had to work really late on Friday? There was someone outside the shop, looking in. I could have sworn it was

Lucas, but they were already across the street before I could get outside. Then, as you know, my car wouldn't start, and I had to call Matthew to help out, since you left your phone in your purse." I only rambled slightly.

"Okay..." she says, drawing out the word. "I get the feeling there's more to the story."

"There is." I pause, unsure how to proceed. I decide to just bulldoze ahead, "Then, you sent Ciaran to bring me lunch today. Thank you for that, by the way. While we were sitting there eating, I looked up, and I could have sworn Lucas was standing at the window. Whoever it was left pretty quickly, but I guess it freaked me out a little. What if Lucas is in town?"

She doesn't answer right away, and there's tense silence between us before she finally speaks. "Why would Lucas be in town? He hasn't wanted anything to do with you or Jo."

"Heavens, Claire, I don't know." I realize my voice is tight and my pitch raised, and I take a deep breath before proceeding. "It probably wasn't him. I'm just asking, what if it was."

"I wouldn't worry about it. If Lucas IS in town and DOES want to talk to you, he'll approach you. But given that he hasn't, chances are it's someone who just looks like him. It's probably someone who works in the same strip of shops." She's right.

"I'm sorry. I just guess I'm still tense, and my mind is probably playing tricks on me," I respond.

"You know I'm right. Put it out of your mind and focus on the now. Speaking of, how is Ciaran? How was your lunch?" She's ready to change the subject, and it's probably best we do.

"Well, other than the fact he probably thinks I'm a lunatic after my possible Lucas sighting, it was good. I asked if he'd like to go on a date some time, and he said yes, if he hasn't changed his mind. How are things on your end?" I hope he hasn't changed his mind.

"Eh, same old, same old. Just waiting on this baby." I hear Jesse in the background. "Listen, I have to go, but before I do, I just want to remind you that you're tied down, whether you're dating or not. You have family here. Family isn't just blood. You have a business and a home. Jo has school and friends. And Grandma Jolene would want you here, so close to where we grew up. She never wanted you to be alone. So, carpe diem or some shit like that." She's right. I already have roots here, although I don't point out that I've never had any issue with the possibility of pulling up those roots if it meant protecting my daughter.

"Okay, okay. I'll call you soon. Tell Jesse hi for me." After I hang up, I actually feel a little better. But I do feel like I need to tell Ciaran a little bit more about the past, even if not everything. Before climbing into bed, I text him and ask what he's doing this weekend. I'm asleep before my head even hits the pillow.

Chapter Twelve

Married life wasn't as blissful as I expected – as I had built it up to be in my dreams, to say the least. Things continued to decline the longer we were home. It was like someone stuck a pin in Lucas, and all the goodwill and positive changes leaked out of him. For the first few weeks after our fight, Lucas actually seemed focused on achieving his writing goals again. He was usually typing away at his laptop, an espresso perched on the table next to him, when I left for work. I'd been picking up more morning and afternoon shifts over the summer, and when I'd come home for dinner, he'd be in nearly the same position. When August rolled around, I had convinced myself that we were over the obstacle that we encountered when we first returned from our honeymoon, and things were really back to normal. Classes started up, and with my heavy coarse load, it didn't take long for my grades to suffer. I knew I'd need to cut back on hours at work if I wanted to graduate. When I brought it up with Lucas, his reaction left me feeling unmoored.

"You can't cut back on your hours. We need that money. How can I focus on writing, when I'm constantly worried about paying the damn bills?" His anger was palpable, the veins in his neck pronounced against the red flush of his skin.

"What are you talking about, Lucas? I thought the money your dad left in the account was going to last until you got a publishing contract for your book."

"It's almost gone. You blew through it with your fancy wedding and expensive honeymoon. It's your fault. You fuck up every-thing." With that, he stormed out the door.

All I could do was sit there, my heart pounding. It was the harshest he'd ever been with me, even when we did fight. I didn't want a big wedding. We only had a few guests, and he picked the honeymoon location. I didn't even care if we had one. My grandma left me money, but I was saving it for when we perma-nently settled down somewhere. I didn't want to put money down on a house and not be able to make the monthly payments. Some of that money needed to be saved too. Maybe once I graduated and had a full-time job, I could do it on my own. But not right then. Who knew where Lucas and I would land after I graduated? The world was open to us. We could go anywhere. But a part of me I didn't want to acknowledge was also screaming at me to save the money. I would swear that I even heard my grandma, telling me to hold on to it.

Although it was still early, I pulled on sweats and crawled into bed. I called Claire from my cell, though I didn't know if I'd be able to speak when she answered. She picked up after one ring.

"Sammi, I was just about to call you. Are you okay?" She al-ways knows. I was crying and couldn't catch my breath to re-spond. "That's it. I'm coming to get you. What the hell did Lucas do? Jesse's going to kill him. No, I'm going to kill him. Are you at your apartment?"

Sniffling, I gasped in air and managed to form words. "Don't. It's okay. We just had a fight about money. He told me that I fuck up everything. Why would he say that, Claire?"

"Because he's an asshole. I should have known... Everything in me said that you'd be better off without him. Come stay with us. Bill and Susan have plenty of room."

"Claire, I can't. I have classes and work. Listen, I'm tired. Can I call you tomorrow?" Even though we'd barely talked, I felt exhausted.

"Don't hang up, Sammi. Are you sure you're really okay? I'll drive there now and pick you up. You don't have to stay."

"Yes, I do. He's my husband. I'll talk to you later, Claire." I thought she was right, but I wasn't ready to go there. What would Lucas do without me? I couldn't abandon him, especially when he was going through a difficult time.

"He doesn't have to be. Call me anytime. I can be there in the blink of an eye." Her voice was louder than normal. I could tell she was trying to rein in her anger before she said something she'd regret.

I disconnected and rubbed my eyes. There was nothing left to do, except cry myself to sleep. When I got up the next morning, Lucas's side of the bed was still cold, the sheet tucked in tight.

On Thursday morning, Ciaran calls and asks if Jo and I would like to go out for pizza on Saturday. My dream of Lucas stirred something deep within, even more determination to keep myself open to this thing with Ciaran, to give him a chance. I deserve more than I had with Lucas. The fact Ciaran includes Jo on his date invitation means a lot to me. After all, we're a set deal. She's my other half. We plan to get together for lunch, knowing that Jo will get tired early, especially given her recent refusal of naps. That makes for a cranky kid by the time late afternoon rolls around.

When Saturday morning arrives, Jo is nearly jumping up and down in excitement, even though I've reminded her, repeatedly, that Fergus won't be there. From what Ciaran told me Thursday, Fergus seems to have himself a lady friend, and I'm incredibly happy for him. I worry a little bit about Jo's excitement to see Ciaran, with everything still so new and fresh in our burgeoning relationship. Over breakfast, she drops a whopper that concerns me even more.

"Mommy, is Ciaran going to be my daddy?"

I choke on my oatmeal and cough loudly, trying to catch my breath. I know I have to give her an answer, and it needs to be well thought out. I'm nowhere near ready for that level of commitment.

Before I respond, she opens her mouth again. "It's just, I don't have a daddy. At school, Mikey said my daddy didn't love me, and I said he does, so Mikey asked me his name. And I didn't know his name."

That damn kid. I'm going to have to call her teacher again. My heart is breaking. I've failed her.

"I'm sorry, Jo. Ciaran is just our friend. We like to do stuff with him and have a good time, but Mommy isn't marrying him. We barely know him. We'll spend some time with him and get to know him better. While we do that, do you think you can just be his friend?"

She frowns and appears to be contemplating my response. Or she's considering my question.

"Yes, Mommy. I can be his friend. I just really like him. And Papa too! But is Ciaran your boyfriend?" It takes me a second to remember that she has been calling Fergus "Papa."

What does she know about boyfriends? Nowadays, kids know far too much, far too soon.

"Fergus is definitely a fun person to be around! I like him too. Ciaran is sort of my boyfriend, but that still doesn't mean we'll get married. As far as your daddy, he had some problems, and he wasn't ready to be a daddy. It was better for us to move here and be closer to Auntie Claire and Uncle Jesse. Don't you like living near them? Soon, you'll have William to play with too. ...Now, finish up your breakfast. We need to run a few errands before lunch."

She's quiet now and is clearly still mulling over things as she chews, but I think I did okay. My response was far from perfect, but I've always been better at explaining things when given time to formulate my response. It's the first time she's directly asked me about her father, and it's a conversation I've dreaded from the day I left. Even when Mikey teased her before, she didn't ask me where her father was. She just mentioned not having a dad, unlike all the other kids. She must be satisfied with my answer, finishing up her meal and skipping off to go pick out clothes for the day. Once breakfast is cleaned up and we're dressed, Jo in a pink explosion of leggings and her favorite sweatshirt, we go to the store for her to pick out a few small gifts from the dollar bins for Claire, Jesse, and Jesse's parents.

Bill and Susan always have gifts for her. I'm grateful for the role they've taken in her life, in the absence of grandparents. I'm not surprised when she asks if she can get something for Ciaran and Fergus too, and I let her. She's so excited, and I don't want to dampen her mood. Plus, it will be nice for her to have something for them when they give her their gifts. We also pick up a few rolls of wrapping paper, and she chooses one with Barbies to use on her newfound presents.

As we wait to pay, I see someone in line at the Starbucks in the front of the store and do a double take. I can only see them from the side, but it looks like Lucas. I keep seeing him, and it can't be a coincidence. Is he following us? It has to be him. This is one time too many. I keep an eye on him in the long line as we check out, but he never turns. He orders as we're finishing up and moves off to wait for his beverage. My anger has continued to amplify as we move past the register, and I wouldn't doubt if steam has begun to roll out from my ears. This is not okay. He's not allowed to pop up in our lives whenever it's convenient for him. He made a choice four years ago, and we haven't heard from him since.

Even though Jo is with me, I know I need to confront him. This may be the only chance, and it has to end now. I place our empty basket back in a stand, and take Jo's hand on one side, bags on my other side. Weaving our way through the Starbucks crowd that keeps growing larger, I approach Lucas, who is staring out the window with his back to me.

"Excuse me," I say, tapping his shoulder, letting go of Jo's hand briefly. He turns to see who's touched him. When he turns around, I can't help but let out a gasp. It's not Lucas. I can see that. "I'm so sorry. I thought you were someone else..."

I'm already backing away, but the large crowd is making movement slow. Why is Starbucks this busy? I need to get out of here, to escape.

"It's okay, no harm done. I have a generic face. Hey, are you okay? You look like you've seen a ghost," the stranger chuckles with the last sentence.

"Yes, thank you, just a mistake." I pick up Jo and push my way through the crowd, nearly running until we reach the safety of our car.

I've just buckled myself in when Jo speaks up from her car seat, "Who was that, Mommy?"

"Oh, Mommy just thought it was someone she knew from college. I was wrong. No big deal. Do you want me to plug in your movie?" She does, and it keeps her busy until we reach home. Crisis averted, once again.

When we get home, Jo insists on wrapping her presents for everyone by herself. We decided to have Ciaran come here, and we'll all ride in my car. Even though it's within walking distance, it's so frigid that driving is the better option. Jo runs up to her bedroom shortly before his expected arrival, and when she comes back down, she's changed into her favorite pair of leggings, with a dress, and she's carrying a purse. It looks like she's brushed her hair, little pieces of frizz sticking out around her face. If she was a teenager, I'd swear she was going on a date for herself. I start to question my own appearance: messy bun, torn jeans, and a well-loved sweater, but Ciaran rings the bell before I can even think of changing. Jo runs to open the door.

"Hi, Jo! Don't you look beautiful? Your dress is so colorful! Are you all ready for some pizza?" He looks up, and his smile is bigger than I've ever seen it. "Sammi, you look lovely."

I'm a little embarrassed at all this. It's been so long since I went on a date, or even a pseudo-date, where I was actually excited. What if I do this all wrong? My blind dates over the last year haven't exactly been good practice. Thinking, I realize that the last time I was excited about a date with someone new was when Lucas and I had our first date, back in 2011. It doesn't make me feel any better. What if I get food stuck in my teeth, or I spill something on him, or I snort when I laugh?

"Thank you. You look nice too." And he does, his legs tall and lean in his dark blue jeans, a light-yellow button-down peeking from under his black parka. We all head out to my car, but I make sure to lock the door behind me, double checking it before I get into my car. When we arrive at the pizza place, Jo picks a booth and insists on sitting next to Ciaran. He doesn't seem to be put out.

"Ciaran, I have to tell you something. I bought you a Christmas present today," Jo says, as she pulls a loosely wrapped package from her purse. So, that's why she wanted a bag... She hands him the gift.

"Wow, thanks, Jo. You shouldn't have. Do I open it now?" Of course, she can't wait for him to open it, and he gingerly pulls apart the taped pieces to find a phone charging cord inside. "This is perfect, Jo! How did you know I needed one of these?"

She's beaming from ear to ear. His reaction was exactly what she wanted. She proceeds to hand him the gift for Fergus and asks him to pass it along, to which he heartily agrees. How did I get so lucky, that of all the kids born every day, Jo is mine?

Our food arrives, and we talk while we eat. Most of the conversation is controlled by Jo, who feels the need to give Ciaran a lengthy description of everything she's done over the last week. He interjects a few times to show he's truly listening, and a little bit more of the wall around my heart chips away. Lunch is done far too soon. Jo is starting to slow down, talking even as her eyes are drooping closed. She must be even more tired than usual.

While riding back to our house, Jo falls asleep. Only a child can doze off in a three-minute car ride. Ciaran carries her in for me and lays her on the couch. We move to the kitchen to avoid waking her.

"Thanks, Ciaran. She's stubborn about not napping lately, and clearly, she still needs one. I had a good time today. Thanks for acting so excited about the phone cord. ...Just a warning, she got a candle for Fergus. It smells like burned cookies, but she liked it."

"Who said I was acting? I'm always losing my charging cords. And Dad will love a candle, no matter the scent." He laughs, and I can't help laughing along with him.

I lean in to kiss him, before stepping back to take a deep breath. "Listen, before you go, I need to talk to you. I told you I was married before, and it didn't end well. But I think I owe you more of an explanation."

"You don't have to tell me anything, Sammi. It won't change the way I feel about you," he promises.

"No, I do need to tell you. I met Lucas when I was eighteen. He was my first boyfriend. ...We got married when I was twenty-one. He had some issues with alcohol, along with the concept of fidelity. I went through some trauma before Jo was born, and while he was great at first, it didn't last. Jo was about six months old when I moved back here, and I haven't talked to him or his family since. ...It's just that, like I told you before, I haven't really dated since then. I've spent a lot of years trying to work through the trauma I experienced and let go of things. I like you, but I won't risk Jo getting hurt. So, I'm not asking you to marry me. I'm nowhere near ready for that, but if you're looking for a quick score, I'm not your girl."

He's silent, watching me as I talk. His face is open, and I dare to think he understands, but I'm so nervous he's going to just walk out. I don't exactly have the best experiences with men to draw on, one of my previous blind dates coming to mind, in which he simply excused himself to the restroom in the middle of the date and never returned to the table.

I can see Ciaran swallow and take his own deep breath before he answers. "I'm sorry, Sammi. Your ex was an asshole. I'm sorry for whatever else you've gone through that has convinced you that everyone is going to hurt you. I'm here for the long haul, if you'll have me. And if you decide you're not in it too, I promise to find a way we can still be friends."

I'm more relieved than I want him to know, and I move closer to him, pressing my head against his chest. He cups my head with one hand and wraps the other around my shoulders. Warmth spreads into me, and with it comes comfort. His lips press against the top of my head, and I pull back to meet him with my own. He lets me lead, and after a minute, I pull away again.

"Thank you for being you." He smiles back at me. "On a different topic, I wanted to ask you something. Are you free next weekend? I have to work Saturday morning, but Claire is having a Christmas party, and I thought you might like to come. ...Like, as my date. Your dad can come too. He can even bring a date of his own." Nervously, I add, "You don't have to come, if you don't want to. You may be tired of our nutty, little group." I laugh anxiously.

"It sounds perfect. Your nutty, little group is exactly where I want to be. What time should we be there? Should I bring any food or gifts?"

"Nope, just yourself." I kiss him again, lingering this time, and his warmth pushes into me once more. What am I getting myself into?

"I should get going. I have to run some errands. But I'll see you tomorrow at church." He leans down for one more kiss before leaving. After, I press my back against the door, a sigh escaping me. I feel like I'm eighteen again.

Chapter Thirteen

It's early on Sunday when the doorbell rings, and my first thought is that maybe Claire has decided to join us. When I peek out the window, Matthew is standing on the porch. What is he doing here so early?

I slowly undo the lock and pull open the door. "Matthew, I wasn't expecting you this morning." I don't ask why he's here, but I hope the question is implied.

"Sorry to just stop in," he begins to apologize. "I was going to go to church this morning and thought I'd see if you would like to join me. Possibly catch a bite to eat after... Jo likes pancakes, doesn't she?"

"Well, actually, Jo and I always go to church. We're about to leave."

"Oh, perfect. Maybe I can join you?" he asks. "Do you go to the same church as Claire? She suggested a place to me, but I don't know how it is."

It seems a little weird, but maybe I'm just overreacting. "Sure, how about we meet you there? I can tell you where it is, if you're not sure."

"Okay. I'm good. We used to run these roads in high school." Sometimes, I forget that Matthew grew up in the city here. Near to us, yet a world away.

As Jo and I drive to church this morning, something feels off, and I'm not convinced that it's Matthew. My anxiety is worked up, and my mind is racing. My body is wired in anticipation of something. I just wish I knew what. I know I have anxiety, but I've never taken medication for it. When my anxiety gets like this, I have a tendency to dwell in the past.

Once I leave Jo in her classroom, Matthew and I move toward my usual spot. Thank goodness, Claire is already seated there. She scoots over to make room for us, and as I sit, I look back to see Ciaran watching. I wave, and he waves back, but it's half-hearted, his eyes barely straying from the hole they're burning in the back of Matthew's head. I can feel his eyes move to me as the pastor begins speaking, and my anxiety intensifies. My leg is bouncing like crazy, and I'm sure I'm shaking Matthew's chair next to mine. Why did Lucas have to mess with my head so much? I can't even enjoy a peaceful Sunday sermon.

I ended up not cutting back on hours at work, and I was struggling to manage all of my responsibilities. To top it off, the transmission on Betty went out, and I couldn't afford to fix her until I could put back money for a few weeks. Lucas wasn't kidding when he said the money was gone, but I still questioned where it really went. I didn't know the password to the bank account anymore, and I didn't dare ask Lucas, still walking on eggshells around him. There were no statements hidden away. The thought of searching for the password was overwhelming. I could have reached out to the bank, but a part of me was afraid to know. It was easier to live in denial.

With Lucas never home, there was no intimacy, and I stopped my birth control. I never liked the way it made me feel and figured if he did show interest, I could simply avoid it around a certain time of the month. I started walking to classes and work most of the time, occasionally getting a ride from Lucas when the weather was poor. It was easier to be gone than home, wondering what would set Lucas off next, where he was, and who he was with when he wasn't home.

Around Labor Day, I kept feeling eyes on me. I heard footsteps behind me as I walked, but I would turn around to see no one there. I convinced myself that all the stress of work, money, and classes was getting to me. My stress level was far too high. After two weeks, I mentioned it to Lucas. He laughed it off, and I burned with shame as we sat there, him chuckling at my expense. "Why would someone be following you, Sammi? It's not like you take care of yourself anymore." So, that's why he never touched me anymore.

Snippets of nasty comments from my childhood played on a loop in my head, and I was embarrassed of myself. Claire had been calling me every night, but I told her, repeatedly, that nothing was wrong. She even tried to visit, unannounced, but I acted as if everything was fine.

I continued to feel watched over the next couple months, even when I took trips to see Claire and Jesse, always without Lucas. The constant feeling of eyes on me was getting out of hand, and I knew it, but I was too scared to admit that I needed help. I was determined to stick it out in my marriage, despite Claire pressuring me to move home. This was just a rough patch. Every marriage went through rough patches. I wouldn't leave Lucas. We belonged together, for better or worse.

I took to wearing headphones and playing music to block out the phantom footsteps that were, apparently, only in my mind. Depression became a serious problem for me. Things at home were tense too, only getting worse every day, and Lucas and I appeared to be in a stalemate. We were barely talking. Our conversations were jilted and shallow. For the first time, I admitted to myself that we may not recover from it. I was determined to ride this out, but there was nothing stopping Lucas from leaving me.

He tried a few times to start something sexual with me, and I pretended to be asleep. It had been so long since he had reached for me like that, and the last thing we needed at that point, with so much unexpressed anger between us, was to have a baby. Then, the Monday night before Halloween, it was as if a flip had magically switched on for Lucas.

We were sitting on the couch, silent. A new fantasy book lay open on my lap, and Lucas was watching the Cowboys game. He turned down the television and turned to me.

"Sammi, we need to talk." His voice was pleading, yet firm. I looked up at him, fully expecting this to be when he asked me for a divorce.

"I'm so sorry for the way I've been behaving. I've been a real jerk. There's just so much anger over my dad, and I keep getting rejections on my book. I realize that I've been taking it out on you." This wasn't the conversation I had expected.

"You've been a real ass, Lucas. I needed you, and you made me feel unloved and crazy." ...Even I was surprised by my words. I'd never been assertive. But I was angry. Angry that he thought an apology would magically make things better. Angry that he shut me out. Angry that he hadn't even told me he finished the book, much less sent it to anyone.

"You're right. I have no excuse. But I don't want to lose you. Can you forgive me?"

He was looking at me expectantly. I wanted to make him wait, to punish him. But I knew I'd forgive him, and I think he knew it too. "Fine, but things have to change around here."

"Name it, and I'll do it," he offered.

"No more drinking. No more late nights. I'm killing myself trying to support us AND finish my classes, and I need you home with me. I barely see you." I could feel my pulse, skittish under my skin.

"Consider it done."

He leaned forward and kissed me, and my steely resolve melted. I found myself back in my place of safety, my place of refuge. We would survive this difficult period in our marriage. Once I graduated, we would move somewhere new, where we could both let go of the baggage we had in St. Louis. His kisses grew more feverish, and all my recent fears of being followed fled from my mind. Right in that moment, I felt whole. Lucas was my biggest weakness. He had been since the day I first saw him.

Afterward, I laid next to him in bed. His snores lightly rumbled through the room and heat poured from his body, warming my feet in our exceptionally chilly apartment. When I woke the next morning, I found a note on his pillow that he went out for coffee and bagels. I rested my head back and closed my eyes, reflecting back on the previous night. Then, it hit me what time of the month it was, and my heart sunk. All I could do, though, was wait.

I come back to myself when we rise to pray. I can still feel Ciaran's presence, him watching me. His eyes bore into me, flitter away, then return. I dash out to pick up Jo, Matthew waiting for us in the vestibule. I suck at social skills, and while I want to see Ciaran, I don't want a confrontation between him and

Matthew. I know they don't care for each other. Claire waits behind with Matthew. When I come back out, they're both standing there with Ciaran. Claire is chattering away, but Ciaran and Matthew are facing off against each other, arms crossed and chests puffed up like peacocks. My heart is racing, and I can feel a thin sheen of sweat bead on my forehead, suddenly roasting in my winter coat. Jo sees everyone and scrambles down from my arms to run to Ciaran, leaping into his arms. Matthew does a double take but doesn't say anything. Jo whispers something to Ciaran, and he laughs.

When I reach them, Ciaran leans down to kiss my cheek, still holding Jo. "Sammi, how are you?" He turns to Matthew, "Matthew, I'm surprised to see you here. I hope you enjoyed the service." While his tone is amicable, his body language is telling a different story.

Matthew is nothing if not polite, responding, "I did. It was nice to experience the message with Sammi. I decided it was time to find a more permanent church home now that I'm not traveling as much, and Claire recommended trying out this one. I think it's a good fit. Now, if you'll excuse us, we have somewhere to be." His dismissal is clear, but Ciaran is not so easily deterred.

"Of course. Just one moment." He turns back to me, "Sammi, I was hoping I could take you and Jo to lunch after. But if you have somewhere to be, perhaps we can have a dinner DATE tonight instead." His emphasis on the word date is clear, his hand lightly rubbing my upper arm through my coat. I can feel his heat searing into me, even through the layers. Matthew bristles next to me, and I wish Claire would open her big mouth right now. I need to defuse the ticking time bomb.

Matthew speaks up, "We're going out for brunch. I already invited Claire to join us. Why don't you come along too, Ciaran? There's always room for one more." I'm surprised, and my head whips to Matthew, but his face seems so sincere. "Sammi is my friend, and if she wants you to come along, you're welcome." He's either really trying hard to be my friend, or he's the best actor I've ever seen.

"Sure, I'd love to." I didn't really expect Ciaran to accept. Apparently, there is a game afoot with two contenders, me stuck in the middle.

Thirty minutes later, the five of us are seated awkwardly around a table. Matthew was sure to snag a seat on one side of me, Claire plopping down next to him. To my surprise, Jo takes Ciaran's hand, guiding him to the seat on my other side and inserting herself next to Claire. A quick glance to my left confirms that Matthew has noticed, but he quickly moves back to perusing the menu. We make small talk while waiting for our food, and a few bites into the meal, Jo climbs into Ciaran's lap, dozing off against his chest. He manages to awkwardly eat his pancakes without disrupting her sleep, and I can't help but think that once upon a time, it's the kind of moment I envisioned us having with Lucas. It leaves a pit in my stomach, thinking of his inability to love my beautiful girl. As we finish eating, the conversation picks up, though Claire and I are primarily observers. Matthew and Ciaran share a game of verbal volleyball, asking questions of one another that range from benign to those meant to dig in some barbs. Claire watches it all with an amused smirk on her face and looks at me with a knowing lift of her eyebrows. When the server asks about the bill, I begin to say how it should be split, but Ciaran speaks up and offers to pay. Matthew insists he will pay because he invited us all out to eat. I think Ciaran will argue, but he doesn't, simply thanking Matthew for his generosity. I'm impressed with his ability to back down and let Matthew take the spotlight. As we're getting ready to go, Matthew gets a text on his phone.

He glances down, then at my face. "I'm sorry, but I need to go. Thanks for spending today with me. I'll talk to you later?" I nod, and he leans in for a quick hug before dashing away. Ciaran easily lifts a still sleeping Jo in his arms, and I grab his coat for him. One-handed, he drapes it over Jo's back to keep her warm.

Outside the door, Claire leans in to me and whispers in my ear, "I'll call you later." Then, she rubs a hand over Jo's head and tells Ciaran bye, going around the corner to her own car. Ciaran buckles Jo into her car seat for me.

"Well, that was interesting." He laughs and runs his hand through his hair, a habit I've observed him doing several times now, usually when he's not sure what else to say.

"Sorry, I know that was weird. He's really trying hard to be friends," I tell Ciaran.

"Sammi, that was not the look of a man who's okay with just being friends. That is a man biding his time until you change your mind," he retorts.

"Don't be ridiculous. He's been perfectly respectable. Maybe you're just jealous." I hope he says he is because I don't want to think that he's right.

He takes a step forward and puts his hands on my waist. He tells me through kisses to my lips, "I. Am. Most. Definitely. Jealous." He takes a step back, "I don't want to be that guy, though. I trust you."

He's too good to be true. I pull him down to me and give him a kiss that should leave him breathless. "Call me later?"

"Absolutely," he says, and he steps away while I get into my car. I wave at him as I pull away, and the smile on my face lifts my spirits. I'm so thankful to be through what may have been the most awkward meal of my entire life.

Chapter Fourteen

The following week drags on. We're usually busier in December than this, but for some reason, this week doesn't have the level of business to which I'm accustomed. A few times, I see someone out the window that looks like Lucas, but I've managed to convince myself to stop being paranoid. Ciaran calls me every night after Jo goes to sleep, and we talk about anything and everything. He tells me more about his ex-girlfriend back in California and trips he'd like to take, and I tell him stories about growing up with Grandma Jolene and Claire. Fergus decided to take the Christmas trip with Fiona and Richard, leaving Christmas Eve and not returning until after New Year's. We make plans for them to come over the Sunday after Claire's party for a Christmas brunch, to give gifts to Jo. I'm not sure if I should get Ciaran a gift, so I text Claire, to which she emphatically tells me I should. I text Matthew again about the car seat, but he still doesn't respond to me. I should have mentioned it when I saw him, but I didn't want to spill the surprise in front of Claire. I haven't heard anything from him since our post-church gathering, and I'm honestly a little relieved. But I also need to get the gift situation for Claire and Jesse sorted out. After a few days, I finally tell him that I'm going to get them something else, if he wants to take care of the car seat on his own. I don't want to be on the hook for his half, and I can't wait for him forever.

Thursday, Ciaran and I are talking again. I decide to ask him if he'd like to come over on Christmas Day, since he's all alone. I hope it's not too forward, but he agrees. Claire and Jesse plan to come over that morning. His parents are flying out to Colorado for the holiday this year, plans made before Claire and Jesse found out about the baby coming around the holiday. I decide I'll do a nice casserole on Christmas Day, to keep it simple, but I want to make a ham for the Christmas meal with Ciaran and Fergus.

I take a long lunch to run to the store for last-minute gifts. For Fergus, I pick out a picture frame and plan to put in a photo of him and Jo that Claire snapped at Fergus's party. For Ciaran, I buy him a sketchbook and a charcoal drawing set. It's time for him to get back into art for himself. Claire also took a picture of us at the same party that I'll slip inside the cover of the sketchbook. We're deep in conversation, oblivious to the people around us, his eyes serious and focused on mine. It's perfect. As a last-minute thought, I throw in a bottle of Jameson Irish Whiskey. I'm not sure if Fergus or Ciaran drinks whiskey, both sticking to non-alcoholic beverages when we've been together, but it might be a nice treat when they come over. Last night, I ordered a gift card to a nice hotel for Jesse and Claire and printed out a coupon for free overnight babysitting services to go with it. I know how much I appreciated a good night's sleep when Jo was little, though I had no one to share my bed for it. With my Christmas shopping done, I stock up on a few essentials in the grocery aisles and check out. On the way to the car, a tingle runs up my spine again, and I can't stop shivering, despite the slightly warmer than normal temperatures. It's a relief to get into my car and pull away, the feeling fading the closer I get back to work.

Ciaran sends me a text Friday morning to let me know he'll be out of town for the day with his dad, taking him on an impromptu drive to see an old friend. It starts unexpectedly snowing early in the morning, and by noon, it's clear that no one will be coming into the shop. I call Josef and tell him not to bother coming in at one. As I tidy up, Jo's preschool sends out a mass text that they're closing early due to the snow, so I put up a closed sign and head out to pick her up. She'll be on break until after New Year's. The tires slip a bit on the pavement, and my knuckles are white the whole crawling drive back to the house. When I go to pull into the driveway's incline, my tires spin. I'm near tears when I see a dark truck turn down the street and slow to a stop before hitting my car. Memories from last month flash in my mind, and I feel sick, double checking the locks. Saliva fills my mouth. To my shock, Matthew climbs out and approaches my Civic. With relief, I crack the door to speak to him.

"Sammi, are you okay? You look like you're about to cry. I just thought I'd check on you guys with the weather, make sure you had plenty of food." His eyes are filled with genuine concern.

"Matthew, I'm so glad you're here. I'm stuck. The tires can't get any traction," I tell him. He motions me over, and I climb into the passenger seat, letting him in the driver's seat. After a minute of no movement, he gets out and moves around the car slowly. When he returns to the driver's seat, he manages to get my car up the drive and into the garage. He heads back to his truck and pulls into the driveway, while I unload Jo into the house. I can see from the window he has a Ford Ranger. Once he's inside, I immediately turn to thank him.

"Thank you so much. I was worried about having to leave the car in the street or digging out the driveway before I could pull it in. You're a lifesaver." I pause, considering his vehicle. "Did you get a new truck, by the way? I thought you have an Audi."

"Yeah, I still have the Audi, but I've been wanting a truck for quite some time. I got it a few weeks ago, but I haven't driven it much. Listen, the snow is supposed to stop in a few hours, but visibility is shit. I didn't expect it to be this bad. Do you mind if I hang out here for a bit until it slows?"

"Of course not. Make yourself welcome. Are you wet or cold? I can make some coffee," I offer. It's a small gesture.

"I'd love some, thank you. You know, I have a snow blower in my truck. I just bought it earlier today. Talk about great timing. I can clean your driveway for you before I head home. I'd just like to move the snow blower into the vacant spot in the garage while we wait, if that's okay." The thought of shoveling snow is certainly unappealing. While he goes outside to move it, I check my phone and have a text from Ciaran checking in on me. I give him a quick call.

"Sammi, thank goodness you're okay. It's nasty out there," he begins.

I'm certainly not going to hide Matthew's assistance from him. Keeping secrets like that is not a great way to start a relationship. "Yeah, we got stuck trying to get in the driveway, but Matthew came by and helped out. Are you trying to come back tonight?" I'm hoping to see him, but I'd much rather he stays out of harm's way.

He's quiet for a minute and I think the call has dropped. He finally speaks, "We're going to crash here tonight. His buddy has a guest room and a recliner that's calling my name. I just don't want to risk the drive when the roads are like this. Are you okay? Is Matthew still there?"

Matthew comes in the door, and I hold up a finger while I reply to Ciaran, "Yes, he's here now. He's going to clear the driveway once it stops in a couple hours, then head home."

"You'll be careful, right?" It's an odd question as it is, but I feel even more awkward with Matthew standing there, waiting for me. I can hear Jo running back to the kitchen too.

"Of course. Listen, I need to go for now, but will you let me know when you leave in the morning?" I'm disappointed he won't be back in town, but their safety is far more important.

"Sure. Be safe, Sammi. Bye." He hangs up before I respond. Matthew's watching me, and I plaster a big grin on my face. Jo asks to go out in the snow. I tell her I don't feel up to it, but Matthew offers to take her out. It's cold, so I give her a twenty-minute time limit and bundle her up in her snow gear. I heat a can of tomato soup on the stove and assemble ingredients for grilled cheese, watching out the window as Matthew helps her build a snowman, snow still falling around them. They come in exactly twenty minutes later, noses and cheeks red, smiles on their faces. Jo runs to me and presses her cold nose against my arm, sending a chill through me, while Matthew laughs. Again, I'm struck feeling like this is another moment she should have with Lucas. Instead, she's having it with someone I'm not even dating. Once I have her in warm, dry clothes, I move to the kitchen to serve up dinner. To my surprise, Matthew's changed into black sweats and a hoodie, and he's at the stove, flipping the grilled cheese sandwiches.

"Thanks," I tell him. "You changed."

"Yeah, I had my gym bag in the cab, and the clothes were clean. I didn't think you'd mind." He raises an eyebrow in my direction.

"Of course, it's fine." We finish the sandwiches and ladle out the soup, the heat spreading through our limbs.

By the time the snow stops, later than anticipated, it's already dark, and the roads are slick. The storm wasn't in the forecast. The news began its coverage early, but accumulations are higher than predicted. We flip on the television to find reports of cars off the road everywhere. It's not safe for driving, even in a four-wheel drive truck. I can't push Matthew out the door in good conscience. I'd never forgive myself if something happened to him.

"Matthew, I think you should crash on the couch tonight. The roads are horrible."

He laughs. "Has anyone told you that you worry too much? I just need to clear your driveway, and then I'll get out of your hair."

His laughter doesn't make me feel any better. "I insist. It'll make me feel better knowing you aren't going to wreck trying to get home. I'm sorry I don't have a spare bed in the guest room, but I have fluffy pillows and blankets, and the couch is more comfortable than you'd expect."

"If it will really make you feel better, I'll stay," he replies, grinning. It's time for Jo to go to bed, so I leave him downstairs with a pillow and a throw while I tuck her into bed. I read her a story, then rock in her room until she falls asleep. The house is eerily quiet. I tiptoe back downstairs, but Matthew is already stretched out, asleep on the couch. I back out quietly, hitting the lights before leaving the room and heading up to my own bedroom. I'm exhausted but can't sleep. I toss and turn all

night, sitting up several times to look around, convinced someone is watching me. There's never anyone there. In the brief moments I sleep, events of the last several months are heavy on
my mind. Overall, I'm feeling better than I have in several weeks,
but something is still digging into my mind, begging to be heard.

*Halloween of 2014 fell on a Friday, and there was excitement
in the air as I proceeded through my classes. Fellow students were
excited for parties that night, but I couldn't wait to get home to
see Lucas. Things with him had been better since earlier in the
week. He was home at night and sober. He was optimistic that
he'd get good news on his book any day. It almost felt like we were
dating again, his spirit lighthearted and free. Things away from
home were still uncomfortable, wound tightly with fear. I continued to hear footsteps and the rustling of clothes behind me, but
I never saw anyone when I turned around. I hesitated to bring it
up to Lucas again, not wanting to tip over the precarious perch
on which we found ourselves. Instead, I tried to convince myself
that I was losing my mind, imagining things that go bump in the
night. The evenings with Lucas were like a balm on my soul. They
soothed and relaxed me, chasing away those imaginary demons
in my mind.*

*That day, I worked for a couple hours but was home by six in
the evening. There were a few kids out in the neighborhood, but
we never handed out candy while living in the apartment complex. It made me long for a home, the chance to greet kids with
a smile, and the opportunity to take my own children around in
their costumes, where we'd return to a quaint little home, both
exhausted and wound on sugar. I was hit with the need to have
Lucas put his arms around me and bounded up the stairs to our
apartment, only to be greeted by silence. I texted him to see when
he'd be home. After five minutes with no response, I called him,*

but it went straight to voicemail. Obviously, tonight wasn't going to go the way I expected, that I had hoped. Changing into sweatpants and my favorite hoodie, I crawled into bed and cried for a while. My phone rang repeatedly, but when I saw Claire's name on the screen, I sent it to voicemail. I just didn't have the heart to get into it with her that night. Finally, around ten, I heard Lucas's key in the lock. For fifteen minutes, he knocked around the kitchen. I could hear the tap running, the pipes groaning in protest. The cabinet doors opened and slammed shut moments later. When he finally stumbled into the bedroom, I could smell alcohol on him. Fury lit up my veins, propelling me into action, causing me to abandon my plan to feign sleep.

"Where have you been? You smell like someone poured a bottle of vodka all over you!"

I clearly startled him, and his eyes locked on me with such disdain that it caused me to shrink back in the bed. They were bloodshot and narrowed to slits. His face was flushed. I'd never been afraid Lucas would hit me before, but I saw something in his eyes that scared me. It was like he was a completely different person.

"Seriously, Sammi? I just got home, and you're already nagging me. Grow up!" His words were slurred as he muttered under his breath, "Why did I even marry you?"

They were the wrong words to say. He asked me to marry him, not the other way around. To hell with the violence simmering on the surface, waiting to boil over. "Screw you, Lucas. I tried texting you and calling you! I was worried. How did you even get home? Please tell me you weren't stupid enough to drive."

His voice dropped. Somehow, there was more threat in his carefully controlled tone than when he was yelling. "You are NOT my mother. If I wanted a babysitter, I'd move back home. Fuck off, Sammi." He spun, weaving his way into the bathroom and slamming the door. A few minutes later, I heard the water turn on. My whole body itched, and I felt like I couldn't stand to be in the apartment for even another minute. I slipped on my running shoes and walked out the door.

My path took me further from the apartment than I normally walked. My body tingled with an unpleasant anticipation, and I could hear Grandma Jolene in my ear, fervently telling me to go home. I turned around but still stewed over the fight. Even angry, I worried about Lucas, about the possibility of something happening to him while I foolishly walked off my anger. I picked up my pace with each step closer to home as it got eerily quiet. While I expected the streets to be bare of costumed children, I anticipated the loud noises of drunken students and parties, not this unsettling silence. My breath pulsed through my ears, and my footsteps sounded like a bass drum against the pavement. Thud, thud, thud. It wasn't far from home when I heard them, a second set of footsteps keeping pace with mine but treading lightly, as if someone didn't want to be heard. There was a short wall to my left, and I paused in front of it, cocking my head to focus on the noises around me. All sound stopped, and I couldn't even hear traffic from the interstate separating our neighborhood from campus. It was as if I had entered a vacuum, and I was suspended from the outside world. With a jolt, Grandma Jolene's voice became frantic in my ear, screaming at me to run. My breathing grew more fevered, and I thought I was having a heart attack, but I knew I had to get away. In only a few steps, I'd be past the wall, my sight open to everything around me. Moments before passing the wall, I turned around, unable to stop myself from checking for someone behind me. But there was no one in sight. Relieved, I stopped and bent down, my hands on my knees, trying to regain my composure. I was hearing things. I was okay.

When I stood back up and spun, a man was set before me, his chest a brick obstacle in my way. A scream ripped from my throat, and he backed away a step, hands up in surrender. Gin was heavy on his breath, and my stomach turned, threatening to expel my lunch from earlier that day. Taking several steps back, I looked him up and down. He had short, black hair neatly trimmed, and his face was clean shaven. He was dressed casually, in jeans and a navy-blue tee, paired with an empty dog leash. The thought popped into my head that in another time and place, I would have found him attractive. But the grin on his face spoke of mischief and deceit, his eyes dark and menacing, glittering with malice. He was the opposite of Lucas, who radiated light, even in his worst moments.

"Sorry to frighten you. My dog slipped his leash, and I can't find him. You haven't seen a brown lab running free by chance, have you?"

Grandma's voice was still there. It was muffled like speaking underwater, but I could still hear her single word, "No, no, no," repeated over and over.

"I'm sorry," I told the man before me. "I haven't seen any stray dogs. I need to be getting home, but I'll keep an eye out. Does he have tags with your number?" My feet itched to run, but I didn't want to be rude.

"He does have tags. His name is Oscar. Are you headed in this direction? I haven't been that way yet. I can walk you wherever you're going. It's not safe around here this late at night. Your boyfriend should be out with you." The offer doesn't feel sincere.

"Thank you, but I'm okay," I replied. "My HUSBAND knows where I am." I placed extra emphasis on the word husband. Everything in me was giving off warning signals. I thought I'd rather turn around and take a long route back to the apartment than to

walk in the same direction as him, but he stepped to the side as if to let me pass. I moved to keep walking, but he grabbed my arm, and every nerve ending in my body lit on fire.

"Are you sure you're okay? I didn't want to tell you this and scare you, but I could have sworn someone was following you. I'd feel better seeing you home safely."

By then, I was completely freaked out and not sure what to conclude. I didn't think there was any way he had been the one following me on the walk, and his words affirmed my belief that someone had been behind me. I had no reason to trust him about that, though. Sticking my hands in my hoodie pocket, I moved to pull out my phone. Surely, if I called Lucas, he'd move heaven and hell to find me. But my pocket was empty, and a memory popped in my head of my phone on the nightstand when I left the bedroom. I looked back over my shoulder, then in front of me.

"I'm Emmitt," he added. "I live just over there." He pointed past the wall to a small bungalow, the porch light soft against the dark night, welcoming and homey. My nerves started to unwind a little more. I'd tell Lucas about this when I got home, and he'd tell me that I have an overactive imagination.

"I'll call you, Emmitt, if I find your dog. I really do need to go. My husband is waiting. Have a good night." I'd barely taken three steps when he started to fall behind me. In five more steps, I was just past the wall into more open space when I felt his left arm wrap around my stomach, his right-hand slapping over my mouth. Panic immediately set in, and my first thought was that he was going to kill me. I was going to die and never see Lucas again. He would be without a mooring. He'd lose himself to the battle with alcohol that I had been still trying to ignore. I'd never see Claire have a baby.

Thoughts were spiraling through my head so quickly that I didn't even have a chance to process most of them, trying to jerk my body from his grip. He had to be close to a foot taller than me and easily had seventy pounds on me. It was useless, but when he easily lifted me from the ground to drag me toward the house he pointed out as his, I kicked my legs and tried to bite his hand. He squeezed my face tighter, his nails digging into my cheeks hard enough to draw blood. I briefly lost my grandma's voice in my ear, but I could hear it again. She was praying. I prayed along with her, for someone to take their dog out for a potty break or a car to drive by, but the street remained hauntingly quiet. I prayed for Lucas to come look for me. The clouds shifted, and the already feeble moonlight disappeared. A new surge of panic rose when he passed the porch of the bungalow and moved toward a shed in the backyard. I couldn't look down to see the ground around me, desperate to find a weapon.

In the doorway, he threw me into the shed and closed the door behind him. A small window let in light from a floodlight in the back of the house. Breathless from my impact with the ground, I could only watch his movements. Dirt scraped against my cheek, but the ground was uncluttered. I couldn't see a weapon within reach and opened my mouth to scream again. His foot connected with my stomach, and my scream escaped as a pained rush of air.

He bent down to my ear, wrapping his hands around my neck, and my muscles tightened, prepared for him to strangle me. Instead, he whispered to me, "If you scream, I'll kill you." I was sure there were any number of tools along the wall he could use to end my life, and the last bit of hope I held onto evaporated. My life was over. My grandma's prayers still played in my head, and I clung to them, my only life preserver in my darkest moment. How could I die in a stranger's shed? I had no energy left to fight. The last thing I registered before sheer darkness was his fist coming toward my face.

The next thing I knew, I was waking up in the hospital. The first thing I saw when I opened my eyes was Claire, seated in a chair next to the bed and crying silently. I just couldn't figure out why she would be crying.

I startle awake in my own bed, my pulse throbbing and a headache brewing behind my eyes. It's three in the morning. I lay there for a few minutes, willing my breathing to calm down. Once I feel like I can move, I creep out of bed to check on Jo. She's sleeping soundly, so I tread lightly on the stairs and check on Matthew. He's asleep as well, and for a brief moment, I consider waking him. But I'm not ready to tell him my story. I check the doors and drag myself back upstairs, popping a couple ibuprofen before returning to my bedroom. I expect to lay in bed for hours with my nightmare still fresh in my mind, but I manage to doze back off, sleeping peacefully. Three hours later, Jo jumps on my bed, and I peel open my sticky eyelids. Matthew stands behind Jo, singing to me to wake up. I can smell my favorite hazelnut coffee, and he hands me a mug. There's a moment of normalcy. This is what it's like to be a family.

Once I'm moving, I take a quick shower and head downstairs where Matthew and Jo have made French toast. The image is one I never thought I'd have, of possibilities, of a future where Jo and I aren't alone like I had always planned, always expected. The only problem is that when I close my eyes, I don't see Matthew sitting at the table. It's not even Lucas in my vision. I picture Ciaran. Jo and I have had four years of wonderful breakfasts together, but I want to make the image I have of Ciaran, sitting where Matthew sits now, a reality. As we eat, she asks why Matthew stayed the night, and he explains that the weather was bad, so he just slept on the couch. It seems to appease her, and I let out a sigh of relief.

While I move the dishes to the dishwasher and wipe up from our meal, Matthew goes out to clean the driveway. The roads are clear, thankfully. I'm supposed to work today, but I'm exhausted and call Josef to see if he can cover me. He's truly great. Today is the party at Claire's, and I need some time to recuperate from my long night before we go over. Matthew comes in after the driveway is clear, disappearing into the living room but returning with two packages. Jo watches him from the table, excited about the possibility of a gift but afraid of being disappointed.

"I hope this is okay. I have gifts for each of you that I picked up and had wrapped yesterday. Since they were in the truck and I'm already here, I thought you might like them now."

"You didn't need to do that. But thank you. And thank you for the driveway. I hope it wasn't too much work."

"Not at all. Anything to help a friend," he replies. We sit at the table, and Jo rips into her present. It's a generic baby doll, but she cuddles it before moving to thank him with a hug. She runs off to her room to get more dolls.

"Again, thank you. She loves babies," I tell him. "You really didn't need to do anything."

"Open yours. You haven't even seen it yet." His knee is bouncing, and he seems eager to see my reaction. I carefully peel the tape from the paper, and inside is a bottle of perfume. I open it to smell the fragrance, and the floral bouquet stings my eyes. I know this perfume, and it turns my stomach, but I thank him anyway.

"This is too much. I can't accept this," I say. If he insists I keep it, I will throw it away after he leaves.

"Please, I insist. I want you to have it. You could even wear it to the party tonight," he suggests. I have to give him something in return if I accept this, and the bottle of Jameson pops into my mind. I excuse myself to retrieve it from the hall closet.

"Here. I'm sorry it's not wrapped, but a gift is the least I can do after you helped us out. I hope you like whiskey." I hand him the bottle, and he politely accepts it.

"Yeah, thanks. I'll bring it tonight. We can all drink a toast." I wonder if he knows Ciaran is coming.

Jo comes back around the corner, her arms barely able to hold her dolls, and introduces her new baby as "Dollie" before engaging them in an elaborate play scene. I look up at Matthew.

"Listen, I just want to let you know that I invited Ciaran to come with me to the party tonight. I think his dad is going to come too. I get the feeling the two of you don't really like each other, so I don't want you to be surprised."

"I don't have a problem with the guy. I don't really trust him, but it's not my choice. You and I are friends. It's cool." I let out the breath I'd been holding. "Listen, I need to get out of here. I have some errands to run. I'll see you tonight?"

"Sure, thank you again. I don't know what I would have done if you hadn't come by last night. I really value your friendship." Once he's gone, I can relax again. I sit and rest my head back against the chair, closing my eyes.

Chapter Fifteen

When I woke up at the hospital, I watched Claire for a minute as she cried. It didn't escape my notice that she was alone. As if she could sense me watching her, she looked up at me and straightened abruptly when she realized I was awake.

"Oh, thank God you're awake! I was so worried about you!" She was choking back tears as she spoke.

My throat was dry and felt like it had been rubbed with coarse sandpaper, but I managed to squeak out, "What happened? Where is Lucas?" My face and head were throbbing, and my stomach roiled.

Her face fell, "You don't remember?" And I didn't, not at first. "The doctor said that might happen. You were injured, and they said there was a good chance you were in shock. I sent Lucas home for a shower. He should be back soon. What's the last thing you remember?"

"I remember being mad at Lucas and going for a walk. He was drunk. I was worried about him, and I was coming home. Then, it's a big blank."

"Maybe I should wait until Lucas is here to tell you what we know."

"No, please tell me." Tears started streaming down my face, partly because I was scared but partly from pain. Claire pressed the button for a nurse, and someone entered just a minute later. I guessed her to be about the age my own mother would have been had she still been alive. She had blond hair, streaked with gray, pulled back into a tight bun. In terms of height, she was about the same as my grandmother, five-foot, and she was slightly plump.

With a huge grin, she greeted me, "Welcome back, dear. How are you feeling? Are you in any pain?"

By then, my tears were a strangled sob. "It hurts so much, my head, my whole body. Why can't I remember what happened?"

"Why don't I see about getting you some more pain medicine from the doctor and having him stop in to see you? I'll get you some water too." Ten minutes later, she administered morphine, and I drifted back to sleep as it slid through my veins.

The next time I woke up, my ears tuned in to the room before I opened my eyes. I could hear urgent whispers, definitely Claire and Lucas.

"Listen, you sorry sack of shit. She's going to need you when she wakes up, and so help me God, if you hurt her anymore, you'll wish for death before I'm done with you." I'd never heard Claire speak to anyone like that.

"I know," he said, and I could hear him crying. "It's my fault. I screwed up. She's never going to forgive me."

"She forgives you every time, whether you deserve it or not. I don't know what your problem is, but grow the fuck up." He didn't answer that time, and I heard light footsteps walking away. I waited a few more minutes, and when Lucas brushed my hair back, I opened my eyes, acting as if I was just waking. The relief on his face was evident.

He leaned down to brush a gentle kiss against my cheek. "Sammi, I was so worried. I'm sorry I wasn't there. I'm sorry I went to bed without you. I had no idea. I would rather die than have anything bad happen to you. Please forgive me." His own tears filled his eyes, but while I understood something bad had happened, I still didn't know what.

"Where's Claire? Did you call her?" I asked.

"She went to get some coffee. She hasn't left since she got here earlier today. She's listed as your secondary emergency contact. The hospital called her."

"What day is it?" He looked stunned that I asked.

"It's Saturday. Don't you remember anything?" As he spoke, Claire came back into the room, a paper cup in hand.

Her response to Lucas was frosty. "She doesn't remember anything. Give her a break." She turned to me, "How are you feeling? Any less pain?" Everything still hurt, but I nodded anyway.

Claire proceeded to tell me what she knew, a story repeated by two police officers who stopped by an hour later. I heard about an elderly homeowner, just down the street from our apartment complex, who found me naked and unconscious in his shed that morning when he went to retrieve a rake. He threw his coat over me and dashed back inside to call for his wife. She covered me with a blanket and sat with me, while he phoned the police and waited for them to arrive. My clothes were found tossed to the ground just around the corner from the shed, my license tucked safely inside my hoodie pocket. I learned that the hospital administered a rape kit, but it would take months to process. I learned from Lucas that after his shower, he went to bed and crashed, not waking until the police pounded on the door. He missed the call from the hospital when I was brought in. He never even knew I didn't come home. He slept while I was violated on the floor of a shed. The hospital offered me emergency contraception, and I accepted. I just wanted to go home and get back to normal.

Slowly, bits and pieces returned. By the next morning, before being released, I was able to give the police a vague description. The part I remembered best in that early aftermath was the missing brown lab, Oscar. They exchanged an odd look when I mentioned it, but I was too tired to ask what it meant. There was a part of me that didn't want to go back to the apartment, but I did. Lucas took care of me at home, and Claire visited every weekend for the first month. I wanted to move, but Lucas suggested we wait until after graduation. He promised we could move anywhere. There was no sense in moving just to move again in May, and that was if a landlord would even let us out of a lease. Amanda came to visit too, just sitting on the couch and watching movies with me while Lucas went for groceries and other errands. His mother never came. For that first month, he drove me to campus each day. He worked on his laptop in the library during my classes. At the end of each class, he'd wait outside, walking me to the next. I continued working, the busyness of my hands keeping my mind from dwelling on things I both wanted and didn't want to remember. At the end of my shifts, Lucas would be waiting on the curb for me, driving me home.

We came up with a code phrase I could send him by text or say on the phone if I ever felt like I was in danger, "Get icing," a reference to his hockey days. It was also innocent enough to avoid alerting a potential threat. I never used it, even when I was scared. By the end of that first month, I was able to tell the police what happened leading up to the point of losing consciousness. Also, at the end of the first month, the stares and whispers started to die out. The police hadn't released my name, but everyone knew it was me. The bruises on my face and neck had made it fairly ob-

vious. My grandma was silent in that month, and I found I missed her voice in my ear.

Eventually, I did start going to classes and work on my own, but I stopped walking. We managed to fix the transmission on Betty, but I didn't want to be alone at night. If I had to work late or had a late-night study group, I insisted that Lucas take me and pick me up. It was also during that all-important first month that I missed my period. Since I had emergency contraceptives, I figured the stress from "the incident" had thrown my cycles off.

The ringing of my phone startles me. Jo is still in the same spot as before, pretending that one of her dolls is Mommy to her newest. Ciaran's name flashes on the screen.

"Hey, Ciaran. How are you? Have you guys left to come back yet?"

"Good morning, beautiful. We have. We're making good time. We just stopped for breakfast, and I thought I'd call before we get back on the road." My eyes flick to the microwave. It's not even eight. "Did Matthew get your driveway cleaned off last night? I'll be home in an hour, so I'll come by and shovel it if needed."

"Yeah, he used the snow blower this morning." He doesn't respond, and I realize that I didn't tell him that Matthew slept on the couch last night. "Sorry, I meant to send you a text. He crashed on the couch. The roads sucked, and I didn't think it was safe for him to drive." Ciaran is still silent, and I'm nervous he's never going to speak to me again.

Finally, his voice comes on the line. "I see. Is he still there?" Yup, he's going to cut me loose.

"No, he left this morning. I promise nothing untoward happened. I miss you. I called into work today, if you want to hang out before Claire's party."

"I'd love to, but I promised Dad I'd help with some projects around the house. Do you want to drive together? I can come by around three. Fergus wants to drive on his own, so he can bring a date." His voice is lighter as he says this, and I'm relieved, even though I worry he's mad about Matthew.

Once we confirm the plan, I hang up and tidy the house. Then, Jo and I set up our Christmas tree. Before we get ready, she asks if she can stay the night at Claire's, so I call to check. Claire gives it the green light, and I pack a bag for Jo, including her new baby doll. I throw on gray slacks with ballet flats and a light-pink, silk blouse with a cardigan over it. Jo decides on black leggings with an emerald-green sweater and cowboy boots. While we dress, I have another conversation with her about Ciaran. I don't want to slip up and kiss him in front of her without explaining exactly what it means for him to be my boyfriend, or whatever he'd be at this point. I could swear she rolls her eyes at me. It starts young.

When I open the door to Ciaran at three on the dot, he leans down to press a kiss against my mouth. "You look amazing." He looks sharp himself, in khakis and a light-blue sweater. Peeking around to see Jo, he smiles and says, "Jo, you look lovely. You have the best cowboy boots I've ever seen." Her bright smile is the best response she could give him. "Are you ladies ready to go?"

I just have to grab the ricotta cheesecake I prepared, a favorite dessert of Jo's. Ciaran settles into the passenger seat, holding it while I strap Jo in. Driving along, the landscape is a beautiful blanket of white, pristine. I feel at peace in the moment, content. Everything is really going to be okay. Claire's house is brightly lit with Christmas lights, and a snowman adorns the front lawn, a yellow scarf wrapped around his neck.

There are already several vehicles in the driveway, including Matthew's new truck, so I drive around to the dirt road that runs from the street down to the field. Ciaran carries Jo and her bag back to the driveway, while I carry dessert. We let ourselves in, and I look around anxiously. Fergus is already here, and his date looks like she'd be sweet as sugar, her short gray hair cut into a pixie and black-framed glasses on her face. She's smiling, and her smile is brilliant, open and sincere. We stop to greet them, and Fergus introduces us as his favorite new people. I excuse myself to put the cheesecake in the kitchen with Jo, promising to come find Ciaran shortly. Claire kisses my cheek and sends Jesse to grab Jo's bag from Ciaran. She starts to ask me what's new, but Susan hobbles into the kitchen and needs her help. I tell her we'll catch up later and go back to find Ciaran.

Jo and I find him talking to Matthew. We're too far away to hear their words, but it looks like a heated discussion. Ciaran is slightly taller than Matthew, leaning into him as he talks, his hands gesturing. I move to approach them, unsure what to expect, but Jo pulls away from me and runs to Ciaran. He immediately stops whatever he's saying and steps back, lifting her by her outstretched arms.

I greet Matthew when I approach. "Hi, Matthew. Glad you could make it tonight. Where's Vanessa?"

He moves forward and hugs me. "You look great, Sammi. Sorry, Vanessa couldn't make it. Her parents unexpectedly came in to town, so they went out to dinner."

"Oh, and you weren't invited?" Ciaran asks. I'm a little taken aback by the hostility in his tone.

It doesn't seem to faze Matthew. "Nah, I told her I'll get lunch with all of them tomorrow. I didn't want to miss the party. Can I get you a drink, Sammi? Or anything for Jo?" I decline politely. "Well, I'll see you around. Enjoy the party." He squeezes my shoulder as he walks by.

I turn to Ciaran, "What was that all about?" He shrugs. "Don't play stupid with me. We'll talk about it later." Bringing it up in front of Jo probably isn't the best idea.

The party is a chaotic swirl of greetings, conversations, and goodbyes. Ciaran stays by my side the entire evening, even holding my hand a few times. Every time his fingers brush against mine, my heart beats out a new pattern, goosebumps spread down my arms, and butterflies dance from my stomach to my chest. I haven't felt this in so long, and I don't want it to end. I don't see much of Matthew the rest of the evening, and I feel relieved. Jo bounces back and forth from Ciaran to Fergus, rarely straying from either one of them. It doesn't escape my notice how closely Ciaran watches her when she's away from us, in a protective way. I can't help also noticing how the three of them look together, like a daughter, father, and grandfather. I'm scared by how happy it makes me. As the party winds down, Ciaran is holding Jo again, her head lolling on his shoulder as she lightly snores. I guide him to the bed Claire has for her in one of the guestrooms, and I rouse her enough to tell her goodnight. She's asleep as soon as her eyes close again. We sneak out and head downstairs.

The party has died down considerably. Only a few stragglers remain. After I say bye to Jesse and Claire, we move toward the door. Fergus left earlier in the night, citing a busy day tomorrow. "You ready to go?" Ciaran asks. I nod. "Give me just a minute to use the restroom?" While I'm waiting for him to return, Matthew comes up.

"Leaving so soon?" he asks.

"Yeah, I'm so tired. You?" It's not a lie. Only three hours of peaceful sleep wears on you quickly.

"I'll probably head out shortly. Where's Ciaran?" The name comes out in a sneer, and he must be able to see from the look on my face that I'm not impressed. "Listen, tell your boyfriend to mind his own business. He needs to worry about himself, and I'll worry about my own stuff."

"What are you talking about?" I ask him, sure he's referencing his earlier conversation with Ciaran.

"Didn't he tell you? He came up and threatened me to stay away from you," Matthew snaps. That doesn't sound like Ciaran, but how well do I really know him?

I open my mouth to respond, but Ciaran is walking back. Matthew sees him, and after throwing me a forceful look, he walks away.

"Do you mind to drive?" I ask. "I'm exhausted and don't trust myself to stay awake". He takes my keys, and on the drive, I broach the subject of the conversation between him and Matthew. "I have to ask you a weird question. Did you threaten Matthew?"

He steals an incredulous look at me. "Is that what he said? Sorry, but that guy is a real piece of work."

"He said you approached him and warned him to leave me alone," I respond.

"That's not what happened at all. He approached me, not the other way around. He wanted to tell me that he knew I was bad news, and I needed to back off." I ponder what Ciaran said for a minute. Nothing in his voice indicates he's lying, though I'm not always the best judge of that, obviously. I certainly couldn't tell when Lucas was feeding me a line. I decide to go with my gut.

"I believe you. I'm sorry. It was just really awkward," I offer.

He nods. "I get it. But I'm not intimidated by him." The rest of the ride is silent, and I can see Ciaran grinding his teeth together. A thought worms its way in, that maybe my gut is wrong. Then, I hear Grandma Jolene, as certain of her voice as I am of anything, telling me to trust.

When he pulls into the driveway, headlights illuminate what looks like footsteps around the porch and windows, the fresh snow disturbed. "Do you see those?" I ask. He nods, leaving the car in park out in the driveway.

"Stay here," he says. "Lock the doors." I nervously watch him approach the house. Restlessly, I observe as he disappears around the side, coming back into view around the other end of the house. He gets back in the car. "All the doors and windows look intact. Did you set the alarm when we left?" I did. He pulls into the garage, and I follow him to the doorway. The alarm wails as he enters the house, and he nods at me to turn it off. "Stay by the door. I'm going to check out the house." Ten minutes later, he's checked all the rooms and closets, and everything is clear. "I think you're okay. Are you comfortable staying here tonight? I can drive you back to Claire's."

I laugh nervously. "Not really. You want to stay with me?" I'm only half joking.

"If you want me to, I will. If you don't want to stay with Claire, I can sleep on the couch."

I hesitate a minute. I do want him to stay, but I don't want him to sleep on the couch. Ready to let go of my inhibitions, I pull him further into the house, making sure to lock the door. I tug his head down and kiss him, my touch more feverish than before. Parting my lips, his tongue darts out to meet mine. His arms come around my back, and he crushes my body to his, lifting me slightly from the ground. My body is hyperaware, tingling from the tips of my toes to my scalp. Right in this moment, I know I'm in trouble. I'm done for. I pull back, my face flushed and my breathing shallow and rushed. The heat between us is an intense pressure that continues to build, even though the kiss has stopped. I trail my hand over his arm lightly, skimming the surface, and goosebumps light up his flesh. He presses his face into my hair, and I can smell him, a mix of pine and bergamot. He lifts my chin and presses his lips to mine again. A premonition of the future flashes through my mind.

I see us next week, next month, even next year. I see our bodies wrapped around one another, followed by quiet moments with Jo, him reading a book to her. I see a Christmas with him and Fergus, us standing in front of a sold sign on a house, my belly swollen. I'm lost to him, forever. He deepens the kiss again, my mouth eagerly responding to him, my tongue joining his.

"Do you want to stop?" he asks. I shake my head and lead him behind me, toward the bedroom. I push him backward, and he sits when his knees hit the side of the bed. Ripping off his shirt, I straddle him, my kisses becoming more desperate and needy. He gently lifts my blouse over my head and peppers my neck and chest with his lips. He lays back, me still poised above him. I'm contemplating pulling off my slacks when something clatters loudly outside the house. I jerk up and look around. Ciaran watches my face and gently lifts me from atop him, setting me back onto the bed.

"What was that?" I ask, all romantic thoughts gone. He gets up and looks out the window.

"I don't see anything. You want me to check out the house?" I do, but I'm too scared to stay here by myself, so I creep behind him as he does another walk through. He opens the front door and scans the outside. "I still don't see anything. You okay?"

"Yeah, it just scared me," I admit.

"I'll make sure nothing happens to you, Sammi. And I won't force you to talk to me, but I wish you'd tell me what has you so scared. Is it your ex-husband?"

I have to take deep breaths to keep from crying. "I will. I promise. But can we do it in the morning?" I don't know that I have the fortitude to get through the story tonight.

We move back upstairs, and somehow, Ciaran knows the moment from earlier is over. We strip off our pants, and I snuggle against him, falling asleep sooner than I expected. When I wake the next morning, he's still wrapped around me, and I realize I didn't have a single dream. I watch him sleeping peacefully, his dark eyelashes brushing against his skin, his mouth softly parted. I lean down and place my lips gently against his forehead, and when I pull back, his brilliant green eyes lock onto my face.

"Good morning," I whisper, still not ready to disturb this fragile place in time. "How did you sleep?"

"Amazing. But please tell me you have coffee. I'd do anything for caffeine right now." Laughing, I slide from his side, tugging on his hand. We dress and brush our teeth, him using an unopened toothbrush from the drawer. Slowly, we move downstairs, working seamlessly together to start the coffee and fry some bacon, words unnecessary. It's as if we've been doing this together all of our lives. In the silence, I'm able to think about how to tell him why I have so much fear of the unknown, and truthfully, fear of him, of losing myself completely in him.

When I missed my second period, I knew it was time to take a test, but I was still hesitant, still in denial. My breasts were fuller, the smell of meat made me nauseous, and I had to pee constantly, but if I just kept telling myself there was nothing to worry about, there wouldn't be. The police came by on a Sunday to tell Lucas and me that they'd arrested someone they thought may be responsible for the incident. They showed me a picture to see if I recognized him, and the instant I laid eyes on his face, I knew. My fears that I'd worked so hard to calm came flooding back. My nerve endings lit up like firecrackers, and I could feel myself starting to shut down. His dark-green eyes bored into me from the photo. All I could do was nod. I vaguely registered the police explaining that a woman was attacked near a bar downtown. By some cosmic twist of fate, a passerby heard her scream, a passerby that just happened to be an off-duty police officer. I cried, feeling relief for this stranger and sorrow that I didn't have the same fortune. Then, they explained that they had some women give the same story in the past, about being attacked by a man claiming to have lost his dog, but they never knew it was him. Finally, maybe there could be closure for all of us.

After they left, we tried to get back to life as normal, but I could feel Lucas pulling away. It was as if the arrest of the perpetrator gave him license to withdraw and leave me on my own again. By the third missed period, I couldn't avoid the test any longer. I needed to know, needed to find out if my marriage was worth fighting for or if I'd be better off walking away. The only problem was that I didn't know whether a pregnancy would mean fight or give up. I waited until Lucas was gone in the middle of the day to take it. When I saw that second pink line appear, my breakfast came up, and I sat in front of the toilet for a long time, pondering. Why didn't the emergency contraceptives work?

The doctor squeezed me in for a last-minute appointment. She told me that I had likely already ovulated, which meant there was a greater chance of emergency contraception not working, but she couldn't tell me exactly which day I conceived. I left with information on abortion, but I didn't know that I could go through with that. I spent the rest of the day waiting for Lucas to return home, wondering how he'd react. What was he going to think? Was it even his baby? We had just started to be intimate again, our encounters infrequent.

That night, I told Lucas over dinner that we needed to talk. "I have something difficult to tell you. I, uh, took a pregnancy test today. It's positive." I fully expected him to yell, but he surprised me.

"Sammi, that's great! I know we weren't planning on it yet, but you're going to be a great mom. This is the start of a new beginning." He was so excited, so happy, and I cringed to tell him anything more.

"Lucas, I'm about three months pregnant," I managed to get out. The words hung in the air.

"Oh, that's..." his voice trailed off. I could see the gears grinding in his head as he did the math. He didn't say anything as he stormed toward the door, his chair clattering against the tile in his hasty departure. The sight of the door closing behind him had become a familiar sight.

"Lucas, wait, we can do a paternity test," I called out, but the sound of the door slamming was my only answer. I was lying in bed when he came in around midnight. I heard the shower running and his footsteps leading back into the living room before the sound of the couch springs reached my ears.

He was gone when I woke up, so I spent some time cleaning the apartment. Claire had called me three times overnight, and I called her back to tell her about the test. She waited to react until I shared how I felt about it. I didn't tell her about Lucas's reaction.

Right then, it was too much for me. With assurances I'd be okay, she made me promise to call her for anything. Before leaving for work, I tossed in a load of laundry, and as I moved Lucas's clothes from the previous night into the washer, I swore I could smell a heavily floral perfume.

When Ciaran and I finally sit down to eat, I know I'm going to have to tell him everything. If this is going to work, I have to be honest.

"I'm ready to tell you the rest. But you need to promise to listen to everything before you respond. You may not want to talk to me again after this, and I'll respect that, but I hope you still give me a chance." I search his eyes, and he nods, so I continue. "Things with Lucas were great at the beginning, when we first started dating. We began having problems even before we got married, especially after his dad passed away, but I kept telling myself we just had to weather the storm. In hindsight, the signs were there, but sometimes the lies we tell ourselves are the most convincing." I pause, and he remains silent, for which I am thankful. If he starts talking now, I may not be able to finish what I have to tell him.

"Halloween of 2014, we had a fight. I went out for a walk, and when I was trying to come home, a man stopped me to ask if I had seen his dog." It's getting hard to speak, to lay myself bare, and the look in his eyes almost stops me. "He knocked me unconscious, and the next thing I knew, I was waking up in the hospital. Needless to say, Lucas did not handle things well when I told him I was pregnant. I tried to make it work for months after Jo was born, but it just got to the point I couldn't stay anymore. It was bad enough that I could smell another woman on his clothes most nights, and he yelled at me when he was home. Or worse, he pretended I didn't exist. I might have been able to live with all that, but I couldn't live with the way he was with Jo. I'd rather raise her alone than stay with someone who doesn't love her. I don't know why Lucas would show up now. I'm not afraid of him, at least not of him physically harming us. But I'm not sure what he could want, and that is what frightens me. He's the reason I'm so hesitant about us. I can't go through that again, and I won't put Jo through it."

I look at him, my eyes pleading for understanding. I've exposed my darkest moments to him, and I don't know how I'll recover if he wants to walk away. He's the first man I've told about this, and his response will stick with me forever. His face is flushed, and his hands are shaking. "He sounds like an idiot. What kind of man turns his back on his wife and daughter, abandons his wife when she needs him more than ever?" He hasn't put two and two together yet.

Here's the lynchpin, the piece of news that holds it all together, the piece that melds my past and my present together... "Jo may not be his daughter."

His face falls, and he's quiet at first. Mentally, I plead with him to respond because the silence is eating me alive. His gaze burns a hole into the wall over my shoulder, and I imagine him putting together my last sentence with the rest of the history I've told him. Finally, his eyes meet mine. "I'm sorry. I'm sorry for you and Jo. And I'm sorry for your ex because he's missing something great. Do you think he's Jo's father?"

"Honestly, I don't know. I wanted him to be, but she doesn't look like Lucas. She looks like him." I don't have to explain to whom I'm referring. Then, I add, "Like you."

"Like me?" It takes a minute before he registers what I'm saying. "The guy who hurt you looks like me?"

"Yes, similar to you. You're both tall, you both have black hair, you both have green eyes, though his are darker. His shoulders are broader than yours. Up close, I can see the differences between you more clearly, but from a distance, it's not so obvious. Surely, you've noticed that Jo looks like she's related to you and Fiona. At first, you intimidated me because of the similarities, but once I got to know you, it was easy to see that the parallels between you and him are physical only, and there are fewer than appear at first glance."

"I see. Did they ever find him?" he inquires.

"Actually, yes. He attacked someone else, and an off-duty cop just happened to be in the area. It was a while before they were able to match his DNA to the rape kit. Turned out that I was one of several. He'd used this lost dog ploy to get women to let down their guard around him before, but they weren't able to conclusively tie him to any others. His parents ponied up a bunch of cash for some hotshot lawyer, who got him a plea bargain, eight years for both attacks. Last I knew, he was still in jail." It still angers me that someone could do something so brutal, yet spend so little time behind bars. It's part of the problem. After what I went through, I understand why some women don't report what's happened to them.

"Are you afraid of him? Are you worried he's going to come after you?" Ciaran asks.

"I'm worried he's going to come after Jo," I admit. "He knows about her. He wanted to see her, but I refused. If I had my way, he'd never know she existed. I don't know for sure that he's her father. Lucas is the only other possibility, and he wouldn't submit to a paternity test."

"Well, this is not what I expected you to be telling me. Thanks for sharing with me. I understand better now."

"Are you going to leave?" I can hear the quiver in my voice, my need for him to stay overpowering.

"Why would I leave?" His voice is disbelieving. "Sammi, what happened was not your fault. You're the victim, not the guilty party. I'm here, unless you want me to leave. I'd actually like to see if I can set you up with a little more security, if that's okay."

Relief floods me that he's staying, but I can't afford to put in extra security measures right now, so close to Christmas. "I don't know, Ciaran. I don't really have the money right now."

"Don't worry about the cost. I can cover it." I lean forward and kiss him on the lips, thankful that he came into our lives, reassured that he's taken everything so well. It's a lot to digest, especially in a relationship that is still so new. I'd been with Lucas forever, and he still couldn't handle it. Ciaran offers to stay behind to put up cameras while I go to pick up Jo, and I give him a key to the front door. He promises to lock up and check the house when he returns from the store. As I leave, it feels like a giant weight has lifted from my chest. I don't know what's going on, if Lucas is in town or not, but I feel like I can get through it now.

Chapter Sixteen

Jo's playing with Oliver when I get to Claire's. We stand there watching her for a minute before I motion to Claire to follow me. Once we're in the other room, I lower my voice to a whisper.

"Ciaran stayed over last night."

That earns a double take from Claire. "What? Did you sleep with him?"

Embarrassment shadows my face. "No. Well, almost. We were making out, and we heard something outside the house. It ended up being nothing, but it ruined the mood. Then, I spent this morning telling him about Lucas and Emmitt and Jo."

I thought her look earlier was funny, but her gaping mouth causes me to giggle, which makes her mad. It's completely inappropriate, but I feel like I can't stop it.

"Stop laughing," she barks. "It's not funny. I can't believe you told him. He seems like a great guy, but you've never let it spill to anyone else. You must really like him."

"I do, Claire, a lot. He's over at the house now, putting in cameras. It's crazy how quickly things change. A month ago, I'd have been ready to pack my bags and run."

"I'm glad you're not running. You belong here. This is home. I want William to grow up with you and Jo around."

"Crap, that reminds me. Is there anything you still need or want? I have a few small gifts for you, but I want to be sure you have everything you want." Now that I'm not going in on a car seat with Matthew, I find myself in need of something else.

"What do you mean?" she asks. "Didn't you and Matthew go in together on the car seat?" What? I told Matthew to go ahead, and I'd get something else.

I must look confused. She adds, "You must be really stressed to forget getting me a car seat. Maybe you need to take some time off and get some rest. Didn't you get my thank you note?" She pauses for a moment before continuing, "Oh crud, I bet it's still sitting in my car, waiting for me to give it to you. Things have been so busy. It must have slipped my mind."

This is all too weird. I haven't given Matthew any money, and he didn't mention that he got the car seat, much less that he put my name on it too. But I don't want to make Claire uncomfortable.

"I must have forgotten, sorry. I've been preoccupied. I need to get back, but I'll see you Wednesday?" This whole thing doesn't set well with me. I'm feeling cornered and need to get out of the house.

Before pulling away with Jo in the backseat, I send Matthew a text asking about the car seat. I don't expect an answer. When Jo and I get home, Ciaran has the cameras set up over the front and back stoops and has checked all the windows and locks. On his recommendation, I change the code for the house alarm and give it to him, even though he doesn't ask. He's even checked all the batteries in the smoke and carbon monoxide detectors. Since he was supposed to come over today anyway, he asks if he can take a shower and change into the clothes he picked up from his apartment while he was out. After, he helps me in the kitchen while waiting for Fergus to arrive, mashing potatoes and assembling a green bean casserole. Jo even gets in on the action, sprinkling the French-fried onions on the casserole with Ciaran's prompt. When Fergus arrives, Jo tows him away to give him a tour, leaving Ciaran and me downstairs.

I'm applying another glaze on the ham when Ciaran asks, "Can I ask you something, Sammi? Is there anything else that's happened that's been bothering you? I know you thought you saw Lucas, and it doesn't make sense. It's unlikely that Emmitt is around."

"How do you know his name?" I ask, apprehension in my voice. "I didn't say it earlier." I have to focus to keep my voice level. Panic starts to rise within me again.

"Sammi, relax. It wasn't hard to figure out who he was. I just did some math and looked back at old news stories."

"Why would you do that? Why wouldn't you just ask me?" I know my anger is irrational, but I feel unreasonably hurt.

"I'm sorry," he whispers, as he wraps his arms around me, and I soften at his touch. He continues in a quiet voice, "It was just driving me crazy, thinking what you've been through, and that you didn't have the support you needed from Lucas. You weren't imagining that sound last night, but it doesn't make sense for it to be Emmitt. He shouldn't be out of jail yet, and you're not on social media. Someone like that doesn't strike me as the type of person to invest a lot in finding someone from the past, not to mention it's been years. Either there were kids playing pranks out there, or something else has to be going on."

His explanation makes sense. "You're going to think I'm really crazy, but back then, I swore someone was following me. I tried talking to Lucas, and he laughed it off. That night, the reason I was rushing to get home was because I thought someone was following me. I know now it had to be Emmitt. It's the only reasonable explanation. Lately, I've been having the same feelings. That, with seeing Lucas, and Halloween, and that incident on Thanksgiving, it's just all very strange. It's had me on edge. ...I've been having nightmares almost every night." I realize that I've rambled toward the end, but everything just came flooding out of me. It's a bit of a relief to let it all out.

"Wait, what? What happened on Halloween?" he asks, an edge of worry in his voice. I forgot that he didn't already know, so I explained the break-in and the missing photo.

"I wish you would have told me sooner. Do you have any other photos of Lucas?" Jo has talked Fergus into playing dolls with her by now, so we sneak down to the basement, where I find the sole box of mementos from my marriage that I kept. He examines the picture of Lucas before putting it back, and we return upstairs.

When he's sure Jo can't hear him, he tells me, "Thanks for sharing that. I'm worried about you both. Promise me that you'll call me if you think you have a prowler. I don't care what time of night it is. I'll be here in a heartbeat. In the meantime, I think you need to watch out for Matthew."

"Matthew? Really? I mean, I know he was interested, but he's dating Vanessa now, and I've been clear with him about you and me. There was that whole car seat thing, but it was probably just a miscommunication. Maybe he didn't get my text." Once again, I'm rambling.

"WHAT car seat thing?" His voice has taken on a protective note, harder, yet not frightening.

I forgot that he doesn't know about this either. He's already so rooted in my mind that I don't think about his life being separate from mine for the most part. "Sorry, it just happened, and

I wasn't thinking about you not knowing about it. Do you re-member when he mentioned going in on a gift together for baby Will? I got tired of waiting for him to get back to me. I sent him a message, telling him I was going to get something else instead. Then, Claire mentions the car seat Matthew and I bought for her. I sent him another message asking about it, but he hasn't responded yet."

"I'm serious, Sammi. There is something off about that guy. I know you're trying to be his friend, and I'm not your boss, but be careful with him. Promise?" Even though I'm annoyed with Matthew, I don't feel like he is a threat. Nevertheless, I appreci-ate Ciaran's concern.

I agree, and we're mostly quiet as we finish preparing dinner, joined by Jo and Fergus. After the meal, we settle in front of the Christmas tree. Jo is disappointed she doesn't have any gifts for Ciaran and Fergus, but I produce the presents I purchased and tell her they're from both of us.

When she hands Fergus the package, he tells her, "I don't know how you could beat that candle you picked. I put it in my bathroom, but let's see what we have here." He's grinning as he opens it, and his eyes water when he sees the frame and photo. "Oh, my sweet Jo, this is the best gift you could ever get me. I'm going to put this up in my living room, so I can show everyone who comes to visit. Thank you, both of you." Love bursts in my heart, love for this man who has been like a grandfather to my daughter, just out of the kindness of his own heart.

Ciaran is as equally enthusiastic about his present and gives us both a hug, then sits and looks at the picture for a moment. As grateful as they both were, he and Fergus are more excited to give Jo her gifts. She's jumping up and down with excitement when she opens her toys, far more there than Ciaran purchased when we were shopping together. While Fergus is helping her open the packaging, Ciaran hands me two packages, one small and light, one larger and heavy. The first is from Fergus and has a beautiful cashmere scarf in a pink and purple plaid pattern that he ordered from Scotland. It's far too much, and I tell him so, but he waves off my concern, telling me he has plenty of money to go around. Ciaran is chewing his lip, his leg jittering as he waits for me to open my gift.

When I open it, I can't believe what he's purchased. Inside is a book series from my favorite author, all signed. "How did you know?"

"I asked Claire for ideas," he admits. She mentioned that you loved this series, but you never purchased any of the books for yourself."

"But there are fourteen books here. This is way too much money, Ciaran." His response is much like that of Fergus, and as I watch him, tracing my finger over the spines of the books, I start to think that maybe I just might love him already.

When he leaves that night, he pauses to give me a smoldering kiss that leaves my knees weak and my heart knocking against my ribs. I lock the door behind him, feeling safer than I ever have in this house.

My pregnancy and Jo's birth ended up being the long, drawn-out tipping point in my marriage. I spent the last two trimesters tiptoeing around Lucas, afraid to even speak. Claire continued to call, but I wouldn't tell her much about what I was experiencing with Lucas. She was becoming concerned that she hadn't gotten pregnant herself, and I didn't want to add to her stress. I made a few trips back home to see her, but they were few and far between with my work schedule and classes. When she offered to come visit me instead, I found excuses, not wanting her to see exactly how bad things had become between Lucas and me. The drinking became more excessive than before, and Lucas would stay out late, stumbling in with a stench like the bottom of a liquor bottle. Our debts grew, and I hated going to the store, never knowing if my debit card would be declined that day or not. I suspected Lucas was sleeping with someone else, but I ignored it, not wanting the truth. Lucas didn't go to the doctor appointments, but Amanda did always call me to check how they went. Claire made day trips for a couple of the appointments, including the sonogram where I learned I would have a daughter, a fact I didn't share with Lucas.

Lucas's mother never spoke to me again. She didn't buy any baby gifts. Even once Jo arrived, she saw her only twice. Once was in the hospital, and she still managed to maintain her outwardly cold demeanor toward me. She saw her the second time when she stopped by to drop off something for Lucas. It lasted all of thirty seconds. Amanda came by a few times after we got home from the hospital, but even she started to cut me out of her life.

Despite my attempts to keep everything from Claire, she wasn't stupid. She could tell something was seriously wrong, and at one point, she again tried to talk me into moving in with her and Jesse, promising to help with the baby. Even though I knew things were over, I wasn't ready to accept it. I wanted to see Lucas be a father to our child, and I prayed nightly that she was his. Anytime I tried to talk to him about a paternity test, he said it didn't matter. But it clearly did matter. Somehow, I managed to finish my bachelor's program, never giving up despite being obviously pregnant. I put off my job search for after the baby arrived, wanting to be able to stay with her when she first came home. My due date was July 23rd, and as it crept ever closer, I was nervous I'd be alone when the baby arrived.

My water broke late on July 13th, and Lucas was nowhere to be found. I tried his cell and couldn't get through to him, striking out with Amanda as well. It was up to me to get myself to the hospital, and to this day, I don't remember the tense drive, just calling Claire on the way and begging her to come. When my darling Jo was born early the next morning, Claire was the only one holding my hand.

I sleep long and hard again, feeling well-rested for once. It helps with the stress I've had lately, and I feel like I can see things more clearly. Jo goes to work with me on Monday. Beatrice and Josef cover the shop in the afternoon, so I can go home with Jo. After a quick trip to the store for groceries, we spend the afternoon making popcorn balls and cookies, reveling in the holiday season. A few times, I think I hear someone prowling outside the house, but I can't see anyone on the cameras and chalk it up to my imagination. Ciaran calls me to check in, and I can't contain my excitement as I tell him about everything Jo and I did together. We spend Tuesday baking even more, even though we already have more desserts than anyone will be able to eat. I check in with Ciaran several times by text, but I don't have a chance to talk to him on the phone. I fall asleep thinking of his touch and wishing he were here with me.

Chapter Seventeen

It was late in the day of Jo's birth when Lucas finally showed up at the hospital. He looked like a wreck, his hair mussed and his clothes wrinkled. He smelled of cheap beer, but I could also detect the same lingering floral perfume I had smelled several times before. When Claire saw him come in, she jumped to her feet, ready to attack.

"Where the hell have you been? I've been calling you all day. You look like shit." She stepped closer to him, where he stood by the bed, and lifted her eyebrows. "Why do you smell like that?" I guessed that secret was out. I could practically see steam gushing from Claire's ears. "You asshole. Your wife is giving birth, and you're out screwing someone else?"

"Relax, I just went to the bar to take a break and lost track of time," he sneered.

I didn't want to listen to this. I didn't want to have this fight in a hospital, in front of my newborn daughter, but Claire wasn't ready to let go, "Who were you with?"

"No one," he replied, but the guilt was written on his face. He flushed crimson where I could see skin, and he looked more sober in that moment than I had seen him possibly in months. He

looked over at Jo in her bassinet as she slept, snugly swaddled, a patch of dark hair on her head... "That's not my daughter."

I was crying too hard to respond. Claire came to my rescue once again. "Get out. And you better pray Sammi allows you in that baby's life because if it was up to me, your ass would be out on the street."

He didn't argue. He just walked out, and I didn't see him again until I returned home. He didn't even come back to the hospital when his mother stopped by the room. She took one look at Jo and left. I told Claire everything at that point, knowing there was no use in continuing to keep secrets. She begged me to pack a bag and come home with her, even temporarily, while Lucas could get some help for his drinking problem.

Claire reluctantly dropped me back at the apartment when I was discharged. Jesse came out to meet Jo. He and Claire had taken my car home for me. Claire made one last plea for me to come home with her, to no avail. We said our goodbyes outside the door to my apartment.

Like a fool, I still couldn't give up on my marriage. While my parents were gone from my childhood for a very different reason, I didn't want Jo to grow up without two parents, and I still held on to hope I'd be able to get Lucas to come around. Why do women always think they can get men to change?

Lucas was inside when I welcomed Jo home for the first time, shockingly sober and apologetic. "Sammi, I'm sorry. I screwed up. I want to be a better husband, a father. It's just so hard. You have to help me."

I needed one question answered first. "Who were you with while I was in labor?"

"It was just some girl," he sputtered. "It didn't mean anything. Please, you have to forgive me. It was a stupid, stupid mistake."

I knew what he was going to say, but it still wasn't the homecoming I envisioned, walking in alone with my daughter, with my husband confessing to what I think he's confessing. "You slept with her? How long has this been going on?"

"I'm sorry, Sammi. It's the worst thing I've ever done. It was just one time. I'll do whatever it takes, if you just forgive me. I can't live without you." I couldn't handle his up and down moods, one minute the perfect husband and the next, spending the night in someone else's bed. Not to mention, I didn't believe for one second that this was an isolated incident.

I took a deep, shuddering breath. "I think I'm going to go to Claire's for a while. I'll let you know what I decide." He sobbed as I called Claire to turn around, while packing a small suitcase. Jo and I spent the first week together at a home that wasn't ours, but Claire helped tremendously. She got up with me as I nursed Jo in the middle of the night, changed diapers, and walked with her while I napped during the day. Lucas called every day. At first, I sent his calls to voicemail. After a few days, I started answering, and we talked about everything, from the good days when we were dating, to the hopes I had for the future, to everything that went wrong. After six days, I decided to give him one more chance, warning him that it was the final straw. I agreed to come home with the contingency that he stopped drinking, get a job, and that we start to look for a house, anywhere other than the city.

For a few months, he honored those contingencies. He took an overnight job at the gas station a few blocks over to help with the bills, but it meant he was gone a good chunk of every night. His absence led to me spending a lot of hours picturing things that turned my stomach and chipped away at my love for him. We started to look at rental houses online, both near St. Louis and back near Boonville, but he asked me to wait a few more months for him to get a publisher before we moved. I reluctantly agreed. I wasn't ready to go back to work yet, and the gas station didn't exactly pay top dollar. I spent some time looking for jobs of my own, trying to convince myself that things were on the rise.

He was gone to work one night when someone knocked on the apartment door. I couldn't see anyone through the peephole, so making sure the chain lock was engaged, I cracked the door to peer out. There was a vase of white roses on the doorstep, but they were already dying, petals falling from the stem even as I watched. There was no card. I left them where I found them, double checking the locks behind me. I called the gas station to talk to Lucas, but the clerk that answered told me that Lucas was off for the night. I spent the entire night awake, sitting on the couch with Jo's bassinet next to me and the phone clutched to my chest, terrified someone was going to break in to the apartment. I left several texts and calls from Claire unanswered. I'm surprised she didn't drive out that night. My eyes were so heavy that they hurt by the time Lucas came home. He pounded on the door when the chain lock stopped his entry, and I let him in before I shuffled back to the couch, sinking down into the cushions, wishing they would swallow me whole.

He was carrying the vase, "What's with the flowers?" I could smell the liquor on him across the room, but I was too tired to fight anymore.

"I have no idea. Whoever left them didn't stay behind. I tried calling you. I've been terrified all night," I admitted.

"Sorry, I left my phone in my locker." Lie.

"I don't believe you," I snapped. He didn't respond, only looked at me with melancholy. "Whatever, I'm exhausted. I'm going to lay down while Jo is napping." I moved her bassinet back into the bedroom, placing it against my side of the bed.

He came in and laid down next to me, but when he threw his arm around me, I shimmied out from under his weight and lay against the edge of the bed. I fell asleep to thoughts of Lucas, sitting in a bar, drinking and kissing someone else.

The memory of Lucas is playing in my head when Jo wakes me the next morning, too excited for Christmas to sleep past five. I trudge out of bed, thankful I preprogrammed the coffee pot for today. Jo and I are decked out in matching pajamas. Per our usual traditions, she opens her stocking, but she waits for everyone else to arrive before opening anything else. I pop in a ham and cheese casserole I put together before bed, and she patiently plays with her stocking gifts. We decide to read *Bad Kitty Searching for Santa* while waiting. We're right at the end when Claire and Jesse let themselves in, arms overflowing with gifts. Ciaran arrives ten minutes later. We spend the next hour dividing up gifts and opening them, before we partake of the food. It hits me that this is the first time since Jo was a baby that there's been a man other than Jesse present on Christmas Day.

While I'm loading the dishwasher, Claire steps away to take a phone call. A few minutes later, she yells out. "The baby is coming. We need to go! I'm sorry, Sammi, Jo. Come by the hospital later?" Jesse and Claire rush out the door moments later to go await the arrival of their son. Ciaran, Jo, and I settle on the couch to watch *Elf*, and she dozes off, her head in my lap and her feet on Ciaran's.

Once the movie is through, we haven't heard from Claire yet, so we load into my car to head to the hospital. The baby still isn't here, and we have a bit of time to sit in the waiting room. Ciaran pulls out his phone and downloads an app for Jo to play with, and while they're occupied, I have time to sit and relax. Tipping my head back against the wall, I close my eyes and focus on my breathing, inhale for four, hold for seven, release for eight. It calms me, and I doze off unintentionally, thinking of another time.

For two more months after Lucas lied about his work schedule, I tried to make things work. I knew things weren't going to get better, but I was still bouncing between disbelief and denial. Anytime I thought I smelled alcohol or the perfume left behind on his clothes and skin, I told myself that I was losing my grip on reality, so afraid to be hurt that I conjured the very things I feared. We went through a dry spell, barely even kissing. I couldn't stand to have Lucas touch me, not knowing where else he'd been.

I knew Lucas was working some, even if he wasn't every time he left for his job. With his overnights, he slept a good chunk of the day, and when he was awake, he was glued to a video game. He barely acknowledged Jo, and the longer I stayed, the more I worried he would never grow to love her. On the rare occasion I asked him to hold her while I took a shower, I'd come back to find her in her pack and play. I was running on fumes spiritually and mentally. Despite my mental state and Lucas's unwillingness to spend time with Jo, she was happy, bubbly, and quiet most of the time. I couldn't have asked for a better baby. The longer I stayed, the angrier I was, but eventually, even that feeling had to pass.

Jo's first Christmas was somber. Lucas spent most of the day silent, barely speaking to me. He didn't have any gifts for me, and almost all of Jo's gifts were ones Claire purchased and delivered because she knew I couldn't buy much. I passed the day playing on the floor with Jo, contemplating where to go from here. I knew the stages of grief and recognized that I had already experienced bargaining, spending so much of our marriage saying that if only various points in time had gone differently, Lucas would be the same person he was when I met him. I had finally accepted the death of my marriage, even though I wasn't ready to be over it, and felt calmer than I had in years. It was time. I needed to get our things ready and spent the next few days after Christmas discretely packing items into my car, things Lucas wouldn't notice were gone. While I didn't think Lucas would lash out physically, I had to admit that I couldn't know what to expect. I never thought he'd cheat on me or lose himself in a bottle either.

On New Year's Eve, Lucas was working when there was a knock on the apartment door. Rather than feel the fear that usually accompanied an unexpected visitor, I felt determination, a need to face what or who was on the other side. Through the peephole, I could see a woman. She was attractive, taller than me, with an athletic build, long brown hair, and icy blue eyes. Looking at her, I knew what she was going to say and who she was, my hackles rising and telling me she was a threat to me, to my mental health. I cracked the door, chain engaged.

"Hi, is Lucas home?" she asked in a sickeningly sweet voice.

"I'm sorry. He's not here. I can tell him you stopped by, if you'd like to leave your name." It was hard for me to get the words out.

"You must be Amanda. I'm Lucas's girlfriend, Tiffany. I can tell he's spent so much time talking about me." She rolled her eyes.

I knew it was coming, and still, my heart sank into the pit of my stomach. I took a deep breath, willing myself to stay calm. "Girlfriend? I didn't know he was seeing anyone. How long have you been dating?" It didn't really matter, but I couldn't stop myself from asking.

She laughs. "That sounds like Lucas. We've been together for about six months. We actually hooked up before that, but we stopped seeing each other for a while. He's told me a lot about you, you know, his brilliant kid sister who's going to change the world."

I didn't correct her. Instead, I inhaled deeply, catching a whiff of her perfume through the open crack. It was definitely her. She was the same woman he slept with when Jo was being born, the same woman whose perfume lingered on his clothes most nights.

"I'm sorry you missed him. I'll be sure to let him know you stopped by." I closed the door before she could respond and watched her walk away through the peephole, after delaying a minute at the door to see if I'd open it again.

This is the woman he was with when he was lying about work. And it had been happening even longer than I knew. He'd still been handling the finances exclusively, but I dug around in his nightstand, looking for the password. Bingo. He never was the most diligent about security. I logged onto the bank account and could see that the deposits were far less than I expected. He was spending more time with her than I even realized. It made the decision to leave so much easier for me. I threw the last of our items in the car and sat down on the couch to wait, Jo in my arms. While I waited, I called Claire and told her I was coming the next day. She offered to come get me with Jesse right then, but I declined.

After a while, I moved Jo into her pack and play and stretched out on the couch, knowing Lucas wouldn't be home until morning if he was being truthful about his work schedule. He walked in around six, fumbling clumsily with the lock. As soon as he stepped through the doorway, I could smell beer on him, and I sat up, ready for this confrontation.

"Shit, Sammi, you scared me. What are you doing out here?" I calmly moved Jo from her pack and play to the car seat, then turned my face to his.

"You had a guest last night. Does Tiffany sound familiar?" His face fell, but he didn't open his mouth to respond. A look of acceptance passed over his face. He knew it was too late to deny

anything, no escaping this moment. "How long?" I asked, a part of me still curious to know if he'd tell the truth, now that it was out in the open.

He was so quiet, I could barely hear him, "about two months."

"Lie. Try again." My voice was tempered, despite the rage coursing through me.

He decided not to answer. There wasn't any point. We entered a standoff, me on the couch, him standing in the doorway. I was sure my eyes were burning a hole right through his traitorous body. "Why?" I finally added, expecting he'd avoid giving me a truthful answer.

"Do you really need to ask, Sammi? You call her our daughter, but anyone who looks at her can tell she's not mine. She looks exactly like him. There's no intimacy between us. Hell, we barely see each other at all. I went back to work so you could stay home with her, but it's never enough. You're not happy, and it's dragging me down. You have no idea how exhausting it is to be married to someone who constantly reminds you that you're a failure. I can't look at you without seeing his face. I can't look at her without seeing him, taunting me."

"How dare you? I didn't ask to be violated. I didn't ask to get pregnant. I asked you to take a paternity test, and you refused. And you've been screwing around long before Jo was born, so don't give me bullshit about it all being because of her."

"It doesn't fucking matter, Sammi. I don't need one to tell me what I already know."

"You're right. It doesn't matter. Jo and I are leaving. Today. Now. I'll be at Claire's if you need something."

He didn't answer me. He just walked into the bedroom and shut the door.

Jesse's voice wakes me from my dream.

"Would you guys like to meet William? Claire's in a room with him." Thoughts of Lucas flee my mind, and all I feel in that moment is love. Love for my daughter, Claire, Jesse, this sweet little boy, and even for Ciaran. Seeing Will is the perfect end to a perfect Christmas.

Chapter Eighteen

The next day, I take Jo to work with me again. Jesse's parents are flying home today, and I'm not about to have Claire watch Jo. I was surprised last night that I didn't see Matthew at the hospital, but he may have stopped by after we left. We stayed for some time, but I didn't want to overextend our welcome. Jo was delighted when she had a chance to hold Will, and I'd be lying if I said that the sight of Ciaran gently bouncing him in his arms wasn't incredibly hot. I caught Ciaran watching me, smiling, several times while I was holding the baby. When Ciaran left last night, he offered to bring lunch by the shop for all of us, so I'm expecting him any time. The bell rings, and I look up, shocked to see Matthew instead.

"Hey, Sammi! Sorry I missed you last night at the hospital. I couldn't get up there until this morning. Exciting stuff, huh?" Jo comes around the corner, but she doesn't greet him as readily as she has in the past. "Hi, Jo! Did you have a good Christmas?" He seems eager and exuberant today.

She doesn't answer, inching backward a fraction. I don't know what's changed, but she isn't happy to see him. "It is definitely exciting," I respond, drawing his attention back to me. "He's perfect. Did Vanessa go with you?"

"Nah, hospitals freak her out." He chuckles at himself, as if there's an inside joke to which only he is privy.

"Listen, you never got back to me about the car seat. How much do I owe you?" Even though I thought it was clear that I wasn't interested in the joint gift anymore, I feel weird about not paying him since he said it was from both of us.

"Don't worry about it. I know things have to be tight, you a single mom and all. I covered your part, no worries." He's not wrong. Finances are always an issue, but it still angers me that he has the audacity to say it, to assume that just because I'm not married means I can't be successful.

He continues, "I actually wanted to stop by for a different reason. I was wondering if you'd like to hang out on New Year's Eve. Vanessa is going to a party with a friend out of town, and I don't want to ring in the New Year alone. We could get some dinner, have a drink, spend it in style." I know the look of disbelief on my face is clear, as he adds, "Just friends, no pressure."

It's not just that. I have Jo to think about too. Besides, I'm not really an out on the town type of person. I'm more comfortable at home, safe on the couch. And I kind of hoped we'd be spending it with Ciaran, the three of us.

"Sorry, I always spend it with Jo," I tell him. "We have an early countdown on Netflix and tuck in before eight. Thanks for the offer, though."

His face falls. "Of course. Maybe another time. I have to get going for a meeting, but I'll text you later?" His whole visit is so abrupt and unexpected.

I really hope he doesn't text. I wanted to try to make the friends thing work, but it's clear it won't. Regardless, I reply, "Sure, I'll talk to you later. Thanks for stopping by."

The bell rings before he responds, and Ciaran steps in. The first thing I feel is relief. The fact Jo didn't say a single word to Matthew concerns me, and it makes me feel a little safer knowing Ciaran is there. Jo steps from behind me, and seeing him, she runs over to him, throwing her arms up for him to lift her.

Matthew watches Ciaran with Jo for a moment before he turns back to me. "I'll get back to you on those drinks. See you later." When the door closes, Ciaran raises his eyebrows to me in a quizzical expression, and I lightly shake my head, an indication I'll tell him later. Ciaran moves his arm up, holding a bag from Firehouse Subs. Jo talks constantly through her bites of food, and Ciaran and I quietly finish our own meals. Once she's done, Jo's eyes grow heavy, and I move her into a sleeping bag in the office for a nap.

Back with Ciaran, I tell him, "Sorry. She's so excited about Will, and she talks a lot when she gets excited."

"It's okay," he replies. "I enjoy listening to her. She's very animated, and her enthusiasm is contagious. Was your sandwich okay?"

"Yes, thank you. We both love Firehouse." I know he's curious about Matthew's visit, but he won't ask. "Sorry about that whole thing with Matthew. He stopped by to invite me out for New Year's, but I didn't accept. You're right. He's never going to be okay with being just friends, so I need to figure out a way to deal with all that."

"And the reference to drinks?" he asks. There's not an ounce of anger in his voice, just curiosity.

I answer honestly. "I don't think he takes no for an answer very well. I'm not getting together with him. That said, I have to be amicable toward him since he's Will's other Godparent.

Hopefully, he gets the hint that it's never going to happen between us."

Ciaran wraps his arms around me. "Good, you're my girl, and I don't share." I feel bubbly with his statement. "So, what ARE you doing for New Year's?"

"Hanging out with Jo and you, I hope." His answer to me is a passionate kiss, one that promises of a night I'll never forget. Once he leaves, my lips tingle for the rest of the day. I yield.

Ciaran has to make a trip out to his employer, based in California, for a few days. I won't see him again until New Year's Eve, but he calls every night, and we text constantly throughout the day. It's an easy week, Jo going to work with me in the morning, then we head home in the afternoons when Josef or Beatrice comes in. We spend several evenings over at Claire's, cuddling with Will, and I help her with meals and other household chores to lighten her load. Will reminds me of Jo as a baby, quiet and observant, taking in the world around him as much as he can. I can picture him in five years, a lisp as he sounds out new words and a backpack bigger than him as he trudges into his first day of school.

One thing I take the time to do before New Year's Eve is run by the store and make sure I'm prepared for the next time Ciaran stays over. Josef offers to close the shop, so I leave after only a few hours. I call Ciaran before I depart and ask if he wants to come early, for dinner. I'm preparing fettucine alfredo, just the way my grandma used to make it.

"Sure," he replies. "How can I turn down fettucine alfredo? What do you say I come over a little early, help you get it ready?" It sounds divine. Lucas wasn't much of a cook and having the extra help is always appreciated. Jo and I spend some time hanging out while we wait for him to arrive, her playing with her new toys from Christmas. It's easy to reflect back on that Christmas four years ago, when I was too poor to buy gifts and determined to make things better for both of us. Things have really changed in those four years...

When I left, I took only the things I could fit in the car, which meant that I had to leave behind the pack and play and Jo's crib. I called Claire on the way, and she told me she already had a guest room set up for the two us. She took care of it all. Our belongings consisted of a suitcase for each of us, a few of my favorite books, mementos from my grandma, and the photos I'd accumulated over the course of my life. I only kept one small box of keepsakes of my time with Lucas, leaving our wedding album behind on the bookshelf. As I left, I dropped a letter I'd written onto the table next to the entry, an apology for allowing our marriage to disintegrate so much that my leaving was the only option left to me. It wasn't an excuse for his part, but I could recognize that by letting him continue to treat me the way that he did, I enabled his behavior. A part of me held out hope that he'd come to his senses, rushing to beg me for forgiveness. But when I tried to picture our lives five years down the road, I couldn't picture him in them, no matter how much I wished for it. I closed by telling him that he was welcome to have a role in his daughter's life, and I would always love him. The last sight I had of our apartment was a cold and desolate living room, full of baby items that would be left to fall apart.

Lucas never got in touch with me. I sent him my new phone number once I settled in and removed myself from the plan we had shared, but his name never lit the screen. He never wrote. After six months of waiting, I filed for divorce under Claire's urging, using a portion of the money I had inherited from Grandma Jolene. The only thing he asked for in the divorce was to sign away his parental rights. That was the moment I knew it was really over. When the divorce was finalized, I heard Grandma Jolene whispering in my ear, once again, "Let it go."

The ringing of the doorbell interrupts my thoughts. Peeking out the window, I see Ciaran and exhale the breath I'd been holding. Some habits die hard. It's the best New Year's Eve I've had in a long time. He counts down with Jo, early, and when she's ready for bed, she asks him to read her a story. He sits on her bed and reads her three books. Finally, her eyes grow heavy, and she falls asleep. We sit down on the couch, and I'm nervous. It's different from the nerves that I feel when I think someone is watching, when I was convinced Lucas was lurking around. It's a feeling of something changing for the better. At first, we're quiet, watching but not really seeing some pre-ball drop show with horrible music and commentary. Slowly, his hand brushes against mine, and it sets an electric charge through me, thrumming deep in my core. I turn to him, and he's watching me, his face serious and his eyes searching for something.

"Thanks for dinner. It was great. It was better than great. You can cook for me anytime."

I laugh. "You sure seem to know your way around a kitchen yourself, cowboy." I don't recall Lucas ever thanking me for dinner. I feel a pressing need to tell Ciaran something that's weighed on me from the minute I realized that I like him. "Promise me that if we don't work out, you and Fergus will stay in Jo's life. She's attached to both of you, and I don't want you to disappear from her life. If you can't do that, it's better to break this off now."

A puff of relief escapes him. I didn't realize he had been holding his breath. "I promise, but it's not going to be an issue. I told you I'm here, as long as you'll have me, and I meant it. If things don't work out between us, it won't be on my behalf. I'm in love with you, and I don't expect you to say it back, but I'm not going to hold back from telling you."

I feel the same way, but I wasn't about to say it to him first. I wonder if I'm rushing things. But Grandma's voice rings through my head, "It's not too soon, Sammi." I tell him how I feel, trusting in her guidance. His eyes brighten, and his grin is bigger than I've ever seen. He leans in for a kiss, soft and gentle at first, becoming more urgent as it goes on.

After a minute, he pulls away. "We have all the time in the world, Sammi," he assures me.

He's right. There's no need to hurry into anything now, but I don't want to wait anymore. I spent years with Lucas, waiting for him to love me the way I deserved, then for him to love Jo as he should, and I spent four years waiting to be able to trust someone new again. When I was with Lucas, for a long time there was a burning need for him, and when we were together, I felt alive and connected. I don't need that type of intimacy with Ciaran to feel connected. There's something tying us together. His touch sends electricity zipping through my body. His kiss leaves me with an exhilarating energy that lasts for a long time after. I realize that with Lucas, we needed that physical intimacy to bond us. But I don't with Ciaran. That bond is already there.

I didn't plan to have Ciaran stay the night when Jo was home, but all my hesitation is gone now. He's my person. There's no doubt lingering in my mind anymore. "Do you want to stay the night?" I ask, adding, "We can just sleep, no pressure."

He smiles, and I lead him to the bedroom. At first, I just lay next to him, my head against his chest and my finger trailing over the sliver of skin between his jeans and his tee. I can hear his breathing quicken and see goosebumps spread across his flesh.

"You smell so good, like honey," he says, his face pressed into my hair. The pressure between us is almost unbearable. I lift my face to his and catch his lips with mine, that smell of pine and bergamot that I love tickling my nose. I'm overcome with a need to feel every inch of him. I strip off my clothes and stand before him, removing his shirt. He stands to slide off his jeans, then pushes me back on to the bed, as I fumble for protection. My body is on fire, and I bury my head in his shoulder to avoid yelling out his name, him not far behind me. We lay there panting after, catching our breath.

"Shower?" I finally ask. With the water beating down on us, he soaps up my back tenderly, and I lean my back into him, heat building again. We're together once again, him holding me up against the wall of the shower until I find release. I've never felt so beautiful or wanted before. We lay down in the bed, and I snuggle against him, his arms wrapped around my body. Just as I drift off to sleep, I think I hear a noise, but I'm too far gone to realize it's not just in my dreams.

I dream of my first time with Lucas, but it's not a dream of romantic reflections. It's a dream of moving past that and sharing something new with Ciaran. My subconscious realizes that my first time with both of the men in my life fell on New Year's Eve, and I'm not really sure what it means, aside from perhaps I've come full circle since my first time. Perhaps I'm finally, really free.

Chapter Nineteen

We all sleep in the next morning, and I jolt awake around half past six. I lay there a moment, listening to the quiet of the house, and trying to figure out exactly what woke me. The dream I had right before comes flashing back to me, and a feeling of terror spreads through me. I can't explain it, but I know something is wrong. There's danger. This is the type of thing that Claire says is my imagination and fear working against me, but I know that it's not that this time. I throw back the covers and nearly run to Jo's room, but she's sound asleep. I've almost convinced myself that my intuition has gone haywire when I hear it. There's definitely someone or something large moving around outside the house. Peeling back the corner of the curtain, I look out, but I can't see anything. I grab Jo from her bed and go back into the bedroom, waking Ciaran. He slides his jeans on under the covers, tugging his shirt over his head, and tells me to stay upstairs while he checks things out. The five-minute wait for him to return is nearly unbearable, but he finally comes through the door and tells me I have a guest. I follow him down the stairs into the kitchen, and the sight I see throws me completely off balance. Lucas is sitting at the table, his finger picking on the skin on his thumb, chewing on his bottom lip in anxiety. Memories flash through my mind of him doing the same things throughout our relationship. I try not to curse in front of Jo, but I can't help the words that come out of my mouth.

"What the hell are you doing here? It's not even seven in the morning, for goodness' sake."

He lifts his hands in surrender, but of what, I'm not sure. "I just want to talk to you." I see him glance at Jo, and I pass her off to Ciaran, giving him a look. He nods, and without speaking, tells me he'll be just around the corner. A moment later, I hear cartoons playing on the TV.

"You better start explaining. How did you even find us?" I ask. I'm both perplexed and angry.

"It wasn't that hard, Sammi," he retorts. I don't respond. "How have you been? You look good, happy. I guess the guy probably has something to do with that. How's Jo? She's getting so big."

"Cut the crap, Lucas. You'd know that if you actually gave a damn about anyone other than yourself," I seethe. "Now, I'm asking you again, why are you here?" My phone rings on the counter, and I walk over to it, seeing Claire's name on the screen. I take two seconds to send her a text that I'll call her shortly.

"You need to call someone? Claire, maybe?" Lucas asks. I shake my head and cross my arms, waiting for him to finally answer the question. Of course, he would know intuitively that Claire was calling.

"Sammi, I know I screwed things up. You and Jo were the best things that ever happened to me, and I threw all that away. I'm sorry. I've cleaned up my life, but I can't let how things ended between us remain unresolved. And I want a chance to be a dad, to be the father Jo deserves.""

For so many years, I wanted nothing more than to hear those words, and now that he's saying them, I realize I don't want that anymore. "Are you serious? You want to reconcile? Because there's no way in hell that's happening. Why would you suddenly want to be in Jo's life? She doesn't even know you." There's no way I'd ever be able to trust him again, with my heart or with Jo's.

"No. I know that ship has sailed, no matter how much I wish it wasn't the case. After you left, I dated Tiffany for a year, but I realized how much I messed everything up. She was just a poor substitute for you. My mom and Amanda convinced me I needed to go to rehab, and I've been sober since. Not a drop of alcohol for over three years now. I spent some time in therapy, working through my issues. And I started writing again. I actually have a publisher. It's a small deal, but everyone has to start somewhere. I can take care of Jo, help with whatever she needs. I tried to come by before Christmas to talk to you, but you weren't home. I actually just moved into an apartment here in town. I'm local now, for pick-ups, drop-offs, whatever you need."

I can only address one thing at a time. There's too much information coming at me at one time. "Wait. That was you? Peeking in windows like a prowler? Who does that?"

At least he looks embarrassed by his behavior. "I'm sorry. I was hoping to see if maybe you were inside and just ignoring the door." All the pieces are falling into place, prompting the next question.

"What are you driving?" I ask.

He seems confused. "Um, I have a small pickup. Why? I got it a year ago or so." Another piece slots into place.

"Have you been following me?" To be honest, I hope his answer is yes. It would take so much of the anxiety from the last few months off my chest.

"I wouldn't say following you, but I did come by your shop a couple times," he admits. "I wanted to come in to see you, but I chickened out. And one day I was driving to the sporting goods store and happened to see you dropping Jo off at Shining Tots Preschool, but I didn't have the guts to approach you. It's taken me a while to work up the nerve to come here."

The final piece fits. I'm not sure how I feel about all of this, a certain mix of relief and frustration coming together. It's not the reunion I once thought we'd have, and I'm okay with that.

I sigh. "I'm glad you cleaned up your life, Lucas, but I don't know what you expect from me or why you moved here. You weren't there for me when I needed you the most. Instead, you made me feel like I had no value, like I was worthless. You were never there for my daughter. You wouldn't even do the damn paternity test before you wrote her off."

"I'm sorry. I'll do the paternity test now if you want, but it doesn't matter. I want her in my life. I can't make up for lost years, but I can spend the rest of my life proving to you that I can be the father she deserves and the friend I used to be. I moved because I want to be closer to you and Jo, whatever that looks like, and I can write anywhere. I always liked coming back here to visit with you, and it's nice to be out of the city. I know I've made it difficult to believe, but I'm not that person who drove you away. Not anymore."

I let out a disbelieving snort, "No. I'm not interested. What difference does it make NOW? You signed away your parental rights. You've never been a part of her life. You've never sent a birthday card. You've never called her. Your own mother and sister completely cut me off when I left, and neither one of them have seen her in four years. I left you a note, told you where I was going if you wanted to keep in touch, and you never even tried. I sent you my number when I changed it. Nothing."

Tears brim his eyes. I'm so angry, but I can also tell he's genuine. He really thinks that we can just be friends again, as if no time has passed, as if nothing ever happened. "There's nothing that I can say or do to make up for it," he nearly whispers. "I can't change the past. But I miss you in my life. Please, won't you at least talk to me about how your life is? How Jo is?" My heart softens a little. This is the Lucas I remember, the one who cared with all of himself. But I don't know how to move past the hurt from before and find a way to have him around. It would be the responsible thing, letting Jo have him in her life, know the man who signed her birth certificate, even begrudgingly. After all, he might be her actual father.

Ciaran comes around the corner and stands against the far wall, hostility pouring off of him. I can hear Jo laughing at the cartoon still playing.

Lucas looks at Ciaran, then back at me. "I tried looking you up a few times on Facebook, but I couldn't find you."

"That's intentional. I have others I don't want finding me. Why should I tell you anything about Jo?" Ciaran still hasn't spoken, simply watching the two of us interact.

"Please, Sammi, I'm begging you." I look to Ciaran again. He clearly outmuscles Lucas, and the look on his face screams that he will remove Lucas's head from his body if he so much as looks at me wrong. Lucas follows my sight back to Ciaran, and the testosterone pouring off the two of them is overwhelming. I walk over and put my hand on Ciaran's arm, my touch seeming to calm him instantly.

"Lucas, this is Ciaran, my boyfriend. Ciaran, this is Lucas, my ex-husband." I can tell Ciaran doesn't want Lucas here, but he moves forward and shakes his hand anyway, deferring to me. I appreciate that he's not trying to take over and rule what happens in my own house. He steps back again, and Jo runs around the corner. She hides her face against his leg, and he lifts her, where she buries her face in his neck, peeking at Lucas from the corners of her eyes. A look of resignation comes over Lucas's face. It's the moment he realizes that I've made a new family and life here. He knows now that even if I let him see Jo, things aren't going to be an easy transition, nothing simple or straightforward. His involvement in her life will be on a trial basis. Whether he's asking me to give him another chance or not, it's clear a part of him still hoped for it.

"Lucas, this is Jo. Jo, this is one of Mommy's old friends, from a long time ago. His name is Lucas."

Lucas studies her. I compare the two of them watching each other.

"It's nice to meet you, Jo," he says, his voice kind and soft. She doesn't respond right away, and I think it's about time for Lucas to leave when she talks.

"You knew my mommy before I was born?" she asks, before pausing. She continues, "She doesn't talk about you."

I can see the sadness in his eyes, but he smiles. "Yes, I did. Your mommy was always so nice to everyone and just a good person."

She nods and wiggles out of Ciaran's hold. "I'll be right back," she says, before tearing off. A moment later, I hear her frantic footsteps running up the stairs. I sit down at the table again,

Ciaran continuing to keep the floor in place from his stance by the basement stairwell.

I lower my voice. "Lucas, I'm not saying you can never be a part of Jo's life. If you want the paternity test, we'll do it. But you have to understand that I can't make you any promises. Jo doesn't know about you or Emmitt, and I don't know when I'll tell her. It's a decision I'll have to make when the time is right. And regardless of what the paternity test says, we can't turn back that clock." The words are hard to get out, but Grandma is speaking up, telling me to give him the chance to be in her life. I'm listening for Jo's footsteps, but she hasn't come back down the stairs yet. My eyes flicker up to Ciaran's, and they reflect back understanding and compassion.

"I get it," Lucas replies. He looks at Ciaran too, then back at me once again. "Are you happy?" It's clear he's sizing up Ciaran, but it's not in a threatening way. It's simply an assessment of the man who took over the role that Lucas was unable to fill.

"Yes, Lucas, I am. I have a future, and I'm not willing to give that up to revisit a past that has a lot of bad memories. The only way now is forward, and that includes Ciaran. That said, I also won't deny Jo the chance to know you, but it will be on my terms. We need to take it slow, and I need to know you're not going to leave her. I won't put her through that."

He looks at Ciaran again. "You promise to take care of Sammi and Jo?" It's a funny question, coming from the man who failed to do exactly that.

Ciaran's posture softens. "Always." There's a moment of silence, and I can hear Jo moving back toward the stairs, but she hasn't started her descent yet. Ciaran adds, "They're everything to me. I'll do whatever it takes to give them the best life. If that means that you take a test, and it comes back that you are Jo's father, I'll step back and let you have a part in that role. But understand that I love her like she's my own. She's my daughter, blood or not." It's the clearest Ciaran has ever been about his intentions, but I don't have time to think about that yet. Feet are pounding down the steps now, and the three of us remain in our awkward triangle, watching for Jo to come around the corner.

She walks to the table and puts a drawing in front of Lucas that I've never seen before. I can see a clear depiction of me standing in the backyard of a house, my belly swollen, but I can't make out everyone else that's in the picture. She points to a figure on my side, holding a little girl that is clearly her. "This is Ciaran. He's going to be my new daddy." Lucas looks over to me in surprise, but my face holds no answers. I'm as shocked as him. Jo points to someone next to Ciaran. "This is my Papa. He's Ciaran's daddy." I'm sure my jaw is on the floor by now, but she's not done. She points to two more figures, standing off to the side in the drawing but with a little distance between us. "And this is you and a girl." I jerk my head up to look at Ciaran, and all he does is shrug. The fact Jo said he will be her father doesn't appear to faze him.

I lean over Jo's picture. "Sweetie, how did you know to draw this? You've never even met Lucas before."

She giggles. "Silly, my great-grandma told me. She told me where to find a picture, so I could draw him." I lock eyes with Lucas. "She told me that he'd visit, and he'd be my friend, and Ciaran would be my daddy."

"What picture are you talking about? When did you talk to Great-Grandma, Jo?" She's seen photos of her, of course, and I've shared plenty of stories, but she's never really said much about her.

"Um, I talk to her all the time. This time was when we met Ciaran at the pizza store. The picture was in the drawer over there." She points to the junk drawer, and chills shudder down my spine. It's time for a little one-way conversation with my deceased grandmother. I have no explanation for what Jo is telling me. I don't have an explanation for the whispers in my ears over the years since she passed either, and I've just come to accept them as real. After all, I'm thinking about talking to a dead person.

Jo speaks once more, "You can keep this. I made it for you."

I can see moisture lining Lucas's eyes. "Thank you, Jo. I'll put it on my fridge. It's a great drawing." He chokes back a sob. We all sit silently for a few minutes, not sure how to go forward after Jo's revelation. Finally, Lucas stands. "Well, I should get going for now, but it was nice to meet you, Jo, Ciaran. Can I text you later, Sammi? Your number is still the same as you sent?" I nod.

"I'll see you out," Ciaran offers. I watch as the two men walk to the door and see Ciaran pull a business card from his jeans pocket, handing it to Lucas. They shake hands, and with that, Lucas is out the door.

I'm not quite ready to discuss the emotional mayhem of the last hour, so we spend some time making breakfast, all three of us in the kitchen together. It's not lost on me how easily we move around, perfectly in sync. Ciaran asks if I'm okay if he runs home, showers, and changes into clean clothes. He has to get some work done, and I have to open the shop. I tell him to pack an overnight bag.

Jo goes to work with me, and we have a perfectly normal day. I send Claire a text and ask if she'd like to come by with Will. She does, stopping over lunch. Jo tells her about our surprise visitor this morning. After some time, she goes into my office and lays down to watch a movie on the little television I bought for her to use on days she comes to work with me. Claire asks if I'm okay, and I realize that I am. I'm really okay. Lucas's surprise visit helped me to see that my fears were misguided. While I certainly was right to be concerned, if I had known all along it was him, my reaction would have been much different. While I feared what he would want with Jo, the alternative of Emmitt was far more frightening to me. In my mind, I had conjured visits from both. The idea of Lucas had been infuriating, but the thought of Emmitt was terrifying.

I'm planning to bring Jo to work with me tomorrow. She won't go back to school until next week. Tina is still back home, but Claire offers to watch her for me. She's family, through and through.

Lucas texts shortly after, and we exchange a volley of messages. He tells me he's going to play hockey here, asks if I'd like to bring Jo to watch a game sometime. I find it easier to talk to him when he's not sitting in front of me. Nevertheless, I'm choosy with what I share, and I feel better after. He shares more about his own journey, and it definitely seems like he's back to himself. I need to talk to Ciaran first, but I'm considering inviting Lucas out for coffee sometime to discuss exactly how to approach things. I don't need Ciaran's permission, but I would like his input.

That night, Ciaran and I talk while we make dinner, and he agrees that it's a good idea to talk to Lucas and make some serious decisions about what his relationship with Jo will look like. I'm still more than slightly perturbed that Lucas moved out here without discussing it with me first, but I can't change that. I have to keep living my life. Ciaran offers to come with me if

I want him to, but I feel like this first discussion is one Lucas and I need to have just between the two of us. There's a lot of baggage to wade through. After dinner, Ciaran reads a stack of books to Jo, and she falls asleep on his lap. He moves her into bed, and we go to my room. Exhausted, we both fall into deep, easy sleeps, and blissful dreams invade my slumber as I see myself walking down the aisle, Ciaran waiting for me at the end.

Chapter Twenty

The next morning, Ciaran heads home after breakfast to work, and I drop off Jo at Claire's so I can go to my own job. The woman amazes me. She has a newborn at home, and still offered to watch a rambunctious four-year-old. When I pull up to the shop shortly after, I'm shocked to find the glass in the doorframe scattered across the floor. I can see a large rock sitting just inside the doorway, and the interior is a mess – flowers, greenery, and home decorations scattered everywhere. Several small garden statues are shattered. I instantly regret not putting in an alarm system when I bought the shop. The first thing I do, remaining in my car, is call the police. While waiting for them to arrive, I call my insurance agent and leave a message. Then, I finally call Ciaran, who offers to come over right away.

Several hours later, the police are done and inform me that the cash register was cleared out. Amazingly, my office was mostly untouched. The only exception is that a picture frame of Jo and me was tossed to the ground, the glass cracked. With the number of people who are in and out of the shop at any given time, there's not much hope in finding anything unusual with fingerprints. It seems likely that someone broke in for the money, and the debris just a parting gift. That said, the police urge me to use caution, and let them know if I think of anything that can help them with the investigation. The fact my home was broken into months ago appears to be an unfortunate coincidence.

Ciaran boards up the door, promising to call about getting a security system installed as soon as possible. We can't open today, and I urge Ciaran to go back home to work. After letting Beatrice and Josef know we'll be closed, and I'd call them as soon as we can open, I head to Claire's to pick up Jo early.

As I'm pulling up to the house, I realize I never even called or texted Claire to let her know what happened. I'm surprised she hasn't reached out to me since she always knows when something is wrong, but maybe she's just been busy trying to care for both kids. I let myself into the house and am greeted by Oliver barking and jumping on my legs. I can hear Will crying in the other room. After petting the dog, I head in to check on everyone. Jo is holding Will, trying to feed him a bottle, while Claire encourages her and issues sweet assurances to the baby. It's bound to be one of my favorite memories of the two of them, Jo caring for Will and looking so grown up.

"Hey, Sammi, what are you doing here so early?" Claire asks.

"Off early today. I can text you later." I give her the look that tells her that I can't discuss it in front of Jo. Instead, I sit, and once Will has eaten, I burp him and rock him in my arms as he falls asleep again. The three of us ladies spend some time talking. Jo dominates the conversation, talking about going back to school next week and how she can't wait to tell her friends about her new cousin. It's soothing to just spend some time with the two people I love most in the world.

After getting home, I text Claire about what happened, and she immediately offers Jesse's help with whatever I need. It strikes me that for the first time, I didn't call Jesse first with a problem. He's been the brother I never had for so long, and the instinct to call him for help is so natural to me. Ciaran sends a text inviting Jo and me to come to his apartment for dinner. As much time as we've spent together, it's the first time I've been there. He lives in a small, one-bedroom apartment, in a nicely kept complex. The walls are painted a generic eggshell color, but I'm taken in by the photographs lining the living room. An assortment of landscapes, usually with water, are hung in a neat pattern.

"These are beautiful, Ciaran. Where did you get all these?" I ask.

"Uh, I took them. These are all places I've been." Blush creeps up his cheeks, though he has no reason to be embarrassed. He definitely has an artistic eye.

I'm awestruck. I've been so few places. One picture in particular catches my eye. It's a small cabin tucked into a wooded area, a body of water shimmering to the side of the frame. "Where's this? It's so peaceful."

"That is actually my parents' cabin up in Door County. They got it when I was about ten, and we spent a lot of time there over the summers when I was a teenager. It's my favorite place, but I haven't been there since I moved away. It's just too far from California. Maybe you and Jo could go up with me this summer, if you're interested. There's this little Swedish restaurant that has live goats on top of the roof. Jo would love it."

I am definitely interested. We spend dinner with Ciaran telling us about the various places in the photos, sharing stories of each that make Jo laugh so hard, she snorts. I have a feeling that a life with Ciaran would mean adventure and new places. In the past, that would scare me. But now, the thought excites me. I can picture the three of us, traveling and discovering together.

After dinner, Jo is getting sleepy. Somehow, without discussing it, Ciaran and I agree that he won't come over tonight. Before I leave, he lets me know the security company will be at the shop the following Tuesday to install. It's a relief, though I'm worried about the few days until then. He walks us out to the car, and I watch him in my rearview mirror as I pull away, full of emotions swirling within me.

On the way home, headlights pop up behind me. Whoever it is drives far too quickly for this stretch of road, and I slow down to let them pass. I don't want them behind me. They slow too, their lights looming in my window, too close for comfort. There's a turn ahead that will take me out of the way to return home, but I'm hoping that the vehicle behind me will stay on this road, and I can get them off my tail. Thankfully, they don't follow me on the turn, but I can vaguely make the outline of what looks like a pickup truck. It's weird, but when I finally pull into my driveway, I shake it off. Strange coincidences.

Friday, the insurance company comes by to look at the shop, so I ask Ciaran to come do the walkthrough with us. I drop Jo off at Claire's again while I take care of it. Once the insurance company is done, Ciaran and I grab a quick bite to eat down the street before he goes back to work on his latest project, and I pick up Jo. Later that day, as Jo and I sit and watch a movie, I hear something outside the house. Immediately, I check the cameras, but all I see is the neighbor's dog using my bushes to relieve herself. Returning to the movie, I text Lucas to see when he can get together. I need to work on cleaning up the shop this weekend. Claire has already offered to watch Jo, and Jesse's parents will be over Saturday to visit with her and Will, so I don't feel bad leaving Jo there. Lucas and I agree on the following Saturday. Tina will be back in town, and hopefully, things with work will be back to normal. Fergus is coming back tonight from his trip. They're flying in to St. Louis, and Ciaran will pick up Fergus from Fiona's house between here and the airport, so I let Jo sleep in bed with me. I realize how silly it sounds, but it makes me feel better to have her close. Despite this, I still sleep poorly, my anxiety clawing its way back. Will it ever leave me for good?

Chapter Twenty-One

Dawn comes on Saturday, far sooner than I'm ready. We start the day before the caffeine has even kicked in. It will take a long time to clean up the shop and get it ready to open on Monday. Ciaran comes by bright and early, and he rides with me to drop off Jo and say a quick hello to Claire. Jesse meets us at the shop, a tingle running up my spine when I realize Matthew is with him. I decided we can't really be friends, but I can be amicable, thanking him for his help. The four of us spend several hours cleaning up glass, straightening things, and tossing debris. Matthew helps Jesse install new glass in the door, and Jesse even takes the time to change the locks for me on the front and office doors. I take some time to go through my office more thoroughly but still don't find anything missing.

By lunch, we've finished. Most of the morning passed quietly, other than discussion on the cleanup process. Ciaran offers to order pizzas for all of us, but Jesse declines. He has work to get back to on the farm. I look to Matthew, but he seems sullen and withdrawn, declining as well. I thank both of them profusely for their help, both shrugging it off before leaving.

Once they're gone, Ciaran turns to me. "I need to talk to you." My heart sinks, sure he's breaking up with me, and I realize how often my mind automatically goes to the worst-case scenario. "I have to go on another trip for work. I'm probably going to be gone all week, but it may not be that long. We just signed on a huge client, and they want me to come work in-house for a few days with their marketing team to get all their new promotional materials designed and ready to go. They're in Utah. But I'm worried about leaving you. Say the word, and I'll tell them to assign it to someone else."

While I'm disappointed he'll be gone so long, he needs to do what's best for his career. "It's okay. I think you should go and do what you have to do. I'll be fine. I don't know why you're worried. I'm not going to fall in love with someone else." But his face tells me that's not what he worried about.

"It's not that, Sammi. I've been thinking about this whole thing with the shop, and I talked to my dad last night about it. Neither one of us thinks this was a simple robbery. I don't want to scare you, but do you think Lucas may have broken in? Maybe some sort of revenge for you moving on?"

"What? No," I splutter. "He wouldn't do that. Why would you even say that? It has to have been a robbery." But how well do I know Lucas? A lot can change in four years. Regardless of what of I say, Ciaran has planted a seed of doubt in my mind.

"It's just weird, Sammi. I know whoever it is cleared out the cash register, but they left your computer. The shop was a mess. It wasn't a simple smash and grab. And the only thing broken in your entire office was a photo with you in it. I'm not saying it definitely wasn't a robbery, but something just doesn't add up." I don't want to consider the alternative. If it wasn't a robbery, it was personal. It's going to take some time to wrap my head around the possibility.

"I know you, Sammi," he continues. "I know you won't call Claire or Jesse if something is bothering you, especially with Will. But if I'm going to make this trip, I need you to promise me you'll be careful. If you feel like something is off, call my dad. He said you and Jo can stay there too, if you feel like you'd be safer."

"Ciaran, I'm not going to call your father every time I get spooked. The police said it was a robbery. I'm sure they're right."

His face falls into resignation. "Just promise me, please, to be careful? I hope you're right, but this whole thing really bothers me."

I lean forward to press a kiss to his lips. "I'll be fine. When do you leave?"

"I'm sorry, Monday morning. I know it's short notice. But I'll call you every night, and if you need something urgent, you can call me during the day. I should be back Saturday night at the latest. I already talked to Jesse, and he said he can come Tuesday for the security system installation if you want."

It's a long time to go without seeing him, but I don't have a choice. I can't, won't ask him not to make the trip.

Ciaran stays the night Saturday, and we spend all day together Sunday. He's still on edge, hyper vigilant around us, but when he leaves Monday morning, he seems a little better, calmer. Jo is back to school, and Tina is around to watch her after school again. It's a relief to get back into a routine, and I keep telling myself the police are right. That little seed is starting to sprout, though.

Chapter Twenty-Two

Monday and Tuesday pass quietly. Jesse comes Tuesday to help oversee the installation of the security system, as promised. Ciaran texts more during the day than I anticipated, but it's nice to hear from him. Unfortunately, his project isn't going well. The client is proving to be rather difficult, and Ciaran has had to scrap several starts. Things are calm on the home front, though, and it seems to reassure him. I even hear from Fergus for a brief five-minute call each night, checking in. It's sweet and very fatherly. Wednesday seems to be a repeat of the previous two days, until I'm hit with a panic attack about Jo. I call the preschool, and they assure me she's fine. I can't go back to being scared all the time. The anxiety will eat me alive. Keeping my hands busy, I go back to work, but I still can't shake the feeling something is off.

That night, I return home with Jo, and there's a vase sitting on the porch with white roses. The memory of all those years ago flashes through my mind, but these roses are vibrant and healthy. I settle Jo in front of a cartoon and move to the porch to retrieve the vase. There's a card with them, and all it says is "To our love." I convince myself that Ciaran must have sent them. He couldn't know the link to my past. I send him a quick thank you text, but I don't hear back right away. About an hour later, he calls.

"What are you thanking me for? Did I do something I don't remember?" he laughs.

"The roses left on the porch. It was sweet. They're gorgeous, although I notice the card is from a different florist." I say the last part with a little bit of playful attitude, but Ciaran is silent. "Did I lose you?"

"No, I'm here." He pauses before speaking again. "I didn't order roses, Sammi. I'm sorry. Are you sure you're okay?" I'm not okay any longer, but I don't want to tell him. "Why don't I call my dad and ask him to stop by?"

I'm tempted to take him up on his offer but don't. The only other person who makes sense is Lucas, and while it's a jerk move to deliver white roses of all things, I still don't believe he'd hurt me. I could call him now and sort things out, but I'll see him in a few days, and I'd rather have this conversation in person.

"Listen, I should be home Friday afternoon. Promise me, if anything else odd happens, you'll go stay with my dad," Ciaran pleads.

"I'll think about it," I tell him. I don't want to give him a definite answer. I don't feel right intruding on Fergus's space because of my anxiety. But if I tell Ciaran no, he won't let it go. He's not happy with my response, but he finally drops it. Knowing him, he'll still call his dad and give him a heads up. Ciaran is nothing if not protective. I end the call quickly and then dial Claire, who texted while I was on the phone, to assure her we are both okay. Before bed that night, I double check the alarm three times, but all in all, it's a surprisingly peaceful night, the knot in my stomach over Lucas dissipating while I sleep.

Thursday morning, I wake up with a determination to sort things out with Lucas and get things back on track. He has to realize that I meant it when I said I was serious about Ciaran, and obviously, it's not going to work for him to be a part of Jo's life. I'm going to encourage him to go back to St. Louis and move on. The work day is going fairly well until Josef leaves for the day. For thirty minutes, the business phone rings repeatedly. Each time I answer, I hear nothing but breathing. As soon as I disconnect, the phone rings again, and the process repeats. After a dozen times of it, I stop answering and let it roll to the machine. The caller breathes heavily through the line to the message before disconnecting and calling again. I'm seriously considering unplugging the phone, but I finally pick up. After the breathing continues, I let loose.

"Lucas, that's enough. I don't know why you're doing this, but it isn't funny." The breathing continues for a minute, and I move to hang up when someone speaks. They're the first words all morning from my persistent caller.

They say only two words. "Lucas who?"

I slam the phone down. He's not being funny. He's being a jerk. It's time to end this. I send him a text that I'll meet him tomorrow at three at the Starbucks. It can't wait for Saturday.

That night, I tell Ciaran of my plans and about the calls. "You shouldn't meet with him alone. Whatever game he's playing, it's not safe. I should be home by then. I'll meet you at the Starbucks a few minutes before three." Despite my earlier stance that I need to have this discussion with Lucas alone, I'm relieved Ciaran offers. Everything changed when Lucas started with all this. After disconnecting with Ciaran, I call Tina to let her know I need her later than usual, but she's already made other plans. Claire has to take Will for a check-up, so she's out. Reluctantly,

I call Fergus. I hate to bother him, but he sounds excited to have Jo come hang out with him. We finalize plans, and I hang up, feeling ready to be done with all of it.

The next morning, I keep getting heavy breather calls again. When Beatrice comes in, the calls stop. Whoever it is must know when I'm alone. It only makes me angrier. Ciaran checks in a few times that morning. He's still planning to be home in the afternoon and meet me at Starbucks. When I drop Jo off with Fergus, he asks if I'm really okay. I appreciate his concern, but I won't tell him I'm not okay at all.

Thirty minutes later, I'm early to Starbucks, waiting on Ciaran and Lucas. I haven't heard from Ciaran since before his flight, and I'm worried. I'm looking at the clock on the wall when Lucas shows up prematurely.

He's smiling broadly and moves to hug me. "Hey, Sammi. Thanks for meeting me." I shrink away, and he frowns a little before pulling out a chair to take a seat. "Is something wrong?"

I really wanted to wait for Ciaran to get here, but I don't have that option anymore. "Lucas, this has to stop. You and I aren't getting back together, and based on your behavior this week, I don't think you should be a part of Jo's life either. You need to go back to St. Louis. Leave us alone."

"What are you talking about? My behavior?" His voice is disbelieving. "I've been in St. Louis all week, packing up my condo to move stuff out here."

I didn't expect that response. "It's not funny, Lucas. No more games. I know you've been calling the shop, breathing into the phone, and I know you left flowers on the doorstep Wednesday. There is no us anymore. You need to move on."

He looks a little angry now. "Sammi, seriously, I have no idea what you're talking about. I told you I've been in St. Louis."

"It doesn't matter where you were," I snap. "You're trying to scare me, and it's cruel."

"I didn't do those things!" He realizes he's shouting and drops his voice again. "I know I've been an ass in the past, but I wouldn't do things to scare you. That's not me. Even when I've been a jerk, I haven't done things to purposely frighten you."

The store is awkwardly silent at Lucas's proclamation, as if every customer and employee have intruded on our private conversation. ...He's right. He's hurt me beyond measure, but he's never tried to scare me. It's never been like this.

"You swear?" I whisper.

"Of course, Sammi. I don't want to say this, but how much do you know about your boyfriend? Is it possible he would be doing it?" He's near whispering too, and I have to strain to hear him.

I almost laugh. Each of them is accusing the other. "Ciaran? No, he's harmless. He's done a lot to protect me physically and mentally in the last month."

"How long have you been dating him?" he persists. "Only a month? Do you really know him that well?"

I sigh. "I know his heart, Lucas. He would never do something to try to scare me. I trust him."

"Well, if it's not Ciaran, and it's not me, it's someone else." Lucas's voice pauses, struggling to verbalize the next question. "Do you think he's out of jail?"

Lucas is voicing the fear that I've carried with me since I moved here. "I don't see how it's possible. I can call the detectives who worked the case back in St. Louis and see. Listen, I know you say it's not you, and I believe you; I think. But I need some time. Can you give me that?"

"Anything you need, Sammi. I promise you, I'm not that same guy you left. I needed help, but I'm better now. I mean it when I say I want you to be happy, whatever that looks like. And I'm telling you now, if you need anything, call me, day or night. It doesn't matter if we're together or not. If you think Emmitt is around, call. I'll be there in minutes."

It sounds familiar, but I'm not sure what to think. I came into this on fire, ready to tear into Lucas and run him out of town. But now, I question everything. Is Lucas telling the truth? What if I'm wrong about Ciaran? I really feel like it can't be him, but I've been fooled before by my heart. And what about Emmitt? I need to call the detectives, but I need to pick up Jo first. I don't feel comfortable leaving her any more. Ciaran still hasn't shown up, and I haven't heard from him. I excuse myself, promising to reach out to Lucas when I'm ready.

I speed all the way to pick up Jo, and Fergus seems relieved to see me. "Sammi, I tried to call you. Ciaran's flight got delayed. But your phone doesn't seem to be working." I pull it from my pocket and have Fergus call it again. It never rings or shows a missed call. "Ciaran tried to call you, but he couldn't get through either. I was tempted to drive to Starbucks, but I didn't have a seat for Jo."

I feel a little foolish for my concern leaving Jo with Fergus. He's clearly concerned for my well-being, though that doesn't mean that Ciaran couldn't have had ulterior motives in anything. I look over my phone again, navigating to settings and realizing the problem right away. It's on airplane mode. When did it get switched to that?

"Thanks, Fergus. I think I figured out my phone. Would you try to call it again?" He does, and it rings this time. I'm relieved.

Suddenly, a volley of texts comes through from both Ciaran and Claire. "When should Ciaran be home?" I ask.

Fergus guesses it will be around six, and I send a text to Ciaran to let him know I'm okay, that I'll call him later. On the way home, I connect Bluetooth and call Claire to let her know how things went with Lucas.

"Do you believe him?" she asks.

I admit, "Honestly, I don't know anymore."

"Do you want to stay the night?" A part of me wants to say yes, but a part of me is tired of running. I don't think I have to worry about anything tonight. I have the alarm system at home, and I can work through things tomorrow, when I'm fresh and rested.

Chapter Twenty-Three

Once we get home, I'm hit by exhaustion. Today has taken a lot out of me. Jo isn't hungry, having talked Fergus into feeding her, and I'm too tired to make myself anything. We head up to my bedroom and stretch out on the bed to watch a movie. I don't intend to fall asleep, but a quick hour later, I'm lost to fantasies of a future with Ciaran when a faint noise registers in my head. It takes me a minute to shake off grogginess and realize it sounds like someone is in the house. I don't immediately register concern because the alarm isn't going off, but it hits me that in my exhaustion earlier, I never set it. It's the first time ever in this house that I haven't engaged the alarm before going to sleep, regardless of the time of day. I almost always have it set, even when we're awake. Ciaran must have let himself in with the spare key I gave him on New Year's Day. I'm still unsure what's going on, but in my gut, I don't think it's him doing all these things to frighten me. I pause again, cocking my head to the side as I listen intently, hearing only Jo's steady breathing.

Feeling paranoid, I settle back onto my pillow. I've spent so long afraid of what could happen. Anytime something is going well, I find myself waiting for the other shoe to drop. Things can't ever just be perfect, and that's something I'll need to work on to be able to truly build a new life with Ciaran. My eyes are just drifting closed again when it feels like someone is shaking me awake. I lurch up in bed and look over, but Jo is still asleep. Then, I hear it, the warning from Grandma Jolene, a single word. "Hide."

I throw back the covers, my legs trembling, and check that the door is locked. Looking for my phone, I can't find it. Maybe I left it downstairs. What am I supposed to do? We're stuck.

Pausing to listen again, I take deep breaths to calm myself. Something clatters downstairs, and Jo jolts awake. I move around and pick her up, and she wraps her arms around my neck. She can feel my panic, and her entire body quakes with fear. Somehow, I manage to calm myself enough to tell her it will be okay. I wish I was as sure of that as I want her to believe.

There's no good place to hide, but there's a small gap between the head of the bed and the wall. I won't fit there, but Jo will. I can still hear noises downstairs, the upstairs seemingly empty of anyone other than the two of us. Whoever is downstairs is not trying to be quiet. Jo's sobs are getting heavier, and I know that I have to save her. There's no one coming to our rescue. The bedroom lock will stall someone, but it won't hold forever. My best chance is to lead them away from Jo and try to get my phone. I look at my daughter, drawing her focus to my face.

"Jo, sweetie, I need you to be brave for me. Can you do that?" She nods hesitantly, unsure but determined. "I need you to be really, really quiet. Crawl into that space near the wall that you like to hide in, okay?" A shout comes from downstairs, and I can't make out who it is, but one thing I can tell for certain is that it isn't Ciaran. "Jo, make yourself as small as possible, and stay as far away from the doorway as you can. No matter what you hear, or who you see, you have to stay there and can't make any noise." I make a split-second decision to trust my gut completely. "You only come out for Mommy, Ciaran, or the police. Okay?" She lets out a whimper, terrified, but she moves to crawl into her favorite hiding place. I bend down to watch her and find my phone laying on the floor, just under the bed. I'm relieved. I do have it. I'm flooded with pride at how Jo is handling the situation. She's clearly scared, but she's so brave too. At four, she's far more courageous than I am at almost twenty-seven. I grab a cardigan, slipping my phone into the pocket. Leaning down again, I tell Jo, "I'm going to go get help. But you have to stay here. Promise me you'll stay here, safe." She nods again. "I love you so much, baby girl. I'll be back for you. I will always be back for you."

I don't know how much time we have left before whoever is in the house comes upstairs. I unlock the door and crack it, listening. The intruder is downstairs still, the sounds of breaking glass reaching my ears. I tiptoe into the hallway and move down to the first room at the top of the stairs, the guest room. I move myself behind the entry to wait out of sight. Footsteps tread up the wooden stairwell, clunking heavily against the grain. A phone call would be too loud, so I text Ciaran to call 911. Whoever is here passes the door of the guest room, and I can hear them move into Jo's room, stomping around. Summoning all my fortitude, I peek around the corner. The light is on in her room, but my door is still closed. I can't see anyone and take a chance, rushing past the hallway onto the stairwell. When I reach the bottom, I make a loud clatter to draw attention back downstairs. I just need to keep them away from my room for a little while longer. Someone is moving toward the stairs, but they don't seem to be in a rush. I slip to the front door and open it, hoping to draw them outside, then dash away to hide in the stairwell to the basement. Someone would only see me if they were on the top of the stairs, and there's no way I'm leaving this house with Jo inside. I don't have time to hit the button on the alarm system in the kitchen, next to the entry from the garage. Ciaran still hasn't called back or texted. Where is he?

There's a shout, but it almost sounds like a song. "Sammi, oh, Sammi, where could you be? It's time to go away with me." I still can't place it. It could be Lucas; it could be Emmitt; it could be a stranger. My blood is thundering in my ears, and I hear the screen door open. I let out a breath. Maybe they'll go outside to look for me. Creeping back up the basement steps, I hear the door close. We're finally in the clear, I think. But I turn to step into the kitchen and hear him again, "Sammi, it's time for you and Jo to come out. I know you're in here." The voice is moving in my direction, and I go the other way, toward the living room. Several framed photos are laying on the floor, the glass broken. I'll need to be careful not to cut myself. Whoever is in my house is unrushed, moving from room to room, so sure that they will find me.

I listen to them open the door to the pantry, and I move further into the living room before they close it. They're moving toward the back of the house, where I'm currently tucked away, behind the wall separating the living room from the stairwell. The living room isn't a good hiding place, and I move to the stairwell leading upstairs. I climb silently up a few steps, so I can still hear from out of sight. The sound of glass crunching reaches me as they cross the floor.

"Sammi, Sammi, Sammi... Can I call you Samantha? It's so much classier. What am I going to do with you? I tried to court you, and here you are, shacking up with another man. Don't worry. I won't hold it against you. You're my wife now, and that's all that matters. But if you don't want me to hunt down your boy toy, you better stop running. I'll give you one thing. You move quick. One day you're not dating, the next day he's sleeping over. That's done now. I expect my wife to be faithful."

It hits me like a sledgehammer. I know that voice. Then, the panic gets worse - I think to myself, "If Ciaran is still on the plane, if his flight was delayed longer than they thought, he won't get my message until he lands. What am I going to do?"

Out of desperation, I fire off a quick text to Lucas, "GET IC-ING". I'm not sure he will remember our code, and if he comes at all, it may not be in time to help me, but all I need to do is stall long enough for someone to help Jo. To keep her safe.

The intruder is still talking, moving around the living room. I can hear him say, "I always wanted a son, but I'll have to make do with her."

Jo's definitely in danger, and I have to take a calculated risk. I peek into the living room to see his back. Then, I move past and wait until he's approaching the stairs I just left, making my way back to the other stairwell that leads down to the basement.

When I reach the bottom, I yell out, "She's not here. The police are on their way."

"Oh, Sammi, you think you're so clever. They won't get here in time. Where is our Jo? Is she with your boyfriend? I'm sure he'll take good care of her. I guess we'll just have to leave her behind. In a few months, you won't even think about either of them anymore." I know I don't have much time, and I crack the door into the basement, slipping through. I find a tall stack of boxes and crouch behind them. It won't be long now.

I hear my grandma in my ear, whispering. She only says one word, "Fight." And fight I will.

Chapter Twenty-Four

Hidden behind the boxes, I look around for any kind of weapon. Then, I see it, a hammer left behind from when I put some shelving down here. I take a breath, run out to grab it, and scramble back to the safety of the boxes.

The voice is closer, possibly just within the entrance to the basement. "Stop hiding. No more games. Let's go."

My phone vibrates. I cringe and look at it, a text from Ciaran. "Called police, OTW, hide." It's too late for that. I can hear the intruder moving around some boxes closer to the entrance to the basement. I know I only have a few minutes, at best, before he reaches me. I may die tonight, but at least it won't be in front of Jo, and maybe I can fight long enough for the police to get here. Footsteps come closer.

"You know, I almost had you more than once. In college, all those years ago, Halloween night. Then, that asshole stepped out and fucked up my plans. This past Halloween... I don't give up easily."

My blood turns to ice. Everything clicks into place, a movie playing in my head from the first time I thought someone was following me, all the way to today. I wasn't imagining it. There was another person following me that night. It was him. He had the chance to stop what happened, and he didn't.

That's when I hear it. It's so faint, it's barely audible. "Mommy?" Oh no, no, no...

I pop from around the boxes, but he's already rushing back to the door. I take the stairs three at a time, faster than ever before, and he's just ahead of me. There's no way I can get to Jo before he will. What happens next takes only a few seconds, but it feels like an eternity. Just steps behind him, I whip around the corner to see Lucas roar out of the entry into the kitchen, between Jo, at the bottom of the stairs, and Matthew.

He swings his hockey stick without hesitation, and it cracks Matthew across the head. "Nobody messes with MY daughter," Lucas roars. Matthew crumples to the floor, and I cry with relief. She's safe.

Lucas picks up Jo, then comes over and wraps me under his other arm. "You're okay," he tells us.

"It was him, Lucas. Always him," I gasp out.

The police tentatively enter the front door, which Matthew left open, and Lucas calls out to them. It's there that Ciaran finds us, and Lucas hands Jo off to him. "Can I just have a minute with you, Sammi?" he requests.

"Uhh, sure," I respond. "Are you okay if I talk to Lucas for a minute, Jo?" I ask her, hesitant to be away from her after such a traumatizing experience. She nods, and Ciaran takes her outside.

"Listen, I know I did a lot of horrible things in the past," Lucas begins. "Things I'm not proud of. Things that have forever altered both our lives. I know it can't ever be the same between us. I've accepted that, and I want you and Jo to be happy. If that's with Ciaran, then so be it. He seems like a great guy. But please, Sammi..." he utters, tears in his eyes. "It's over between us, but regardless of what a paternity test shows, I want to be a dad to Jo. I want to be the dad I should have been all along. Just think about it, please?"

It's all I wanted to hear for so many years, and yet it's completely different. It's like Grams used to say, "God works in mysterious ways, Sammi. Sometimes, what seems like an unanswered prayer at the moment ends up being exactly what we need in the future."

"I'll think about it, Lucas," I tell him, and with that, he smiles.

"Thank you, Sammi." An officer approaches and asks Lucas to give a statement. "You should probably go check on Jo," Lucas says, before walking away to tell his story about what happened.

I step outside, and I see Jo, giggling in Ciaran's arms. She's going to be okay. It's finally over.

Chapter Twenty-Five

Eighteen months later, I sit on the couch, feeling as big as a house, knitting baby booties for the little boy about to become Jo's brother. My wedding band reflects the sunlight streaming through the window, casting brilliant light around the room. Fiona comes into the room. "It's time, Sis. Everyone is here."

She offers me a hand, tugging me to my feet, and I walk into the backyard of the house that Ciaran and I purchased six months ago in our whirlwind relationship. We married a year ago, followed by a surprise pregnancy shortly thereafter. There's a big, fenced backyard for the kids to play, the kitchen I've always dreamed of, and best of all, no tarnished memories.

Ciaran is holding Jo, and when she sees me, she tells him, "Look, Daddy, Mommy's here." I walk up to him and stop to rest my head against his shoulder. Claire is standing out in the yard, surrounded by folding tables and blue balloons, one table covered in gifts. Jesse is out further in the backyard, chasing Will, who toddles around at an unbelievable speed. I stand there, taking in the scene around me. Fergus stands next to Ciaran, looking proud.

When I look to my left, I see Lucas come in through the open gate of the fence. He pauses there for a moment, looking at everything around us. A woman is next to him, looking very much like the woman in Jo's picture. Lucas takes a breath and moves forward, but Rachel nervously hesitates. She hasn't met any of us yet. The moment is perfect. Jo's drawing from all those months ago is coming to fruition.

As I stand there, soaking in the scene around me, I can feel my grandma's spirit next to me, but she doesn't speak. She doesn't need to say anything, I can feel her words in my heart. I've finally done the only thing she ever wanted me to do. I found my happy ending.

ACKNOWLEDGEMENTS

When I first set out to write this book, I had an entirely different vision for it. In my head, it was a story about a couple who goes through something unthinkable and how they manage to work through this event. As so often happens, as I began to write, Sammi's story took on a life of its own. Even in its final form, this is not meant to have a shocking, mind blowing ending. At its heart, this is the story of a girl who must find the strength to carry on with a life that takes a turn she never anticipated. For me, writing the story has been a truly cathartic experience.

Thank you to my husband, David, for his countless rereads and suggestions on this book, as well as the multitude of hours spent entertaining the kids so I could achieve some peace in my writing. Thank you to my children for letting Mama take the time to get this story on paper and polish it into what it is today. Everything I do is for you. Remember that you can achieve anything, as long as you are willing to do the work.

Thank you to my parents, Robert and Diana, for everything. You are the reason I love reading and love to express myself through words. Without your constant encouragement and support, this would never have become a reality. One of my earliest memories is sitting on Dad's lap, reading *The Hobbit* to each other. A huge thank you to my sister, Mandi, who let me bounce a million ideas off of her throughout the process.

Finally, thank you to my siblings, Steven and Paige, and my dear friend, Mandi Figueroa, for taking the time to read this and provide constructive feedback. Your encouragement means the world to me.

Last, but not least, thank you to everyone who takes the time to read this book. Words cannot adequately convey my appreciation for you.

9 780578 807263